Bello:
hidden talent rediscovered

Bello is a digital-only imprint of Pan Macmillan,
established to breathe new life into previously published,
classic books.

At Bello we believe in the timeless power of the imagination,
of a good story, narrative and entertainment, and we want to
use digital technology to ensure that many more readers
can enjoy these books into the future.

We publish in ebook and print-on-demand formats
to bring these wonderful books to new audiences.

www.panmacmillan.co.uk/bello

Richmal Crompton

Richmal Crompton (1890–1969) is best known for her thirty-eight books featuring William Brown, which were published between 1922 and 1970. Born in Lancashire, Crompton won a scholarship to Royal Holloway in London, where she trained as a schoolteacher, graduating in 1914, before turning to writing full-time. Alongside the *William* novels, Crompton wrote forty-one novels for adults, as well as nine collections of short stories.

Richmal Crompton

JOURNEYING
WAVE

First published 1938 by Bello

This edition published 2015 by Bello
an imprint of Pan Macmillan
20 New Wharf Road, London N1 9RR
Basingstoke and Oxford
Associated companies throughout the world

www.panmacmillan.co.uk/bello

ISBN 978-1-5098-1015-4 EPUB
ISBN 978-1-5098-1013-0 HB
ISBN 978-1-5098-1014-7 PB

A CIP catalogue record for this book is available from the British Library.

Typeset by Ellipsis Digital Limited, Glasgow

Visit **www.panmacmillan.com** to read more about all our books
and to buy them. You will also find features, author interviews and
news of any author events, and you can sign up for e-newsletters
so that you're always first to hear about our new releases.

Chapter One

THE light filtered softly through the drawn curtains, grew stronger, and flooded the big square bedroom, which, despite the up-to-date furnishings, still retained a vague suggestion of Victorianism. The bay window, the high ceiling, the ornate marble mantelpiece, struck the note of more settled spacious days, and the chintz pelmeted curtains and chintz skirted dressing-table seemed tactfully to bridge the gap between the old and the new.

Viola had disliked Elm Lodge when first she came to live in it after her marriage. Compared with Campions, where she had spent her youth, it was vulgar and ostentatious. Its mock turrets and battlements, its balustrades and gables, proclaimed the fact that it had been built by a Victorian merchant who had made money and wanted everyone to know it. Humphrey, on the contrary, was proud of the house, but Humphrey's taste had always been deplorable. Oddly enough, that was one of the things she had loved in him. It made him seem pathetic and vulnerable. . . . And he was never hurt, when, as often happened, she showed amusement or dismay at the outrageous presents he chose for her—the Derbyshire-spa inkwell, the voluminous lace collar, the brooch made in the shape of a bird's claw.

"But what's wrong with it?" he would ask, puzzled.

"Nothing," she would reply, struck with compunction at having appeared ungrateful. "It's lovely."

"It's not," he said. "I'll get you to choose it yourself next time."

But he never did, because he enjoyed surprising her with unexpected presents, and on each occasion he was sure that this time, at any rate, she would approve his choice. He had a child's love of garishness and bright colours, and with it a child's disarming humility, a child's ready, if wondering, acceptance of other incomprehensible standards. He was in a way even proud of his lack of taste, because it emphasised the perfection of hers.

"It's all my wife's choice," he would smile, when people praised the arrangements and furnishings of the house. "She tells me that my taste is atrocious."

The only time she had felt ashamed of him (and even then she had been ashamed of her shame) was when he had stayed at her home before their marriage. In the quiet aristocratic atmosphere of Campions he had seemed irremediably common. He had been, she could see, a great shock to her parents. Physically there was nothing to be ashamed of in him. He was tall and powerfully built, with rough-hewn features, a wide mouth, and level grey eyes. But his well-proportioned, slow-moving figure held an ungainliness that he had inherited from his labouring forebears, and that no amount of good tailoring could quite hide. There was a Midland burr to his speech, and he was immensely proud of his ownership of "Lessington's"—a draper's shop in a small Midland town. He had been expansively affectionate to her parents, mistaking their distant politeness for approval. Outside his own business (in which he was shrewdness itself) he was simple and gullible. There was nothing of the snob about him. He considered himself infinitely beneath her, but not because her mother was Sir Frank Overton's daughter and her father's family had lived at Campions for more than two hundred years. Despite his humility, he had inherited the sturdy independence that is the mark of the English working-classes. Her parents had raised no objection to the marriage.

"Of course, dear, if you like him ..." her mother had said with a shrug.

"I love him," Viola had retorted. "That's why I'm marrying him."

Her father had said nothing, but his very silence told Viola that he shared his wife's feelings. She knew, however, that beneath their contempt was a certain relief. She was a young widow with a very small income and a child to bring up, and their own means were straitened, the old house mortgaged, their capital sadly depreciated.

They had looked forward with secret apprehension to the years of their grandson's education. Now, of course, they need not worry. A stepfather had appeared to relieve them of the responsibility, and they had a vague idea that it did not behove them to look too closely into his social qualifications. Besides, it was not as if Viola were a young girl. She had been married and widowed, and, presumably, knew her own mind.

Already, before she met Humphrey, her brief married life with Gray had taken on a remote dream-like quality in her mind, had become something that she had read in a book or seen in a play, not something that had actually happened to her. Gray had been the opposite of Humphrey in every way—vivid, mercurial, artistic, as well as socially irreproachable. He painted vividly impressionist landscapes, and, everyone said, would have made a name for himself if he had lived. He died, however, only four years after their marriage, but not before she had glimpsed the irresponsibility that underlay his charm, and the fickleness of his swiftly changing enthusiasms. It was Humphrey's very unlikeness to Gray that had first attracted her, his lack of those spectacular qualities that—before marriage, at any rate—had made Gray resemble the Prince Charming of her dreams. Her love for him, too, was very different from her love for Gray. Her love for Gray had been a tumultuous ecstasy, her love for Humphrey a deep quiet contentment.

Hilary had been eight years old when she married Humphrey, and she had hoped that it would be as if he were Humphrey's own son, but in that she had been disappointed. Hilary was Gray's son both in appearance and in temperament. He had Gray's slender build, his restlessness, his talent, his moodiness, his volatile enthusiasm. He had Gray's sideways mocking glance and sensitive, rather weak mouth. He professed exaggerated admiration for his father's talent, hanging the few pictures that Gray had left conspicuously on his bedroom wall, but Viola suspected that this was a glorification of himself rather than of Gray.

He and Humphrey had never quarrelled. They treated each other, indeed, with punctilious courtesy, but Hilary had always made it quite clear that he merely tolerated Humphrey as his mother's husband and did not accept him in his father's place. He had spent few of his school and college holidays at home—staying generally with school friends, Gray's people, or her own parents at Campions. Perhaps that had been a mistake. Neither her people nor Gray's liked Humphrey. When Hilary did come home he wore the air of one belonging to another and superior world. This never seemed to irritate Humphrey. Even the boy's occasional deliberate attempt to rile him passed over his head, apparently unperceived. Hilary was now at Oxford in his last year, highbrow, dilettante, self-conscious, self-assured, already the author of a small volume of modern verse that Viola had read with ever-increasing bewilderment.

The light shone full upon her now. Still half asleep, she opened her eyes ... then closed them again and lay motionless, relaxed.

She was dimly aware that some unwelcome piece of knowledge was waiting to spring upon her as soon as she returned fully to consciousness, but that as long as she could keep her memory dulled and drowsed she need not know what it was. She tried to escape it by drifting off again on the warm tides of sleep, but sleep in its turn evaded her. Desperately she forced her mind to turn to trivial domestic matters. ... There had been a bad fall of soot from the dining-room chimney yesterday. She must ring up the sweep this morning. (It was typical of the times that the sweep was on the telephone and came in a car.) Then she must see about the new loose covers for the drawing-room. The old ones were worn and faded. Her thoughts went back to the day when she had chosen them. She had met Humphrey for lunch in Burchester and they had gone to the shop together. She had teased him because he had been attracted by a pattern of vivid red roses on a black ground, but he had approved her final choice of a soft blue-and-grey linen. He had—— She opened her eyes, and a cold shiver crept through her. It wasn't any use. She couldn't fight it off any longer. Everything led straight to it. It was no use thinking of the chimney-sweep or the new loose covers, because there would be no need of either. She was leaving Elm Lodge and Humphrey for ever. ... She made a little gesture of surrender and let the knowledge flood her mind in wave upon black wave. It was like a physical onset, leaving her bruised and shaken.

Even now she couldn't believe it. She could remember Humphrey's telling her about it last night, but she couldn't believe it. Humphrey had had an affair with a girl, and the girl was going to have a baby. Her first feeling had been one of anger and humiliation. She had from the beginning half unconsciously shared the attitude of her friends and relations with regard to Humphrey, seeing herself as a princess who has stooped to marry a commoner. She had been a woman of breeding and culture, and he was a man of little education and no social background. Of her interest in art, music, literature, he had understood nothing. One part of her had been starved throughout the long years of her marriage. She had deliberately confined herself in all their intercourse to his narrow limits. And yet through it all she had been happy. And she had thought that he was happy. Indeed, he had told her last night that he had been happy, but she had cut him short.

"Please don't try to explain," she had said. "I don't understand, and I don't want to. Do you love the girl?"

"Yes," he had said, after a slight hesitation.

"Then you must marry her, of course. I'll divorce you."

Beneath the pain at his desertion had been a deeper pain, because another woman was giving him the child she had always longed to give him.

She would have liked to know more about the affair, but her pride forbade her to ask him. He had met the girl casually, she gathered, when he was in London on business.

It was her pride, of course, that suffered most deeply. She had, she felt, deliberately renounced her birthright for him, and he had repaid her sacrifice by throwing it back at her contemptuously. No, she had to be fair. There had been no contempt. There had been compunction and unhappiness in his expression last night, though his voice was, as usual, slow and deliberate. He had made no excuses or protestations, simply told her the facts and left her to judge. The contempt had been, naturally, on her side, though she had said very little, merely turned her head away and cut him short with a quick movement of her hand.

"Please don't try to explain. . . . I don't want to understand."

He had left her soon after that. It was fortunate that he was, in any case, going to London, so that the servants need suspect nothing for the present. They would have to know soon enough. . . . She had told him that she would go down to Campions today to break the news to her people. They would take it hard, of course. They were old-fashioned and divorce did not come into their scheme of things. A wife must suffer any indignity rather than divorce her husband. Well, the day of those ideas was over, thank God. It wouldn't have mattered so much, of course, if it hadn't been for the child. Again the thought of that sent a sharp pang through her heart. She turned away from it quickly to think of her own child, Hilary. Hilary and she must draw nearer to each other now. She remembered that when Gray died she had vowed to herself that she would never marry again, that she would devote the rest of her life to Hilary. Perhaps this was her punishment for marrying Humphrey. It was Humphrey who had, without, of course, meaning to—she did him so much justice—stood between them from the beginning. And Hilary was interested in the things that she had been interested in before she married Humphrey. She and Hilary. She applied the thought as if it had been healing balm to the wound of Humphrey's disloyalty. Oh, there would be compensations. She wasn't the kind of wife whose life was left empty by a husband's defection. She had always despised women like that. She would go away from Reddington for one thing—Reddington, with its narrow provincialism, its dullness, its pettiness, its lack of interest in anything beyond money-making and its own parochial affairs.

And again came the thought of how much she had sacrificed for Humphrey—living for so many years among people who were socially and mentally her inferiors, making herself pleasant to his impossible relations, losing touch with all her old friends. Deliberately she whipped up her anger against him. It made her feel less hurt and bewildered and lonely. . . .

There came a knock at the door, and Evelyn, the housemaid,

entered with her morning tea. Viola glanced at her sharply, wondering if she guessed anything. There wasn't any reason why she should, but it was odd how servants always did seem to know when anything untoward had happened in a household, whether they were told or not.

The woman met her gaze disingenuously enough as she set down the tray on the table by the bed, then went to the window to draw the curtains.

"A lovely day, madam," she said.

"Yes, isn't it?" said Viola, sitting up and straightening the coverlet. She felt that in trying to speak ordinarily she had spoken just a little too brightly. She thought that Evelyn glanced at her curiously. Perhaps she knew—she and Cook and all of them, even the tradesmen. Perhaps they had known for some time. The wife was always the last to find out. She'd read that somewhere—in a book or a play. ... No, that was silly. They couldn't possibly know. It wasn't as if the girl lived in Reddington. But she must try to be more natural or they'd suspect something.

"Did I tell you I was going over to see my mother today, Evelyn?" she said.

That sounded almost too natural, because she didn't often go to see her people (she'd never quite forgiven them for their attitude to Humphrey), and she would not ordinarily have been quite so casual about it.

"No, madam," said Evelyn.

"She's not been very well lately, and I'm rather anxious about her."

That sounded just right—concerned, but not too concerned.

"I'm sorry to hear that, madam," said Evelyn.

Viola looked at her, wondering what she would say when she knew. Would she take her side or Humphrey's when they talked the affair over in the kitchen? She had always been on good terms with the servants, but so had Humphrey. Evelyn was middle aged and matter of fact, kindly and capable and reserved, rather plain and with no nonsense about her. She could keep the tradesmen in their places, and even Cook, who was inclined to be a martinet, stood in awe of her. Suddenly Viola longed to confide the whole story in her, tell her how hurt and unhappy she was, sob her heart out on the clean starched bosom. ... But she merely said, "Oh, nothing really serious," as she took the tray on her knee.

"How long will you be staying, madam?" said Evelyn.

"Just a few days," said Viola. "If you'll get my small suitcase out now, I'll put a few things into it when I've dressed."

Evelyn got the suitcase from the boxroom and went down to the kitchen, and Viola poured out the tea, frowning abstractedly. She wondered whether, when the news was public, Evelyn would say, "I could see something was the matter that morning," or "She seemed just as usual the morning after the master went." Oh well, she'd be out of it all soon, and, anyway, it didn't matter what they thought. Her mind turned to the practical aspect of the situation. She must consult her solicitor. But he was Humphrey's solicitor, too. He couldn't act for them both. Or could he—as Humphrey would not be defending the suit? She felt resentfully that Humphrey ought to be seeing to the whole thing. He always had seen to her business—interviewed her bank manager, filled in her income-tax form, looked out her trains.

Her mind went back over the years of their life together. Their relations had long ago, of course, become stereotyped, had long ago settled down into a humdrum jog-trot of compromise, as did the lives of most married couples. The glamour that had invested him when she married had long since faded. She had discovered unsuspected limitations in him. She had begun to take all his good qualities for granted. His admiration of her she had always taken for granted. She had even felt a little complacent at having hidden from him her occasional boredom, and at having, when with him, confined her interests so entirely within the narrow circle of his, accompanying him to revues and musical comedies when they were in London, patiently listening to his recounting of the plots of the detective novels that were his only reading. It had never occurred to her till now that he might have found any deficiency or limitation in her, and the discovery of his unfaithfulness had been a shock to her self-esteem.

She hugged her righteous anger to her as a breastplate. Anything rather than admit the feeling of loneliness and desolation that was lying in wait for her. . . . She raised the teacup to her lips. She had left it too long, and it was cold. She drank it with an effort. She didn't want to give Evelyn any fuel for suspicion. ("She left her tea, too, that morning. I thought there was something queer.")

She got out of bed, put on her dressing-gown, and went to the looking-glass. That side of the question, too, had to be faced. She was forty-three. Sexually, she knew—and was rather proud of the knowledge—she had always been cold. Once they had given up hope of a child, she and Humphrey had lived more or less apart. But she had always prided herself, too, on the fact that the real basis of their marriage had not been one of sexual attraction. It had been one of understanding and friendship. Well, there also she had evidently been living in a fool's paradise. Humphrey was like any other man in that respect. The girl was probably young and fresh and seductive. She herself was none of these things. She examined her reflection critically in the glass. She had been lovely enough as a young girl, but she was not a young girl any longer. She was still slender, but there were faint lines graven from nose to mouth, grey threads in the dark hair. She had always been pale, and her face had always been thin, but it was thinner, less shapely, now—her cheeks hollow, shadows beneath her eyes. She was a good-looking, well-preserved woman, but that was all. She summoned an imaginary picture of a girl, soft, rosy, dewy with youth, saw her and Humphrey together . . . and turned sharply from the mirror, trembling, her cheeks hotly flushed. It was horrible. The whole thing was horrible. She must get away from it as quickly as she could.

Chapter Two

WATCHING fields, houses, woodlands flash by the carriage window, she felt indescribably relieved to have left Reddington behind her. Her thoughts went to Humphrey's family—his twin aunts who lived together in a little house just outside the town, his sister, his sister in-law, his nieces and nephew. She wondered whether he would tell them about the divorce now or wait till the case came on. It would give them all something to talk about, she thought with a twisted smile, and that was a godsend in Reddington. ...

The aunts would be horrified. Their lives consisted of a monotonous round of trivial interests and duties—a round in which any unusual detail, however small, assumed colossal proportions.

Harriet, the elder by half an hour, would break the news to Hester very gently, as if Hester were a young girl whose innocence might be sullied by the knowledge. And, despite her sixty-odd years, there was something suggestive of a young girl about Hester. She was timid and withdrawn and always looked faintly perplexed. They both gave Humphrey the unquestioning, unqualified admiration that women of their generation gave as a matter of course to the man of the family, and the news would shock them deeply. But they would rally to his side none the less. Their family loyalty would triumph over their strict Evangelical upbringing. Reddington was a great place for family loyalty. My people, right or wrong. Hester would perhaps look a little more perplexed than usual for a few weeks. ...

Then there was Humphrey's sister, Doreen. She had married a Parish Church curate, who had obtained a living in Guilford shortly after the marriage and had died a few years later. After his death

Doreen had returned to Reddington with her baby, very smart and sophisticated, "putting on airs," as Reddington said, making frequent references to the bishop and St. Chad's and the more aristocratic members of her husband's congregation. In her short experience as a vicar's wife she had acquired a gracious manner and a somewhat exaggerated idea of her own importance. She patronised her old friends and set to work to win a footing in the small exclusive set that represented the local "county." She was partially successful, for she was good-looking, pleasant, ready to make herself useful, and quite impervious to snubs. She had sent Bridget, her daughter, to a "finishing" school in Harrogate for a year after she left Reddington High School, in order that she might be a social asset to her, but so far Bridget was turning out somewhat of a disappointment. She was pretty enough and her manners were charming, but she was shy and curiously obtuse with regard to her mother's plans. Doreen would give an impressive performance of grief and horror when she heard the news of Humphrey's divorce, but inwardly she would rejoice. She had always believed that Viola could have helped her more than she did in her social campaign, and she looked on Viola's avoidance of Reddington's smart set as a deliberate affront to herself.

And Bridget ... That was quite another matter. Bridget had adored Humphrey from childhood, putting him in the place of the father she did not remember, while Humphrey, on his part, seemed to put her in the place of the daughter he had never had. Their relationship—of adoration and trust on Bridget's side and of tender protectiveness on his—had often made Viola feel secretly hurt and resentful. It seemed to shut her out and reproach her for not having given him a daughter. But her heart grew heavy as she thought of Bridget now. There was nothing of the modern girl about Bridget. This would hurt her terribly. ...

Aggie, Humphrey's sister-in-law, would be very little affected by the news. She would merely enjoy the sensation it caused, just as she enjoyed a good murder case in the newspaper or one of the cheap novelettes she was so fond of. Aggie was plump, slovenly, good-tempered, and ineradicably feckless. People said that Mark,

Humphrey's brother, might have done better for himself if he hadn't married her, but Mark had been fully as shiftless and incapable of sustained effort as his wife. He had always hated the shop, and had realised his share of the business a few years after their father died, buying, against everyone's advice, a farm that had never paid its way and had ultimately to be sold up. Mark had been ill at the time of the sale and had died a few days later. Aggie had returned to Reddington and lived on an allowance made by Humphrey. It was a generous allowance, but money ran through Aggie's fingers like water and she never had anything to show for it. Her shiftlessness infuriated Elaine, her elder daughter. Elaine was smart and hard and pretty and extremely capable, and Aggie stood very much in awe of her. Joey, the boy, had left school last year and gone into Lessington's, and Monica, the younger girl, had won a scholarship to St. Margaret's, Oxford. Monica's interests were bounded on all sides by the limits of the scholastic world, and the news would affect her hardly at all.

As the train drew farther away from Reddington Humphrey's family became less real, and her own—Father, Mother, Frances—took on a new compelling reality. She felt a faint compunction at having given so little thought to them since her marriage, at having let herself be alienated from them by their critical attitude to Humphrey. Experience had proved that they were right and she was wrong. . . . Again the feeling of desolation threatened to sweep over her, and again she struggled against it, drawing her armour of superiority about her, telling herself that she must look on what had happened as an honourable release. She had done her duty by Humphrey all these years, denying her real self, burying her life in that dreadful little Midland town, and now she was free. Campions. . . . Her heart turned to it with a nostalgia that took her by surprise. She had felt something like this, she remembered, when she had returned to it after Gray's death—as if she were a ship coming to harbour after a long and stormy voyage. She remembered how Mother had clasped her in her arms and said, "Your home is here now, dearest, with us," and Father had said, "You'll give two old people great happiness, my dear, if you and the child will make your home here." For even then Frances had been remote from them, wrapped in her memories of Robin, living only for those brief ecstatic moments when she felt his presence as plainly, she said, as if he had been actually there. The same thing would happen again, of course. She had not formed any definite plans till now, but now she decided suddenly that she would make Campions her home again. She had always loved the place. Hilary, too, had always loved it. She need not ever return to Reddington. Evelyn could pack her things and send them on to her. Humphrey could do what he liked about Elm Lodge. He could take his new wife to live there if he pleased. Its vulgar ostentation would probably suit her, she thought sardonically, but a pang shot through her heart as she thought of Humphrey and the girl (she didn't even know her name) living together in the square high-ceilinged rooms that she had furnished with such care. Still, that didn't matter now. She'd finished with all that. As to the divorce, Father and his solicitor would see to it. There was nothing for her to worry about any more.

She glanced at her watch, then took the mirror from her hand-bag and began to powder her face and tidy her hair. She had dressed with unusual care, putting on a new two-piece of a soft grey woollen material, the loose sleeves of the three-quarter-length coat edged with fur. She didn't want them—or anyone—to think that she had lost her husband by letting herself go, by no longer taking pains over her appearance. Something of her usual self-confidence had dropped from her. She had ceased to feel quite sure of herself. And now came a sudden nervous fear lest her costume should seem too elaborate for Campions. She shrugged impatiently and lifted her suitcase from the rack. She was usually so poised and assured. This affair had thrown her out of her bearings. . . .

Her heart began to beat more quickly as the train slowed down at the country station, its name, Thorneham, almost hidden by climbing roses. She remembered the wild joy with which she used to leap out of the carriage into her mother's arms when she was a little girl returning from school. Frances had followed more slowly and sedately. The old station-master, having checked her impetuous exit ("Wait a bit, missie, wait a bit. Wait till it stops"), would stand in the background, smiling indulgently. There was a new station-master now, a young man who was suspected of communistic tendencies and had what her father, who disliked him intensely, called a "damned independent manner." The old station-master had knocked his wife about and spent a large proportion of his wages on drink, but he never forgot to touch his cap to the "gentry," and would never let anyone else carry her father's bags to and from the train. It would be rather amusing to be back again among the little interests of village life, to discover the cross-currents of intrigue that only those who lived among them could feel. She must try to enter into Frances's interests—the Women's Institute and Girl Guides and Village Clubs.

"The car's here," the station-master was saying.

She felt a momentary disappointment that no one had come to meet her, but, of course, she had not wished to disturb them unduly, and so had said nothing in her letter about being in any trouble. And Frances had no time for meeting trains. She was endlessly busy with all those village affairs in which she, Viola, would now take her part.

As she drove along the country road the sense of home-coming deepened, bringing a lump to her throat and a sudden mist to her eyes. ... What a tragic mistake her marriage had been from the beginning! She should never have left her own world. She needn't have done. ... Gray had belonged to her own world. And even after Gray there had been Adrian Basset. Adrian had admired her since she was a child. He had proposed to her when she was eighteen, and had tried to propose again after Gray died, but she had given him clearly to understand that it would be useless. Adrian, sensitive, artistic, fine-drawn, with his thin aristocratic features and quick perceptions. ... And instead she had married Humphrey, coarsegrained, insensitive.

The wrought-iron gates in the high brick wall were open, and the car turned into them adroitly from the narrow road. The house stood at the end of a short drive immediately in front of the gate. It was one of the smaller Elizabethan manor-houses, low and unpretentious, the brick-work mellowed to a soft rose tint. The inside had been freely reconstructed, but the frontage had always been considered sacred and, except for necessary repairs, had never been altered.

Viola had to wait for a few moments at the front door before it was opened. That, too, slightly chilled the ardour of the home-coming. She couldn't help feeling that Mother ought to have been there waiting with outspread arms to receive her. ... A housemaid with a rather forbidding expression, whom Viola had not seen before, came at last and showed her into the hall. Carlo, her mother's Pekinese, sat on a cushion on the hearthrug, while Sean, the red setter, lay dozing beneath the refectory table. Deep easy-chairs and a settee were ranged round the fireplace. On the floor against the wall was an old copper cauldron filled with sweet-peas, bowls of roses stood on tables and window-sills, and on the oak chest was a tall jar of delphiniums. A work-basket and half-finished piece of tapestry lay on the settee. Over all hung the faint elusive scent, composed of roses, pot-pourri, tweeds, dogs, tobacco, and leather bindings, that Viola had always associated with her home.

"I'll tell madam you've come," said the maid.

Viola took off her hat and threw it on to the table, running her fingers through her soft brown hair.

Sean, the red setter, rose, stretched, and came towards her, wagging his tail. Carlo turned his head in her direction with a plaintive wheeze. Viola stood, gazing in front of her, one hand caressing Sean's silky ears.

The door opened suddenly and Mrs. Ellison entered.

"Darling," she said, "how nice of you to come down! It's such a long time since we saw you." She gave Viola a quick light kiss, and drew her down on to the settee beside her, taking up her needlework at the same time. "Now we can have a cosy time together till tea, and you can tell me all your news. Father's down at the farm, and Frances is having a rehearsal for the Girl Guides' concert in the village hall. She'll be there all the evening, I think, because it's the last full rehearsal, and you know how keen she is.

The performance is on Saturday, so these few days are very anxious ones. It was sweet of you to run down and see the old folk, dear." She patted Viola's hand. "Are you quite well?"

"Mother——" began Viola, but Mrs. Ellison had laid down her needlework and was on her knees beside the wheezing Pekinese.

"Poor little Carlo! How are you, my sweet?" She raised her gentle blue eyes to Viola. "I'm so worried about him, dear. He seems so ill. He eats hardly anything. I had Mr. Mellor to him yesterday and he couldn't find anything wrong, but there must be something wrong, mustn't there, my pet?" she said caressingly, as she drew her hand over his soft coat. "No, go away, Sean dear. Carlo isn't well. Don't worry him." She resumed her seat on the settee and took up her needlework again, putting on a pair of spectacles. "You know, I think I must go and have my eyes seen to, dear. I really think they're getting worse."

"You do such fine work, Mother," said Viola absently.

She had imagined herself pouring out the story of Humphrey's unfaithfulness in her mother's arms the first moment of their meeting, but somehow or other that hadn't happened, so she must now wait for a more suitable opportunity. She couldn't blurt it out in the middle of her mother's confidences about her eyes and Carlo. ... Her mother was holding up the piece of needlework with a pleased smile.

"Well, it *is* rather lovely—isn't it?" she said, "—for an old woman of my age. What do you think about that blue bit, dear? I was in two minds about doing it in orange. I could easily undo it. ..."

"No, it's lovely in blue," said Viola mechanically.

Her father would be coming in any minute. She must tell her mother before then. ...

"Mother——" she began again, but Carlo had wheezed more loudly, and Mrs. Ellison bent down and picked him up, laying aside her embroidery.

"There, then! Come and sit on Missis' lap and tell her all about it. What is it, then? No, Sean dear, go away. Poor little Carlo's ill. You know what a fuss we made of you when you got your leg caught in the trap, don't you? It's Carlo's turn now and you must be a good boy and try not to feel jealous. Make a fuss of him, Viola, dear. He's very sensitive. ... I *am* so worried about Carlo. They say that Mr. Fenton over at Hanley's very good, but I don't want to hurt Mr. Mellor's feelings by calling in anyone else. Of course, it *may* just be a liver chill. He's had them before, but never as bad as this. ... I don't think you've seen that fire-screen since I finished it, have you, dear? It's made up much better than I thought it would. And it goes so well with the chairs, don't you think?"

Viola got up and knelt by the fire-screen, pretending to examine it. Every moment she didn't tell Mother about Humphrey made it more difficult to introduce the subject. She hadn't even asked after him. That, at any rate, would have given her an opening. She looked at her as she sat on the settee, bending over Carlo, one hand resting on Sean's head, as if to assure him, too, of her affection—a small, compact, pretty old lady with white hair that still had a soft natural wave, skin that was still pink and white despite the many wrinkles, and eyes that were still brightly blue behind her horn-rimmed glasses.

Mrs. Ellison looked up and met her daughter's gaze.

"Like it, darling?" she said, with a charming air of modest gratification.

"It's lovely," said Viola, rising to her feet.

"I did get a little tired of it before the end," confessed Mrs. Ellison, "and I was a wee bit tempted to leave out that top spray of leaves, but I knew that it would have worried me all the rest of my life if I did. And then I had that bad cold—you remember? I told you about it in my letter—and couldn't go out for a fortnight, so I simply set to and got it done."

Of course, thought Viola, I could make myself say it. Just blurt it out. "Mother, Humphrey's left me for another woman. I'm divorcing him." But there would be something cruel in breaking up the atmosphere of gentle passionless serenity in which the old woman lived. It would be like striking a child.

Surely, if she waited, an opportunity would come. Her mother would be bound to mention Humphrey sooner or later. And there was all the rest of the day. No need to hurry things. Better, perhaps, to wait till her father came in and tell them both together. The housemaid entered, set out the low tea-table, then returned with a laden tray.

"*Such* a nice girl," said Mrs. Ellison when the door closed on her. "Her father rents Beck Farm, you know."

Mrs. Ellison always got on well with her servants—constituting herself the unofficial guardian of each, knowing all their private affairs, helping the more unfortunate members of their families. To her own class and to the class that is known as the "working-class" Mrs. Ellison was uniformly kind and friendly. To the class immediately beneath her own she was, for some reason she didn't quite understand, haughty and distant.

She always made the tea herself from a spirit-kettle, doing it slowly and absorbedly as if it were some solemn rite—warming the silver teapot, measuring out the tea from the silver caddy, and leaving it to stand for the exact time before she began to pour out. Viola remembered how her mother's leisurely way of doing things used to irritate her when she was a girl. It belonged to the days when women had little to do except "fill in their time."

"No sugar—isn't it, darling?—and very little milk," she said as she poured out Viola's cup.

She had always been rather proud of remembering the tea-time requirements of her friends and relations.

She put down a saucer of weak tea for Carlo on the hearthrug, and then Colonel Ellison came in. He was short, like his wife, with white hair, a weather-beaten face, and twinkling grey eyes.

He lived in the open air, making the management of his small estate the excuse for constant activity on foot or horseback. He hunted regularly, shot whenever he got the chance (he had had to sell most of his own shooting), and adored his wife, home, and family. He was good-tempered, generous, starkly loyal and honest, somewhat childish in his interests, and very narrow in his opinions. He had a limited, if hearty, sense of humour and loved to tease his daughters about nursery and schoolroom incidents that they had long since forgotten. His wife humoured him and managed him and hid from him anything that she thought he wouldn't like to know.

He kissed Viola affectionately, said, "Well, Buntikins, what about the mangel wurzels?" (an old nursery joke whose origin she had quite forgotten), laughed whole-heartedly at the memory (whatever it was), took a cup of tea from his wife, and sank down with a sigh of content into his favourite armchair. He did remember to say, "Humphrey all right?" but he didn't wait for an answer. He was—naturally, perhaps—far more concerned about Carlo.

"Poor little chap!" he kept saying. "Poor little chap!"

He thought the best plan would be to tell Mellor quite firmly that they wanted a second opinion.

Two spaniels had come in with him, but they were sternly ordered away from the tea-table and went to lie down together on the rug by the door. They were working dogs, to be kept fit and disciplined. Carlo and Sean, on the other hand, were lilies of the field. He poured out his bits of news to the accompaniment of little noises of interest and concern from his wife. There was dry-rot in Rose Cottage. He couldn't understand it. He'd stipulated most emphatically on well-seasoned wood, and seen it himself. He'd get Carroway to go into the matter. It was most unsatisfactory. He didn't like making changes, but he'd a good mind to try Fleet's for the next piece of building he wanted done.

Then her mother told Viola the local news, Colonel Ellison joining in occasionally with correction or amplification.

"The Jenkinses have had another baby, dear. Their eighth. Such a sweet little thing, though it's very improvident of them."

"The eldest son's working now and that helps a little, of course."

"Your, father paid for Sarah to go to Droitwich for her rheumatism, but really it's not much better."

"It was better at first, my dear."

"Yes. Then it seemed to get bad again. Such a pity. It makes her quite helpless."

"She has a good deal of pain, I'm afraid, poor soul!"

"I told you in my letter that little Dorrie Hampton had married, didn't I, dear? Such a pretty wedding. To young Morrison, you know, of Hurst Farm."

"Your mother gave her her wedding-dress."

"Quite a sensible one, you know, that she could wear afterwards. She was so grateful. . . ."

Viola thought: It's the only world that exists for them—old Sarah's rheumatism and the Jenkinses' children and Dorrie Hampton's wedding. The trouble that had driven her to them for comfort began to seem far-off and unreal. She felt more an alien here than she had felt even in Reddington. She didn't belong anywhere. Something of the panic that seizes a child when it suddenly realises that it is lost swept over her. . . .

"Now, darling, you must come and see the garden," said her mother, when they had finished tea. "I dare say poor little Carlo would get a sleep if he were left quiet. What about you, dear? Will you come with us?"

"No, thank you, my dear," answered her husband. "I'll go to the study. I have a few letters to write."

Colonel Ellison generally spent the morning and afternoon in strenuous exercise and dozed in his study between tea and dinner, but the fiction of "a few letters to write" was always faithfully maintained by everyone in the house.

Viola followed her mother slowly into the garden. Perhaps it would be easier to tell her in the garden, now that the slight constraint of their meeting had worn off and they were alone together. Surely she must *see* that she was unhappy. After all, they were mother and daughter. There was surely a strong enough bond between them for that. She was sure that if her mother had been unhappy or afraid she would have known. Perhaps she did know, and that was why she had asked her to come into the garden. "What's the matter, darling?" she would say in that tender caressing voice that was one of Viola's most precious memories of childhood, and then she would be able to tell her everything.

But Mrs. Ellison, leading her slowly along the herbaceous borders, did not, after all, seem to have noticed her daughter's unhappiness. There was plenty of tender solicitude in her voice and manner, but, just as indoors it had been given to Carlo, so outdoors it was given to any plant that was putting up a hard fight or had suffered during the recent drought. Mrs. Ellison knew and loved every one of her plants. She felt for them the same protective interest that she felt for her servants and for the villagers.

"I believe that really it ought to have more sun, but it does quite well here. So pretty, and I'm so fond of it. . . . I lost that new double daisy I had here last summer. I *was* sorry. It wasn't really a hard winter, but it was all that rain. . . . Isn't that helenium lovely? I only put it in in the spring. It's wonderful to have done so well the first year."

There were gay formal beds of antirrhinums and stocks and marigolds, but Mrs. Ellison took very little interest in those. It was her herbaceous borders that she loved and cherished, looking on each plant as an old friend, watching over it anxiously, welcoming it tenderly after the winter, grieving over the casualties, hoeing and staking and giving little mulches of leaf-mould and grass cuttings and fertiliser. Her "pottering" exasperated Matthews, the gardener, who could have done effectively in five minutes what she did ineffectively in as many hours, but Mrs. Ellison went twice a week to sit with his bedridden wife, and so he tried to hide his irritation even from himself.

Once she said, "Is Hilary getting on all right? We haven't seen him since Easter," but, even while Viola was gathering breath to seize the opening and tell her about Humphrey, she had gone on to describe how most of her catmint had died during the winter and she had had to raise a fresh lot from seed.

"I think it makes *such* a lovely edging, don't you, darling?"

They inspected the Buff Orpingtons in the orchard, then went back to the house. Colonel Ellison came out of his study, yawning and flushed with sleep, as they entered the hall, and his wife said, "Finished your letters, dear?" not with any intention of sarcasm, but because she always said it. It seemed to round off their little fiction, and make it real and satisfying to both of them.

Frances didn't come in till after dinner. Examining her with new interest, Viola thought that she looked older than her years, but the suggestion of dreamy innocence, which had belonged to her girlhood, still hung about her, and she still wore the dark dresses with touches of white—vaguely suggestive of widowhood—that she had worn ever since Robin's death. Viola remembered the exultation with which she had once said, "He seems nearer to me now even than he was when he was alive."

She greeted Viola with her faint smile, answered her mother's questions about the concert mechanically, and went into the dining-room for her dinner, which had been kept hot for her.

"Frances is always so busy," said Mrs. Ellison proudly. "I simply don't know what they'd do without her in the village. The Women's Institute gave her a rose-bowl in the summer. *So* sweet of them, but, as I said at the time, she really does deserve it."

She made coffee in her new coffee-machine that Hilary had sent her last Christmas. She was secretly afraid of it, as she was of everything "new-fangled," and had a vague suspicion that it might explode at any moment, but she always used it because she liked to be able to tell people that Hilary had given it to her. ("Such a dear boy. He's up at Oxford now and doing so well.")

After they had finished coffee, Mrs. Ellison took up her embroidery, and Colonel Ellison settled down to read aloud to her. They did this every evening. ("You don't mind, do you, darling?" murmured Mrs. Ellison apologetically as he opened the book.) They never read modern novels. ("Yes, dear, I know there must be some nice ones. I don't say there aren't. But it's so distressing for your father to come across the language they use in them. Of course, he can't read it aloud to me and it does embarrass him so.")

Their reading consisted almost entirely of *David Copperfield, Pickwick Papers*, the Barchester novels, and *Forrocks*. Colonel Ellison read very badly, but he thoroughly enjoyed it, and the better he knew a book the more he enjoyed it. They were reading *Pickwick Papers* now, and his laugh kept ringing out as much in anticipation of the joke that he knew was coming as of appreciation of the one he was actually reading. Mrs. Ellison's smile accompanied all the laughter, but Viola knew that she wasn't listening. She never did listen. She was absorbed in her own thoughts—planning the colours of her embroidery (just a touch of bright red in the centre. Not too much), rearranging the border that didn't get enough sun (one *couldn't* cut that elm tree down, and there are quite a lot of flowers that grow in the shade. I must talk to Matthews about it), worrying over Carlo's mysterious illness (I *must* stop them giving him tit-bits in the kitchen. I've told them not to, but I'm sure they still do. It must be something he's eaten there that has upset him. I'm always so careful with his diet. Poor little darling! Poor little *darling*!).

Colonel Ellison was reading in a voice choked with laughter: " 'What makes him go side-ways?' said Mr. Snodgrass in the bin to Mr. Winkle in the saddle. 'I can't imagine,' said Mr. Winkle. His horse was drifting up the street in the most mysterious manner—side first with his head towards one side of the way, and his tail towards the other.' "

He was laughing so much that he had to put the book down. "I think that's one of the most humorous passages in the whole of English literature," he said.

"Yes, isn't it, dear?" replied Mrs. Ellison.

He went on reading and she went on dreaming placidly. She had long ago learnt to make appropriate comments and rejoinders without knowing what he had said. (Campanulas grow in the shade, of course, and so do Michaelmas daisies. . . . Will that blue look a bit too bright by daylight? I think not. . . . I'll get Mr. Mellor to draw up a strict diet for Carlo, and tell the servants they must not feed him on any account. Of course, visitors are a nuisance. They will give him bits of bread and butter and he *is* inclined to be just a little greedy, poor darling! . . . How nice to have Viola home again! *Such* a dear child. . . .)

Viola watched them, wondering if her father had ever been unfaithful to her mother, knowing that if he had, her mother would have turned a blind eye to it. She belonged to the generation that was trained to turn a blind eye. Ought she to have turned a blind eye to Humphrey? But Humphrey hadn't given her the chance—even if she'd wanted to. Besides, the child made things difficult. Humphrey had always longed for a child. She tried to steel herself against that thought, closing her eyes and compressing her lips till they were a thin line.

" 'By whatever motives the animal was actuated,' " read Colonel Ellison, " 'certain it is that Mr. Winkle had no sooner touched the reins than he slipped them over his head, and darted backwards to their full length.' "

Mrs. Ellison smiled across at Viola.

"Quite comfortable, dear?"

"Yes, thank you," said Viola.

She'd tell her tonight in her bedroom. She always looked in to pat her pillow and smooth the coverlet and rearrange the bowl of flowers on the dressing-table and ask her if she was quite sure she had everything she wanted.

Frances came in from the dining-room and went to the bureau, taking a ledger and note-book from a drawer. There she sat, mysteriously withdrawn and aloof from the others, entering the minutes of one of her many meetings in her small neat handwriting.

Chapter Three

MRS. ELLISON fluttered about the bedroom with gentle birdlike movements.

"I wondered whether to put you here, dear, or in one of the bigger rooms, but I remembered how you used to love this little room."

"Yes, I remember . . ." said Viola, sitting on the bed and looking round her.

The room, which had been hers as a child, was in the oldest part of the house. It was small and rather dark and had two steps just inside the door, which had always given her a pleasant sense of privacy. People couldn't come into the room just anyhow. They had to come slowly and carefully, and, if strangers, they had to be warned. ("Mind the two steps into Viola's room.") There was a heavy oak beam across the low ceiling, too, which she used to imagine was full of hidden treasure. Once she had stood on her bed and bored a hole in it with a penknife, half expecting a rain of pearls and doubloons to fall on her.

On wet afternoons she would curl upon the cushioned window-seat (made in the thickness of the wall) by the little casement window and read her beloved Red Fairy Book till it was too dark to see. She had lain awake in that small bed under the pale blue coverlet the night before her marriage to Gray, excited and half afraid. The moonlight had shone full upon the wreath of orange-blossom that lay on her dressing-table. The door of the wardrobe cupboard in the wall was ajar, and she could see the white satin wedding-dress hanging inside. Her marriage to Humphrey had been a different and more sober affair—an affair of navy blue charmeuse and a faint damping atmosphere of disapproval.

"If only he could get a good night's rest, I'm sure he'd be better," Mrs. Ellison was saying. "I've had him in my room since he was ill, and I hear his little basket creak, creak, creak. He's restless even in his sleep. . . . What would you do about Mr. Mellor, dear? Would you ask him to let Mr. Fenton see him?"

"Yes . . ." said Viola absently.

"I'll write to him tomorrow, then. I can put it quite tactfully. . . . How do you think your father's looking?"

"Very well."

"I think he is quite well, on the whole. Except for a little rheumatism now and then. It's the winter I dread for him. He will go out in all weathers. He won't realise that he's not as young as he was."

She flitted to the dressing-table, rearranged the bowl of roses and examined the cover with little caressing touches. "These *have* lasted well, haven't they? They were a wedding present from Aunt Florrie. She did all that drawn-thread work herself. . . . They've not been in general use, of course. I've always kept them for visitors. . . ." She came towards Viola with arms outstretched. "Well, my darling, I must say goodnight. Are you sure you have everything you want?"

Viola looked at her for a moment in silence, then said slowly, "Mother, I'm going to divorce Humphrey."

Mrs. Ellison's arms dropped to her sides and the smile faded from her face.

"*Divorce* him, darling?" she said incredulously. "Not *divorce* him!"

"Yes," said Viola. "Another woman is going to have a child by him. They want to get married."

Mrs. Ellison sat down on the bed, her face a mask of horror.

"Oh, *darling!*" she said. "Do you think you're wise?"

"I don't think I've any choice in the matter," said Viola stonily. "I can't hold him against his will."

Mrs. Ellison sighed.

"I never liked him," she said. "I shall never forget that common aunt of his at the wedding. Really, she might have been a charwoman."

"That's not the point——" began Viola wearily, but Mrs. Ellison interrupted her.

"I think it is, dear. I remember I was quite ashamed of our friends' meeting them. They quite definitely weren't gentlefolk. I remember the aunt spoke just like a comedian."

Mrs. Ellison's chief experience of the more northerly dialects had been in connection with comedians, and she could never dissociate the two.

"But, Mother," said Viola unhappily. "Humphrey and I . . ."

She wanted to tell her mother about the long years of companionship, of, as she had thought, happiness, of how cruelly Humphrey's desertion had hurt her. She remembered her mother's tender sympathy when Gray died. But the years had separated them, and the older woman's world had closed round her so that she couldn't see anything beyond it.

"Of course, darling," she was saying, "I know that people *do* get divorced nowadays."

She classed divorce with flying and ribbon roads and cocktail parties and people combing their hair in public. There had been divorces in her day, of course, but they had been portentous affairs of which one spoke in whispers, and the participants were branded for ever afterwards. Nowadays it was different. She didn't try to understand it, any more than she would have tried to learn to fly.

"And you'd get rid of those dreadful relations," she went on. "I don't know how you've endured them all these years."

"I wondered if Father . . ." began Viola, then stopped.

Before she came it had seemed so obvious that Father should take over the business of the divorce for her, interview the lawyer, manage everything. . . . It seemed less obvious now.

"Oh, darling," said Mrs. Ellison, dismayed, "I don't think we'd better tell Father about it. It might upset him."

"I don't think it would," said Viola a little bitterly.

"It might," said Mrs. Ellison. "He's getting old, you know, dear.

Things do upset him. He was awfully upset really about that dry-rot in Rose Cottage."

"But he'll see it in the papers," protested Viola.

"No, he won't, dear. He never reads that sort of thing. Neither of us do."

"But someone else might see it and tell him."

"In that case, of course, he'd have to know, but we needn't tell him. He never liked Humphrey either, dear. He often said that there was absolutely nothing one could talk to him about."

There was a short silence.

She doesn't want him to know because she doesn't want to know herself, thought Viola. As long as he doesn't know she can pretend not to. ... In any case it's not real to her. Nothing outside her house and garden is real to her. ...

Mrs. Ellison rose from her seat on the bed.

"Now, darling," she said affectionately, "you mustn't worry about it. You're doing what you think right and that's all that matters. Things are quite different from what they were when I was young, and it isn't as if Humphrey were anyone we really *knew*. I mean, we aren't likely ever to run into his people or anything of that sort. That would have made it a bit awkward, I suppose. ... That *dreadful* aunt!"

Viola smiled wanly. She was trying not to feel resentful. She knew that if she had broken her leg or were going to have a baby, no one would have been kinder and more helpful than her mother. It was just that this lay outside her line of vision.

"Goodnight, my darling."

"Goodnight, Mother."

"And don't worry, my pet. ... You're *sure* there's nothing else you'd like? Not a nice glass of hot milk?"

"No, thank you."

Mrs. Ellison kissed her again and went back along the corridor to her own room.'

She was thinking of this divorce of Viola's, conscientiously trying to feel as worried about it as she was about Carlo's illness, but somehow she couldn't.

Viola still sat on the bed, staring in front of her.

A few hours ago she had taken for granted that she would make her future home here, but she realised now how impossible that was. It had never even occurred to her mother to suggest it. There was no place for her in the enclosed ordered life of this house. Her mother's lack of sympathy had hurt her deeply, but she realised that it was natural. Her mother was an old woman. She had forgotten how cruelly things hurt when you were young. Her thoughts turned to Frances. Frances belonged to her own generation. Though she had now won through to peace, she must have suffered acutely at Robin's death. During their girlhood in this old house they had shared every joy and sorrow. Surely Frances would understand. . . . She had heard Frances come to her room while she and her mother were talking. She went along the passage and tapped softly at the door.

"Come in."

Viola entered. The room was plain and austere, like a schoolgirl's room—no fallals or frivolities, no pots of face cream or bottles of lotion. The dressing-table was bare except for brush and comb, hand-mirror, and pin-cushion. Some old school groups—prefects, hockey elevens—hung on the wall. On her chest of drawers was a large framed photograph of Robin in uniform. It had been taken on his first leave, just after Frances got engaged to him. He had had only one more leave after that before he was killed by a sniper as he was entering his dug-out. Frances had locked herself in her room—this room—on hearing the news, and for two days had refused to come out or speak to anyone. Then she had come out—white and worn-looking, but with a kind of radiance about her.

"He's nearer to me even than he was when he was alive," she had said to Viola. "He's with me all the time. . . ."

And through the long years the conviction had remained.

"Only Robin's real to me," she said. "Other people are just like shadows."

She was standing at her dressing-table now, in her plain tailored dressing-gown, brushing the hair that had once been luxuriant and

29

glossy, the colour of burnished copper, but was now thin and faded. It was characteristic of Frances that she stood—never sat—at her dressing-table. As Viola looked at her, a rush of envy swept over her. Life couldn't hurt Frances any more. She was secure in her remote mysterious happiness.

"Hallo," said Frances, with faint surprise.

She laid down her brush, plaited her hair into a thin greyish plait, then carefully drew the comb across the brush, made the combings into a neat ball, and dropped it into the old-fashioned "hair tidy" that hung from the looking-glass.

Viola, sat down on the cretonne-covered box-ottoman at the foot of the bed and watched her. It was going to be harder than she had thought it would be to confide in Frances. She had never realised till now how terribly and imperceptibly the years separated people—made them strangers to each other, though once they had known each other's every feeling. One glance would have told the old Frances that she was in trouble. This Frances looked at her indifferently, slightly bored by her presence, wondering, without much interest, why she had come, and how long she was going to stay. But she was still Frances, thought Viola rebelliously, the elder sister who had comforted her in all her childish troubles. Surely she would comfort her now if she knew she needed it more than she had ever needed it in her life before.

"Haven't you started going to bed yet?" said Frances, glancing at the black dinner-dress that Viola still wore.

"No. . . . Frances, were you surprised when you heard that I was coming over today?"

"No," said Frances, after a slight pause. "I don't think I was. You do come over sometimes, you know."

"I've not been lately. . . . Frances, I'm going to divorce Humphrey."

Frances gave her a baffling expressionless glance.

"Why?"

"Another woman is having a child by him."

"Do you care?"

"Of course I care."

Frances took up the dress that she had worn during the day and that lay over a chair, put it on a hanger, and hung it up in the wardrobe without speaking.

"You might be nice to me, Frances," said Viola unsteadily. She knew that she was speaking like the spoilt little girl who had once claimed Frances's sympathy as a right, but she couldn't help it. She had never dreamed that her homecoming would be like this. "I thought you'd be sure to understand."

Frances turned round from the wardrobe.

"Why should I?" she said.

Viola stared at her.

"I don't know. I thought . . . I mean—you've had your happiness, and nothing can take it away from you. You've still got Robin. I've lost Humphrey for ever."

Frances's lips took on a tight line.

"What do you mean, I've still got Robin?" she said.

"Well, you said—you've always said——"

Frances caught her up, speaking in a harsh angry voice that Viola had never heard from her before.

"I know I have. I made my bed and I must lie on it. I'm not complaining, am I? I don't go running about crying for sympathy, so why should you?"

Viola looked at her, bewildered and aghast. "I don't know what you mean," she faltered.

Frances sat down, wrapping her dressing-gown about her, staring straight in front of her. Her face looked worn and haggard under the hard electric light.

"I'll tell you, then," she said, speaking still in that hard angry voice. "At first it was—as I said. Robin did seem to be with me all the time. Nothing and no one else in the whole world existed. And then—very gradually—it all went. So I started pretending. Year after year. Pretending that he was still real to me, and trying to make myself believe it. Mother and Father and everyone takes for granted, even now, that it's still the same, that I'm still quite 'happy with my memories.' " Her lips twisted bitterly. "That's the way they put it. I'm still pointed out as a monument of constancy and faithfulness."

"And don't you——?" gasped Viola.

"I don't even remember what he looked like. I shouldn't know him if I met him in the street tomorrow." She turned to the photograph of the pleasant characterless young face—regular features, a small moustache, cap at the correct angle. "It's just a photograph. It might be anyone. I don't remember anything about him or even want to. He's much less real than the postman or the village policeman. I know that I was once engaged to him, but it means nothing. I don't want to meet him again. I'd hate to."

"But, Frances," said Viola, "when—it went, why did you—pretend——"

"I had to," said Frances defiantly. "There was nothing else to do. I'd shut myself in a sort of prison, and I couldn't get out. There wasn't any other sort of life left for me. No one in the whole world needed me. No one *has* needed me for years."

"Mother and Father have, surely," protested Viola.

"No, they haven't. They've never really needed anyone except each other."

Viola considered this in silence. It was true. They had always been tender, considerate, indulgent parents, but they had never really needed anyone except each other.

"But your work——" she said. "Your Women's Institute and Girl Guides and——"

"I *hate* them," burst out Frances in a voice that quivered with pent-up emotion, "but I've got to do something. I can't just sit and think what a blasted fool I've been. So I go on pretending that I love it all and that I'm faithful to Robin. . . . And, of course, I *am* faithful to him. I've got to be, whether I want to or not. . . . When I think how I've wasted my life I could kill myself. Did you know that Brian Harvey proposed to me the year after Robin was killed?"

"Yes. I remember. . . ."

"And Martin Howard proposed just after you married. I could have married half a dozen times in those years if I'd wanted to. I might have had children. I might have had a son of Hilary's age. But it's too late for anything now." She turned on Viola. "And you come moaning and bleating that you're unhappy. Well, you've come to the wrong quarter for sympathy. I envy you. You're lucky to have something to be unhappy about. I wish to God I had. . . ."

She dropped her head suddenly into her hands.

Viola fell on her knees beside her and tried to gather her into her arms. "Francie. . . . Francie, darling . . ." But Frances shrank from her, keeping her face still hidden.

"Go away," she said in a stifled voice. "I don't want you. I don't want anyone. . . . Please go."

Viola got up and went slowly, dazedly, to her own room. The whole world seemed to be full of unhappiness.

Chapter Four

BRIDGET stood in front of her dressing-table mirror examining her reflection, an anxious frown on her round childish face. No, she *didn't* look as she knew Mother wanted her to look.

It was an expensive dress, but somehow expensive dresses never looked expensive on her. She was too plump and dumpy, and there was something incurably schoolgirlish about her appearance, though she had left school now more than a year ago.

The dress was of printed crêpe-de-chine with a soft cowl collar and short sleeves. It would have looked very smart on Elaine. Everything Elaine wore looked smart. She had quick clever fingers, and could make a dress for a few shillings that you would have thought cost six or seven pounds. It was maddening for Mother, because Aunt Aggie took no trouble at all over Elaine's clothes, and Mother took endless trouble over hers, and Elaine always looked the smarter.

Today's, fortunately, wasn't an important tea-party, because only the family was coming—Aunt Hester, Aunt Harriet, Aunt Aggie, Elaine, and Monica, and perhaps Aunt Viola. Uncle Humphrey, of course, was always too busy to go out to tea, and in any case he was in London on business just now. Aunt Viola had been home on Thursday to see her mother (who was not very well) but she had only stayed one night and had returned to Reddington yesterday. She had sent a message this morning to say that she had a headache and might not be able to come. Bridget hoped that she would come. She was so different from the others. . . . Bridget had admired her ever since she could remember, but her admiration made her even more shy and tongue-tied with her than she was with other people. It was only with Uncle Humphrey that she lost the feeling of uncertainty and bewilderment that was her usual attitude to life. Her shyness didn't seem to matter with him. He, too, was silent and reserved, never saying more than was necessary. You were aware of his kindness and understanding all the time, but there was no need of words. She had only been a few months old when her own father died, and the photograph of the somewhat sharp-featured man with high forehead and clerical collar meant nothing to her, but she had often comforted herself in her childish troubles by pretending that she was Uncle Humphrey's little girl. And Aunt Viola—beautiful, remote, like someone from another world—added the final touch of glamour. They were both perfect, and it was inevitable that their love for each other should be the perfect love of legend and romance. The prince and princess in her fairy tales had always been Uncle Humphrey and Aunt Viola. Later they had become Richard and Berengaria, Dante and Beatrice, Tristram and Iseult—all the lovers she had ever read or heard of.

Then her thoughts went back to Mother, and the cloud settled again on the smooth young brow. The root of the trouble with Mother, of course, was her failure to become the sort of person that Mother wanted her to be. Things hadn't been so bad before she went to the school in Harrogate, because she had been too young to have any place in Mother's life, and Mother had been too busy to take much notice of her. It was after she went to Harrogate that the trouble began. Her shyness and diffidence prevented her making friends easily, and this annoyed Mother, who was very anxious for her to make friends—to make friends, that is, with the right people. It was for this reason, Bridget gathered, that she had been sent to an expensive school, and the money would be wasted if she failed to play her part. Mother certainly didn't fail to play hers. She would swoop down on flying visits, choose out girls whose parents were wealthy or influential, make herself devastatingly charming to them, then depart, leaving the rest to Bridget. Even after she returned to Reddington her letters would be full of affectionate messages and flattering allusions that Bridget knew she was meant to show to the chosen "friends," but never did. Invariably the friendships, so carefully engineered, would lapse. For one reason the girls were seldom the type of girls that Bridget would herself have selected as friends. They were smart, assured, rather like Mother. And the shy slow friendships that Bridget formed naturally with more congenial girls were never allowed to ripen. Either Mother disapproved and did all she could to discourage them (and there was a quiet persistence beneath her sweetness that was almost impossible to resist), or she approved and was so gushingly affectionate that it made Bridget ashamed.

She was acutely aware of her mother's disappointment when she left school without having made any friends that could be described as "useful." And the situation was even more difficult when she came to live at home. Evidently the grown-up world of Reddington contained mysterious social boundaries and demarcations whose existence Bridget had never before suspected. There were the people who "belonged" to the town, who had been born and bred in it, who worked in it and loved it and were proud of it, who were Councillors and J.P.s and Aldermen, and subscribed large sums to its charities. Uncle Humphrey was one of these, and Bridget had always thought that they were the most important people in the town. But now she discovered that there was another more exclusive set who despised Reddington and sneered at it, though circumstances compelled them to live there. They formed the local "smart set," looked upon themselves, in the Midland manufacturing town, as Royalty in exile, "ran up to Town" on every possible excuse, and found their chief recreation in bridge and the gossip of London clubs.

Bridget preferred Uncle Humphrey and his friends. They were kind and easy-going and generous and understanding, even if they dressed badly and spoke with a Midland accent. But Mother disliked them, and despised Aunt Viola for being content to remain among them when she might so easily have entered the other set, and, what was more important, have helped Mother to enter it. It was a shock to Bridget to realise, on leaving school, that she was expected to play her part in this social campaign. Mother had managed, with some difficulty, to get her elected to the most select tennis and badminton clubs of the district, and Bridget conscientiously attended them, but, as in her schooldays, the knowledge that she was expected to make "useful" friends paralysed her. The girls were all of the same type—hard and bright and sophisticated—and she felt awkward and ill-at-ease with them, aware always of Mother waiting at home to catechise her on her return. ("Whom did you talk to, dear?" . . . "What did you say?")

Mother had discouraged all the friendships she had formed before she went to Harrogate, and the only one that she had managed to retain was with Lucy Wheeler. Lucy had been her greatest friend at the Reddington High School, and Bridget had refused to give up the friendship despite all Mother's tacit opposition.

It was not that she was particularly fond of Lucy—indeed the glamour that had invested Lucy in the old days had disconcertingly faded—but a sense of dogged loyalty made her cling to the friendship. She wouldn't drop Lucy just because she wasn't grand enough for Mother. Actually, now, her friendship was more with Terry, Lucy's brother, than with Lucy, though she met him seldom and neither had much to say to the other when they did meet. She had with him the same feeling of security and peace that she had with Uncle Humphrey, a feeling that seemed to her, strangely, to be one of home-coming, though it had nothing to do with her own home. The thought of him brought with it a sense of happiness so fragile and tenuous that she dared not examine it too closely for fear it should vanish. Often, when she would have turned to it for comfort she refused, because she was afraid of finding that it was no longer there. Terry, who had a post as junior clerk in a not very flourishing insurance society, was shy and rather stupid, just as she was herself, and though Bridget didn't think him ugly most other people did.

Mother disliked him intensely, especially since she had got to know Roy Hamwell. Roy was the only son of Robert Hamwell, who was a cousin of Lord Fernhurst and managed his Reddington property for him. Lord Fernhurst himself lived in feudal glory in Somerset, and the glory was fully reflected by his Reddington kinsman and representative. The Hamwells lived at Furness House, three miles outside Reddington, and were County in all its implications. Acquaintanceship with them was the uttermost goal of the local social climbers, just as marriage with Roy was the secret dream of most of Reddington's unmarried girls. Roy had met Bridget first at the tennis club and had pursued the acquaintance zestfully, despite her obvious avoidance of him. He was thin and dark and handsome, with a touch of arrogance in his manner and an almost feline grace in his movements. Moreover, he was good company—gay, witty, and pleasantly cynical—and even Bridget, though she avoided him and was paralysed by nervousness when with him, felt beneath her nervousness a certain secret excitement that she would not admit even to herself. She didn't like it or understand it. It was quite different from the happiness that she felt when she was with Terry. . . .

She took up her hand-glass and anxiously studied the back of her head. Other people's hair seemed to go into place easily and stay there docilely, but hers was straight and thick and difficult to manage. It irritated Mother when ends escaped from the roll and fell untidily about her neck. It didn't matter so much today, however, she reminded herself again, because it was only the family. Yesterday had been dreadful. The guests had been Mother's smartest friends. She had felt nervous and inadequate from the beginning. "Do try to talk to people more," Mother had said before they came. "It's ridiculous to be so shy at your age. You ought to be able to help me entertain. Remember you're grown-up now."

The trouble was that Bridget didn't feel grownup. She still felt a little girl—perplexed and awkward and afraid. She had tried very hard yesterday to be bright and sophisticated as Mother wanted her to be, and it had been a hopeless failure. She had been even more tongue-tied than usual, and the frown with which Mother watched her only increased her nervousness. To make matters worse, Roy had been there. He did not usually attend bridge parties, and his presence yesterday had been considered "pointed" by the other guests. He had watched Bridget all the time and tried to talk to her whenever he got an opportunity, but she had avoided him in a panic-like access of shyness. When he said goodbye he had asked her to go to the pictures with him the following Wednesday, but she had said (quite truly) that she was going to tea with Lucy Wheeler (Mother's frown had deepened at that) and he had made no further suggestion.

Bridget started as the door opened and Doreen entered.

"Aren't you ready yet, dear?" said Doreen.

She spoke sweetly as ever, but with a sweetness that hardly attempted to conceal the irritation beneath it. There the child was, dawdling and mooning about her bedroom as if there was nothing to do downstairs. . . .

Everything about Bridget, even her clumsiness of build, exasperated Doreen, who was herself small and graceful and vivacious, as quick in mind as in movement. In her black-and-red dress she suggested some darting, brilliantly coloured bird. She looked at Bridget with the familiar critical frown. The child had some quite good points—the thick glossy blond hair, blue eyes, and clear complexion—but she simply wouldn't learn to make the best of them, and it was so disheartening trying to teach her, like whoever it was who kept rolling a heavy stone up a hill only to see it roll down again.

By a piece of good luck she had managed to attract young Hamwell (Heaven only knew how) and she behaved with him as if he were a table or a chair. She could have slapped her yesterday—telling him she couldn't go to the pictures with him because she was going to tea with Lucy Wheeler! Lucy Wheeler of all people! A feeling of pathos invaded Doreen's irritation. She worked herself to skin and bone for the child, trying to give her a chance in life, and she got no help or thanks or encouragement. After all, it was only Bridget she was working for. She assured herself of this quite frequently. All the trouble she took to get to know the right people was only a mother's self-sacrifice for her child. She wouldn't have grudged the trouble if only Bridget would help, would, at any rate, try to cultivate an ordinary sense of social values.

She began to pull the dress into shape on the shoulders and about the waist. Beside her mother's neat trim figure Bridget always felt uncomfortably large and clumsy and unfinished.

"I'm rather disappointed in this dress, dear," said Doreen, still quite pleasantly.

She prided herself on never letting the child see the exasperation she so frequently caused her.

"I'm afraid it's me," said Bridget apologetically. "I'm too fat."

She wished that Mother would be cross straight out about things. It would be so much better than pretending to be nice about them.

"Have you got your new corset-belt on?"

"No, not the new one."

The new one was made of rubber, and Bridget always tried to get out of wearing it because it was too long and too tight.

"Oh well, I suppose it doesn't matter today."

She smoothed Bridget's gleaming hair back into the little roll, flattening it tightly against her head. Her hard bright eyes were unusually soft. She was dreaming that Bridget was Roy Hamwell's wife. She'd be able to pay back Mrs. Hamwell then for some of the snubs she'd endured so patiently in the past few years.

"Darling," she said suddenly, "I wish you'd ask Roy to propose you for the dramatic society. The one his sister's got up."

Bridget's heart sank in sudden dismay. "But, Mother, I can't act, and I—I hardly know his sister or any of them."

"Well, really, Bridget," said Doreen pathetically, "when I'm doing all I possibly can for you I do think you might help just a little."

A familiar feeling of shame swept over Bridget. She remembered having had the feeling first when she was quite a little girl. She had been brought down to the drawing-room after tea, and the visitors had praised her dress and appearance and manners, while Mother had sat with a complacent smile on her lips. And in a sudden illuminating flash Bridget had known that her mother's much-vaunted love of her was in reality a love of herself, and that she existed in her mother's eyes solely to reflect credit on her. She had hated the knowledge, fought against it, refused to recognise it, but it had been there, hidden at the back of her mind, ever since.

"I'm sorry ..." she said unhappily.

"Well, never mind, darling," said Doreen cheerfully. "Let's go downstairs now, shall we?"

She went briskly down the staircase, followed more slowly by Bridget.

The house was small, but light and airy and pleasantly furnished. By dint of various makeshifts it managed to create an atmosphere of ample means, even of luxury. There was a large number of "best" things that were only put out when visitors were expected and so never got worn or shabby—the blue satin cushions, the white hearthrug, the table-runner of Chinese embroidery, the hand-painted vellum lampshade, the elaborate doll telephone-cover. Mrs. Hamwell had once called to see Doreen, three or four years ago, about the arrangements for a Church bazaar that she was to open, and Doreen still kept her card on the top of all the others on the silver salver on the hall table.

The general servant, Annie, was on her knees on the hearthrug, putting a light to the fire, for though it was summer by the calendar the day was cold and raw. Doreen engaged a general servant and an occasional charwoman, whose working hours were carefully selected so as not to include a meal, but she always referred to "the maids," and tried to give the impression that she kept at least a cook and housemaid.

"I told you that was to be done by half-past three," said Doreen sharply.

The tone in which Doreen addressed her servants always made Bridget feel hotly uncomfortable. Doreen had an odd hatred of her servants that she never understood or tried to understand. She hated them just for being servants. She resented the consideration that one was forced to show them nowadays. She would have liked to live in the days when you could make them sleep anywhere and eat anything, and keep them hard at work all day long for a few pounds a year. She approached the standards of those days as nearly as she dared. She bought food of inferior quality for them, doled it out sparingly, and kept all food locked up between meals. She never spoke to them except to find fault or give orders. She tried to hide her dislike of them, but it showed in every word and look—a deep, unreasoning, vicious dislike. They were constantly giving notice, and she was finding it more and more difficult to get new ones. She had a "bad name" at the local registry offices. Exaggerated stories of her meanness were exchanged at G.F.S. meetings and over tradesmen's counters.

The girl muttered sulkily and rose from her knees.

"Don't speak to me like that," snapped Doreen. "Go into the kitchen and cut the bread and butter."

The girl went out, slamming the door behind her.

"Insolence!" said Doreen angrily.

She looked round the room and moved a vase of marigolds from the mantelpiece where the heat of the fire might make them fade sooner. She never bought flowers unless she was expecting visitors. Every penny of her income was budgeted, and the whole object of her expenditure was to appear to have twice as large an income as she actually had. It involved a hundred little make-shifts and meannesses and subterfuges and lies, but these Doreen enjoyed. They added a zest to life. She often wished she had a daughter who would help and understand better than Bridget did. . . .

She sat down in an armchair with a faint sigh. It would be a dull afternoon, and she'd be glad to get it over. She generally had the family to tea on the day after she'd given a party. It served the twofold purpose of disposing of the surplus food and of disarming criticism. People couldn't say that she was ashamed of her own people if she had them to tea at regular intervals like this. After all, it wasn't her fault that they were all so unpresentable. . . . The only presentable one was Viola, and Doreen's small tight mouth tightened still further when she thought of her. Viola could so easily have helped her to know the people she wanted to know—the fact that she was an Ellison and a baronet's granddaughter counted tremendously in Reddington—but she had remained impervious to all her hints. . . . Stupid, spiteful, and conceited. She, Doreen, had never liked her, even in those early days when everyone else had been raving about her. Funny that she never asked any of those grand relations of hers to stay with her in Reddington. Hilary, too. . . . A conceited young puppy. Hardly ever condescended to visit Reddington at all. . . . She wondered if Viola would come to tea today. That message about a headache was probably only an excuse, though, to do Viola justice, she generally came to family gatherings. It was Doreen's invitations to other parties that she always refused.

"Here's Aunt Viola," said Bridget suddenly, starting up from her seat and going to the door.

"Sit down, Bridget," said Doreen sharply, "and let Annie show her in properly."

She had noticed with annoyance the look of pleasure that had flashed onto Bridget's face. Ridiculous, the fuss she made of Humphrey and Viola, running off to their house whenever she got the chance! It wasn't as if they ever made the slightest effort to be of use to her socially.

Annie threw open the door and muttered sulkily, "Mrs. Lessington."

Viola entered, and Doreen's eyes ran sharply over her figure. A new coat, but not one of those really fashionable ones. A hat that might have been last year's, though it probably wasn't. She didn't wear smart clothes, and yet somehow she always looked smart. This annoyed Doreen, who herself could only achieve an appearance of smartness by some striking exaggeration of the fashionable mode. Her sharp eyes noticed, too, that Viola looked pale and tired.

She rose from her chair with a bright smile and an elaborate affectation of graciousness. Doreen always flattered herself on knowing how to play the hostess.

"So glad you could come, dear," she gushed. "I *do* hope the headache's better. Sit down, won't you?"

Viola sat down and began to draw off her gloves absently.

"I'm afraid I can't stay long, Doreen," she said, "but I thought I'd just drop in and see you before the others came."

She was looking at Doreen with a curious remote interest. It was strange that the small tight mouth and sharp hard eyes should give the effect of prettiness, but they did. At first sight you would have called Doreen a pretty woman. ... It had always surprised her that she should be Humphrey's sister. There was nothing vulgar about Humphrey, for all his uncouthness and the Midland burr of his speech, but this little woman, with her clipped refined speech and elegant manners, was vulgarity itself. As she looked at her she had a sudden irrelevant memory of meeting her for lunch once in London in the early days of her marriage. Doreen had been shopping at Parnell's, but she had brought out with her a paper carrier of Debenham & Freebody's in order to slip the Parnell purchases into it.

"Did you enjoy your visit home, dear?" said Doreen. "Quite a short visit, wasn't it? I should have thought you'd have stayed longer."

"I only went for the one night."

"Did you find your mother better?"

"Yes, thank you."

Viola turned to Bridget, and the unguarded love and admiration in the child's eyes caught suddenly at her heart. She had always been faintly antagonistic to Bridget—resenting, almost unconsciously, Humphrey's affection for her—and the stab of tender compunction took her by surprise. Bridget had put Humphrey on a pedestal, and his fall from it would kill something that might never come to life again.

She drew a letter from her bag and handed it to Bridget.

"Bridget, dear," she said, "will you just run to the post with this for me? It'll save my going on to the end of the road. Do you mind?"

"I'd love to," said Bridget, springing to her feet.

Her heart was singing happily. With Aunt Viola's entrance had come the something of serenity and gentleness that always accompanied her, that had its being, Bridget thought shyly, in the love between her and Uncle Humphrey. Fears and bewilderments melted away in the warmth and light of it.

When she had gone Viola turned to her sister-in-law.

"I sent Bridget away, Doreen, because I wanted to speak to you alone."

"Yes?" said Doreen.

Viola went on, speaking as if with an effort, her pale face set and strained.

"You'll have to know sooner or later, and I thought I'd better tell you now. Perhaps you'll tell the others, will you? I'm divorcing

Humphrey. He's in love with another woman and she is going to have a child by him."

Doreen looked at her in silence, while a great triumph surged in her heart. So this was what it all came to—her airs and graces, her superiority and grand relations! She hadn't been able to hold even an ordinary man like Humphrey. Behind the triumph was an avid relish. She leant forward and put her hand on Viola's.

"Darling," she said, "do tell me all about it."

Viola pulled her hand away with a jerk and stood up. She was trembling. The futile pretence of sympathy, the morbid gloating curiosity, nauseated her, and the old longing for Humphrey, which the presence of anyone uncongenial always brought to her, swept over her, together with the knowledge that this refuge for her hurt of spirit was closed for ever. Doreen was watching her narrowly.

"Let me get you some water," she said, starting up from her seat.

Viola mastered the sudden faintness that had made the room swim before her eyes.

"No ... please ... I'm all right. You'll tell the others, won't you? ... But"—she hesitated—"please don't tell Bridget just yet. Don't let her know till she has to. Will you do this for me, Doreen?"

"Yes, of course," said Doreen, pursing her lips primly and assuming an expression of extreme fastidiousness. "I've always tried to keep that sort of thing away from her."

Chapter Five

HARRIET LESSINGTON opened the oven door and cast an experienced eye upon its contents—a stew bubbling invitingly in a small casserole and a bread-and-butter pudding just nicely browning. A savoury smell and a wave of heated air was wafted into the kitchen, which shone with almost ostentatious cleanliness.

The "woman" came to do the rough work on Tuesdays and Fridays, but Harriet much preferred the days when she had the little house to herself and could potter about at her leisure. The little house was Harriet's hobby, her pride and comfort and delight. She loved polishing and scouring and cleaning and cooking. She loved to see it spotless and shipshape—the surface of furniture and linoleum reflecting the light from a gleaming sheath of polish. Hester did her share of the work, of course, but Hester was delicate and dreamy and not very much interested in housework, and Harriet would often do her work over again, but secretly, so that Hester should not be hurt.

Hester had a slight cold today, and Harriet wasn't quite sure that she ought to go to tea to Doreen's this afternoon. Hester's slight colds so soon became bad ones, and then they went to her chest, and it was a case of linseed poultices and camphorated oil and two or three days in bed. Harriet had looked after her ever since their childhood, making her change her things when she had been out in the rain, anxiously fending off her coughs with doses and chest-rubbings, darning her stockings, seeing to her clothes, scolding her affectionately for her vagueness and absent-mindedness. To Harriet, Hester was still the little girl whose hand she always held on the way to school, and who had to be piloted carefully

46

over crossings and sheltered from anything that might distress or harm her.

The door opened, and Hester came in.

"I'm so sorry, Harriet," she said. "I'd forgotten the time. Can I help?"

"There are the potatoes to pour, dear," said Harriet, "and then that's all. I'm just going to get the stew out."

She turned off the gas, took the oven-cloth from the nail by the oven, and lifted the casserole on to the earthenware dish, set ready on the table.

Hester poured the potatoes into a colander at the sink.

"We'd better go in our grey costumes this afternoon—don't you think?" said Harriet. "It's really none too warm."

"I suppose so," said Hester in a slightly constrained voice.

Harriet glanced at her. Hester was sometimes a little moody. One just ignored it and she soon came round.

They carried the dishes into the dining-room, Harriet slipped off her apron, and they sat down to the meal.

The room was furnished in middle-class Victorian style. There was the inevitable dining-room suite, the chairs upholstered in leather, the sideboard supporting an elaborately carved back. The overmantel, too, was elaborately carved and consisted of one large mirror, several small ones, and half a dozen tiny shelves, each of which was occupied by a china ornament. In the centre of the mantel-piece was an ormulu clock, which Harriet always kept ten minutes fast so as to be on the safe side, and, flanking it, two bronze figures in a state of semi-nudity engaged in an apparently unequal struggle with refractory steeds. An ink-pot stood by one horse's head and a mug of spills by the other, as if to prevent them from plunging from the shelf on to the hearthrug, which Harriet had made twenty years ago from a job-lot of mixed thrums. At the window was a basket-work fern-stand that held four ferns, and on the wall hung a framed Testimonial that had been presented to the twins' father by his Bible Class on his marriage.

This was the sisters' living-room. The drawing-room (furnished with a green plush suite) was only used on the rare occasions when they entertained.

"It's a very good stew, Harriet," said Hester.

There was an apologetic note in her voice. She was feeling a familiar sense of compunction at the memory of her recent moodiness. It was so wicked to let herself be irritated by Harriet, who was so good and kind and loved her so dearly.

"Yes, it's quite good, isn't it?" said Harriet.

She felt warmly gratified by Hester's approval. She took a lot of trouble to prepare nourishing appetising meals, and as often as not Hester didn't even notice what she was eating.

There was a silence, then Harriet said, "I think we might let Miss Porter make up that navy blue silk soon. We really need another summer dress."

The twins had dressed alike all their lives. It was Harriet, of course, who had charge of their wardrobe, who decided when they were to discard old dresses and have new ones made; Harriet who bought lengths of dark good material at reduced prices during the sales and kept them in the bottom drawer of the big chest of drawers till they were needed.

Their dresses were always made in the same style—straight skirts, and bodices with small V necks, in which they wore little fronts of net.

"Yes," said Hester. "That will be very nice."

She spoke absently. She wasn't thinking of the new dresses. She was wondering who would be at Doreen's this afternoon. Viola had gone home on Thursday and would hardly have got back yet. Humphrey never came to tea-parties except just to call for Viola on his way from the shop and take her home. And, anyway, he was in London on business just now. Bridget would be there, of course, and Aggie and Monica and perhaps Elaine. Hester was secretly a little afraid of Elaine. She was always very polite, but she made Hester feel old and plain and slightly ridiculous. Elaine worked at Randolph's, a firm of patent medicine manufacturers in Burchester, but would be free this afternoon as it was Saturday.

"I suppose Elaine will be there," she said.

"Yes," said Harriet grimly. "Bossing Aggie about as usual. Really, Aggie has brought up those children very badly."

Harriet was always saying that people had brought up their children badly. Hester thought it rather silly of her, but she'd noticed that people who had no children always knew how they ought to be brought up.

The twins went on with their meal in silence. In their childhood they had been generally supposed to be so much alike that it was impossible to recognise them apart, and the idea still persisted, though the likeness was now only a superficial one. Both had thin faces, small decisive features, brown eyes, and mouse-coloured hair turning grey, strained into small neat buns at the back of their heads. But, whereas Harriet's eyes were sharp and shrewd, Hester's were vague and dreamy; whereas Harriet's mouth was, though quite kindly, tight and firm, Hester's was tremulous and sensitive. When they were young you would have thought Hester pretty if you'd seen her alone, but, when they were together, she was so like Harriet that you knew she couldn't be.

"I'm glad we left Gilchrist's," Harriet was saying. "Warne's meat is so much better."

"Yes, isn't it?" said Hester, trying conscientiously to be interested in Warne's meat.

"But I shouldn't have left him, of course, if he hadn't kept on charging as much for two or three ounces over the pound as for a whole quarter. And not just once or twice, either. It couldn't have been a mistake."

"Of course not," agreed Hester.

She was wondering whether to take refuge in her Escape, but decided not to—not just yet, anyway. To know that it was there and yet not to go to it made the final going to it all the more satisfying.

Hester changed the plates, and Harriet brought in the pudding, throwing a complacent glance at the gleaming sideboard as she did so.

"It really is worth while making polish from that recipe of

Mother's," she said. "It's a lot of trouble, but nothing you can buy is as good."

Hester was back in the little shop in Parker Street where they had spent their childhood. Mother was making polish in the kitchen, and the mingled smell of bees-wax, ammonia, and turpentine hung over everything. Customers would smell it and wrinkle up their noses and say, "Whatever's that?" and Father would smile and say, "It's the wife making furniture polish. She won't have any tinned stuff. Not even furniture polish."

The kitchen was in the basement, and the living-room on the first floor. (The little room behind the shop was used as a store-room.) At the bend in the staircase was a plant in a bamboo plant-stand, with long pale leaves, which Mother sponged with milk on Wednesday mornings when she did the stairs. The shop was small and dark and crowded. Bales of materials overflowed the counter and were piled on the floor. Garishly loloured tablecloths and antimacassars hung from strings stretched across the ceiling. The space behind the counter was full of boxes of buttons, hooks and eyes, tapes, sewing cotton, needles, pins, ribbon, embroidery silks, and darning wools. The window—a heterogeneous jumble of odds and ends—was never altered from year's end to year's end, and inside the shop it was so dark even at midday that you had to take things to the door in order to be quite sure of the colour. The two gas jets, though they made the atmosphere friendly and cosy and emitted a pleasant little popping sound at regular intervals, gave very little light. In the darkest corner of the shop stood a headless dummy, dressed in a maid's print dress and white apron. This figure played its part in all Hester's imaginary games, and sometimes invaded her dreams, a beneficent protective presence. Hester had always loved the shop, but Josiah, their brother, had hated it. He had no patience with their father's shiftless easy-going ways and the higgledy-piggledy place where nothing was where it should be and you had to hunt through endless drawers and boxes to find anything. He disapproved of the select band of their father's cronies, who used to foregather in the evening and talk politics over the counter. It wasn't Business, he said sternly. It kept Real

Custom away. Both Father and Mother stood in awe of Josiah. He was so capable and efficient, so impatient of the small horizon that had always satisfied them.

Mother had been short and stout and shiningly clean and neat. The kitchen was the centre of her world. Like Harriet, she loved to cook and pickle and preserve and scour and polish and bustle about, wearing the large blue-and-white check apron that had always seemed an inseparable part of her. She hardly ever went out of doors. When she wanted a change from her housework, she would go down into the shop and gossip with the customers. Both she and her husband used to let their, friends have anything they liked from the shop. "Pay when you like," they would say. "Any time will do."

As soon as Father died this state of things came abruptly to an end. Josiah turned Mother and the twins out of the shop and set them up in this little house at the other end of the town. He wanted them to be as far away from the business as possible.

"But Josiah, dear," Mother had pleaded tearfully, "we can help. We can all serve in the shop. I know the business through and through."

"You may have known my father's business," said Josiah grimly, "but you don't know mine. And I don't want any of you messing about in the shop."

So they had departed from the warm, dark, hugger-mugger little place to this brand new villa, and Mother had busied herself in the kitchen here—cooking, cleaning, scouring, pickling, preserving—but the heart had gone out of it all. She missed her affectionate easy-going husband. She missed the cheerful gossips with the customers. She even missed Josiah, harsh and critical though he had been. She died before the end of the year, and Harriet and Hester settled down to the life they had lived ever since. Josiah had visited them occasionally—short perfunctory visits in which he told them very little about himself or the business.

But news of it reached them from one source or another. Lessington's was prospering. The old shop was closed and a new one opened in Peel Street, overlooking the Market Square. The new one gradually expanded, absorbing the shops on either side as the leases fell vacant, till now Lessington's dominated the town—a great "store," with more than twenty departments and a tearoom where the whole of fashionable Reddington gathered for coffee at eleven on Saturday morning. People who formerly would only shop in Burchester (the large manufacturing town ten miles away) now did their shopping regularly at Lessington's. It was, in fact, so grand that the twins, who had presided happily over the little shop in Parker Street, were afraid to enter it and preferred the smaller, more friendly shops at the cheaper end of the town. Humphrey had inherited Josiah's business acumen, but there was in him, too, something of his grandfather's easy-going kindliness. Or perhaps he had inherited that side of him from his mother—a sweet delicate woman who had served in the millinery department. The ambitious side of Josiah had never quite forgiven the sentimental side of him, till then unsuspected, for tricking him into this marriage. He might have done so much better for himself if he'd kept his head. . . . She had died when Humphrey was nineteen.

The sound of Harriet's voice brought Hester abruptly back to the present.

"I think we'd better take our umbrellas this afternoon," she was saying. "It doesn't look too settled."

Hester winced at the "our." It always made her feel as if she were shut up in a sort of prison with Harriet and would never, never get out. She had felt like that ever since she could remember. It would have been unbearable if she hadn't had her Escape.

Harriet was chewing with her front teeth in quick short rapid movements. She always ate like that. Sometimes it irritated Hester almost more than she could endure. Now with the irritation came the familiar pang of remorse. All her life Harriet's kindness and thoughtfulness and tenderness had surrounded her, and, instead of feeling grateful, instead of loving Harriet as much as she, Harriet, loved her, she hid this bitter resentment at her heart. She tried to conquer it, but she couldn't. It was wicked, so wicked that she sometimes felt she could have no possible hope of salvation in the world to come. Often she looked forward with dismay to the time when the secrets of all hearts should be revealed and Harriet, in her spotless robes of saintliness, should realise with what black ingratitude Hester had repaid her lifelong devotion.

"Do you remember," said Harriet suddenly, "how that old yellow cat we used to have at the shop—what was its name?"

"Tiger," supplied Hester.

"Yes, of course. . . . Tiger. Do you remember how he used to love bread-and-butter pudding? He'd stand by our chairs and mew whenever we had it."

Hester smiled faintly. It was strange to think that every single memory in her life was shared by Harriet. All except one, of course. And that was her Escape. She didn't want to think of that just now. She wanted to wait till she was alone. Somehow, even to think of it when Harriet was there made it no longer quite her own. . . .

Harriet was opening Hester's bottle of indigestion capsules and handing her one. Hester swallowed it obediently. Her indigestion and the colds she caught so easily always seemed to belong more to Harriet than to herself. Harriet took possession of them, managed them and organised them. Sometimes, when they persisted in spite of Harriet's efforts, Hester had a guilty feeling of harbouring a rebel against Harriet's authority.

The sisters washed up—Harriet washed the dishes and Hester dried—then Harriet cleaned the saucepans, while Hester put the china away. Harriet never trusted Hester with the saucepans. She never really trusted anyone but herself with the saucepans. There was something deceptive about a saucepan. It was so easy to think it was clean when it wasn't.

"And now, dear," she said, when they had taken off their aprons, folded them up, and put them in the drawer in the dresser, "you'll have time for a nice little rest before you change to go to Doreen's."

A tea-party of any sort was a social event to the sisters, and Harriet always tried to see that Hester had a rest before it, just as she had had a rest before going to a party in their childhood.

"Very well," said Hester and turned to go upstairs.

"Take your corsets off, dear," counselled Harriet solicitously from the hall, "and lie right down on your bed. We needn't start till nearly four."

Hester went into her bedroom and closed the door, but, instead of lying on the bed, she crossed to the window and sat there, gazing out over the little suburban garden.

For a few moments she surrendered herself to the exquisite relief of being alone. . . . She drew a deep breath, and a slight shiver ran through her. It was like being able to breathe after being suffocated, it held something of the ecstasy of the sudden cessation of physical pain. Her Escape was there waiting for her, but there was no hurry. Harriet would take for granted that she was trying to sleep and would be very careful not to disturb her.

At the bottom of the garden a poplar tree stood, graceful and tapering against the pale blue sky, and just at the top, as if balancing on it, was a tiny lilac-coloured cloud. Hester caught her breath as she looked at it. It was incredibly beautiful, but it wouldn't have been beautiful if Harriet had been there. Beauty could never give her its message in Harriet's presence.

Then slowly, with an almost sensuous pleasure, she turned to her Escape. Her Escape was a six-weeks' visit that Humphrey had paid her more than forty years ago, when he was five years old. Harriet had caught scarlet fever and had been removed to the Reddington fever hospital, and at the same time Janet (Josiah's wife) had to go into hospital for an operation. So it had been arranged that Mark and Doreen should go to stay with one of Janet's sisters and that Humphrey should come to Hester. So Humphrey had arrived—small, sturdy, solemn, shy. The two had got on together excellently from the beginning. There was something essentially childlike about Hester herself. She could enter his world as her right—the strange jumbled child world of fantastic adventure. He used to creep into her bed in the early morning—tousle-headed and sleepy-eyed in his miniature sleeping suit—and she would tell him stories and give him sugar biscuits from a tin that she kept for the purpose on a table by her bed.

After breakfast they would go up to Wealden Moor, carrying their lunch in a basket—egg sandwiches and the crumbly sponge-cake that Humphrey loved and lemonade in a bottle. There they would walk over the springy upland, and Humphrey would talk in the slow deliberate voice that used to irritate Josiah but that Hester loved. He held her hand, lifting small bare legs high over the big tussocks of heather.

"Let's pretend we're the only people in the world, shall we? What shall we do first?"

Such "pretending" never seemed foolish to Hester. She was almost as interested in them as Humphrey himself.

"We can take all the toys out of the toy-shops 'cause there's no one in the world but us. . . ."

"Now let's go on the sea. We can take any of the ships we like. There's no one to stop us."

They acted his favourite stories together, and Hester would be dwarf, prince, Viking, or talking animal as the story demanded. Sometimes they would eat their lunch in the garden, sitting under the poplar tree and pretending that they were Red Indians or explorers. When it rained they played in the attic—a room that fascinated Humphrey, chiefly because the water tank was there and made sudden gurgling noises. Once he had a terrifying dream in the night and came to her for comfort, clinging to her tightly, hiding his face on her breast.

The passion of protective tenderness that Hester felt for him was something quite new to her. It was the first and only time in her life that she had escaped from the prison of Harriet's possessive love. Instead of being guarded, protected, she in her turn had guarded, protected. Moreover, she had ordered her days as she pleased. She had gone out without Harriet's "Where are you going, dear?" She had read a book without Harriet's "What are you reading, dear?" She had even enjoyed having indigestion without Harriet to give her little pills after every meal. . . .

She had cried herself to sleep the night that Humphrey went home. After that, Harriet's anxious elder-sister solicitude again enclosed her, and she returned to the routine from which they had never deviated for a single day since. Her whole life seemed to have been completely uneventful except for those weeks. Her whole life seemed to have belonged more to Harriet than to herself except for that one episode. She had never told Harriet anything about those weeks. Harriet had taken for granted that she had continued their routine, and that Humphrey had played his undistinguished part in it as a child who was seen and not heard.

As the years passed by, the visit assumed an exaggerated importance in her life. The memory of it was her only outlet from Harriet's dominating care and affection. She could still go over every incident of it in her mind. She remembered exactly what Humphrey had done, exactly what he had said, on each of the separate days. When Harriet's solicitude seemed to close round her so tightly that she could scarcely breathe, she would escape from it to the moors, to the garden, to the attic, with Humphrey. It gave her a secret sense of triumph to say silently, "You think you know everything that's ever happened to me, but you don't. You don't know anything about that time when Humphrey stayed here."

She was just lacing Humphrey's shoes on the first Tuesday morning, ready to take him up to the moor (it was the day they'd found a little pool and had pretended to be an inch high and made little boats of twigs to sail across), when she heard Harriet coming upstairs. Hastily she lay down on the bed and closed her eyes.

Harriet opened the door and looked in with her kind loving smile.

"I think it's time you got up now, dear," she said. "So glad you've had a little nap."

Chapter Six

AGGIE sat with her elbows on the kitchen table and her hands clasping a large earthenware cup from which she sipped at intervals. She wore a faded overall, stained down the front and torn under the arm. Her large good-natured face was flushed with the hot tea. Her thick greying hair was bunched untidily at the back of her head. On the other side of the table sat Mrs. Mumbles, the charwoman—a thin, sharp, knife-like little woman with keen grey eyes, grey skin, and a long tight mouth. On her head was a once-black straw hat, which many years' wear and accumulation of dust had transformed (trimming and all) to a uniform grey. No one ever saw Mrs. Mumbles without her hat. She arrived in it, worked in it, departed in it, and, presumably, slept in it, for the skewer-like pin that fastened it had rusted into the straw.

Between them on the table stood a loaf of bread, a jar of jam, a bottle of milk, a bowl of sugar (for Mrs. Mumbles), and the big brown tea-pot. They were having their "elevenses."

Aggie always enjoyed her "elevenses" with Mrs. Mumbles, though it exasperated Elaine that she should sit and drink tea at the kitchen table with a charwoman. "Surely she can bring you a cup into the sitting-room on a tray, Mother, if you must have it," she would say in that short impatient tone in which she generally addressed Aggie. Aggie would have hated to have a cup on a tray in the sitting-room. What she enjoyed was this intimate little meal at the kitchen table, with the turbid stream of Mrs. Mumbles' anecdotes flowing around her. There seemed to be no end to them. Mrs. Mumbles had worked for her now for nearly a year, and the stream still flowed on, as rich and varied and dramatic as ever—every detail personally vouched for by Mrs. Mumbles.

"She may 'ave died nacheral or she may not," she was saying darkly. "That's as it may be. There's wheels within wheels an' there's a sayin' that dead men tell no tales. All I can say is that it was as measly a funeral as ever I see an' that I sor 'im only two nights after with a dressed-up piece in the Blue Lion."

"But you don't think he actually killed her?" gasped Agnes.

"Least said soonest mended," said Mrs. Mumbles. "I'm namin' no names. Let them as the cap fits put it on. But that's not the only case I could tell you of *to* my own knowledge. There's poisons that leave no trace, as the sayin' is, an' it's a funny thing if you notice how many wives die before their 'usbands. Look at me own uncle 'Orace's wife up 'Endon way. Died quite sudden, she did, an' the doctor said 'eart same as what they always say when they don't know what it really was, but if ever I see a guilty look on anyone's face it was on 'is at that funeral. Spent no end on it, 'e did, too, to keep orf suspicion. An' 'e was married again before the year was out."

When other subjects failed Mrs. Mumbles fell back upon her husband—a furtive-looking little man, with protruding teeth and watery eyes, whom Mrs. Mumbles regarded as a veritable Lothario. His "tricks" and the measures Mrs. Mumbles took to circumvent them formed a never-ending Odyssey.

"I'd 'eard 'e was up to 'is tricks again an' nieetin' 'er that night at the Square an' Compass," she said, "so I goes there at op'nin' time to wait for 'em an' ..."

Death and sex, operation and illness (generally of a peculiarly distressing nature) were the ever-recurring motifs of Mrs. Mumbles' recital. Not only herself but all her friends and acquaintances seemed to live lives of almost incredible stress and strain.

She had passed on to the description of her next-door neighbour's daughter.

"Mind you," she was saying, "she's allus bin queer on account of an earwig gettin' into 'er ear when she was a child an' workin' its way to 'er brain. They 'ad it took out, o' course, but she was never the same after it. Unlucky family, they are, as the sayin' is. 'Er sister died an 'orrible death. ...."

Nero had jumped on to Aggie's knee and was rubbing himself against her overall. Nero was a black cat—scraggy, mangy, and with a permanently bald spot on the top of his head—which Elaine had had as a kitten on her sixth birthday. She had been devotedly attached to him in those days, but, now that his charm had waned, disliked him and wanted to have him destroyed. Aggie, however, who loved him in his battered old age as she had never loved him in his winsome kitten-hood, protected him and kept him out of the way when Elaine was at home.

The presence of Nero on her knee reminded Aggie of Elaine, and she thought again guiltily how annoyed Elaine would be if she could see her now. Elaine found Mrs. Mumbles' stories, such thrilling slices of life to Aggie, "low" and "disgusting," and Mrs. Mumbles herself "familiar." When Elaine was there, Aggie tried to adopt a distant authoritative tone to Mrs. Mumbles, as befitted employer to employed, but it was not very successful, and Mrs. Mumbles herself did little to sustain the fiction.

"Well," said Mrs. Mumbles, draining the last drop of her third cup of tea and rising to her feet. "Time I was gettin' ...."

The "elevenses" sometimes lasted till nearly twelve o'clock (especially when Mrs. Mumbles had something particularly interesting to relate), and Mrs. Mumbles was always the first to move.

"I suppose so," said Agnes dreamily. Her mind was a pleasant haze of poisoned wives and unfaithful husbands and the mental ravages of earwigs.

Then suddenly she remembered Monica. Monica was upstairs in her bedroom studying for an exam. (Monica was always studying for an exam, and Aggie had long since given up trying to remember what exam, it was, because, by the time she'd got it into her head, Monica had passed it and was studying for another.) She'd better take her up a cup of tea. It was a bit stewed, but probably Monica wouldn't notice. Monica didn't notice things. Aggie felt vaguely sorry for Monica. It seemed such an unnatural life for a girl of that age. Still—it was the only thing she wanted to do, and Humphrey paid all her fees at Oxford that were not covered by the scholarship, and everyone seemed to think it was all right. Sometimes Aggie thought wistfully how nice it would have been if one of the girls had been more like herself at their age—content to stay at home and help with the house-work and look at the shop windows and gossip about the neighbours and go to the pictures occasionally. But there was Elaine setting off every morning for Mr. Randolph's office and so strict and disapproving about everything when she did come home, and Monica lost and remote in her world of studying and exams., and Joey, who had a good post in Lessington's and yet was always discontented. . . .

She poured out a cup of the strong stewed tea and put some milk into it. As she did so, she caught sight of her torn overall in the kitchen mirror. "I must mend that," she said to herself. She'd torn it several weeks ago and always said that to herself when she caught sight of it in the glass.

Monica was sitting at her desk, writing in a note-book, when Aggie entered. The room was furnished as a bed-sitting-room—desk, chair, and dressing chest of unstained wood, curtains and divan-cover of a material that always reminded Aggie of sacking, and walls of the same shade. It had been a bright little room when Monica was a schoolgirl, with pink curtains, a pretty flowered wallpaper, and nice cheerful pictures—"When Did You Last See Your Father?" and "The Little Princes in the Tower"—on the walls.

Aggie could never understand why Monica had wanted to change it; but, when she went to college, Humphrey and Viola had given her some money towards her outfit and she had spent it instead on her room. Aggie had offered to buy her some coloured vases to help liven it up, but Monica had refused the offer. Aggie couldn't understand this modern craze for drabness. Even the carpet was a plain brown without any pattern on it. Surely life was dull enough (except for Mrs. Mumbles) without wanting to surround yourself with things that gave you the hump.

"I'm sorry to interrupt you, dear," she said, "but I thought perhaps you'd like a cup of tea."

Monica turned round. Her dark hair was parted in the centre and taken back into a small neat knot. She was really quite as pretty as Elaine, thought Aggie, but she made herself look so school-mistressy. She generally wore tweed suits and jumpers and was always immaculately neat and tidy. Her fastidiousness was instinctive and unconscious. Slovenliness in other people did not offend her, because it did not impinge upon her consciousness. She moved in a world of her own and saw little beyond it. People who didn't know her well thought that she was shy, but Aggie knew that she wasn't shy. She was self-contained, austere, aloof. The narrow world of scholarship seemed to satisfy her every need. Over her desk hung a piece of paper that looked like a temperature chart, but that really registered the hours of work she did each day.

"Thank you, Mummy," she said as Aggie poured the slops in the saucer back into the cup and set it down on the desk. "How nice of you!

She didn't smile, but her voice was kind and pleasant. She was never irritated or angry, as Elaine frequently was, but her pleasantness was so uniform and impersonal that it meant much less than did Elaine's rare good-humour.

Aggie went downstairs to the sitting-room. She had better dust and tidy it. It annoyed Elaine to find it unswept and undusted when she came back from work. She wandered about vaguely, putting some socks of Joey's that she had been darning behind a cushion, and hiding her sewing materials behind the big photograph of Mark on top of the bookshelves. Then she caught sight of her reflection in the glass, thought "I must mend that" again, and ran her fingers through her hair to tidy it—a process in which she had a pathetically misplaced trust. She straightened Mark's photograph, thinking for the hundredth time that there was a look of Humphrey about it. But, of course, Mark hadn't been strong and capable like Humphrey. He had been weak and ineffective but very, very kind. He was the only person in the world, Aggie sometimes thought, who had ever really loved her. Her vagueness and forgetfulness and untidiness had never troubled him, because he had been like that himself. They had muddled along together somehow, finding comfort in each other when things went wrong, as they invariably did. Mark had hated Lessington's and persuaded Humphrey to buy him out as soon as old Josiah died. Heaven only knew from what distant ancestor he had inherited his passion for farming, and how he had managed to persuade even himself that he could make a success of it. He had lost in it literally every penny he had. And it wasn't that he hadn't worked. He was up before dawn and out working till late at night. . . . He'd had bad luck from the beginning. Everything he touched seemed to go wrong. For her part, she had loved the life on the farm—the fluffy little chickens and baby calves, the big flagged kitchen, the orchard, roofed with apple-blossom in spring, where the little pigs chased each other round the trees. The children had run wild there. It didn't matter what they did or what they wore. . . . Those had been four very happy years for Aggie and Mark in spite of the debts and worries, the foot-and-mouth disease, and the blights on everything that could possibly harbour a blight. And now Joey was going the same way—fretting and grumbling and saying that he hated Lessington's and that he couldn't breathe in a town and that he wanted to go out to the colonies. But Aggie was very firm about it. Humphrey paid her a regular allowance and had always been kind to them, and, as Joey was the only boy in the family (Hilary, of course, was far too grand even to consider it), he ought to go into Lessington's. They owed it to Humphrey, she told Joey emphatically. They all knew, she said, what farming led to. . . . He must just settle down to business and make the best of it. One couldn't pick and choose—not in this life, at any rate.

She fetched a duster from the kitchen and flicked it about in a dreamy hit-or-miss fashion over the surface of the furniture. Elaine was always saying that they could afford a properly trained maid on Uncle Humphrey's allowance if only Aggie managed better, and Aggie knew that this was true, but she didn't want a properly trained maid, and, anyway, she couldn't manage better. She'd often tried. The money just vanished, and, as she could never remember what she'd spent it on, she couldn't keep accounts.

She supposed she'd have to wear her navy blue at Doreen's this afternoon. Elaine always made her dress in dark colours—navy blue or nigger brown or black. She never let her choose any of her clothes herself, but always insisted on accompanying her to the shop to see that she didn't buy anything "dressy." Aggie loved bright colours and, though officially she only wore the clothes that Elaine chose for her, she had had one or two furtive outbreaks in the shape of a red blouse, a green hat, and a highly variegated scarf, which she kept carefully locked up and only wore when there was no possibility of Elaine's seeing her.

She also kept hidden from Elaine the many things she bought from men at the door. She never could refuse men at the door. They only had to go on talking long enough and she'd buy whatever they were trying to sell whether she wanted it or not. They knew it—and she knew that they knew it—after one glance at her good-natured credulous face.

She wondered whether she dared pin on to her coat the buttonhole she had bought in the town the other day—an ingenious little bunch of fir cones painted red and green and blue and gold. It was very pretty ... but perhaps she'd better not wear it today. Elaine's temper was sometimes a bit raggy on Saturdays. Aggie was quite looking forward to going out to tea, in spite of the fact that it would only be the family—Doreen, who was so stuck-up because she'd married a Parish Church curate (though Aggie knew for a fact that she was the third woman in Reddington alone he'd proposed to); and Bridget, poor child, whom Doreen was trying to turn into a bright young thing, though she was more like a suet pudding; and the twins, Harriet fussing all the time as to whether Hester were sitting in a draught, and Hester so dreamy and absent-minded that she didn't hear half you said to her; and perhaps Viola—though someone had told Aggie in the town that Viola had gone home on a visit. Aggie was always a little aggressive in her manner to Viola, imagining that Viola must secretly be criticising her for not managing better on Humphrey's allowance. Viola was supposed to be rather grand, but she never looked half as smart as Elaine. ... That brought Aggie's thoughts back to Elaine. People called Elaine hard and "bossy," but they didn't know about the other Elaine—no one but Aggie knew about her—the Elaine who would wake in the night, obsessed by mysterious terror and despair, and who would go to Aggie for comfort, the Elaine who sobbed and clung to her and said, "Oh, Mummy, let me stay with you ... I can't bear it alone." The next morning she would be more cold and distant than ever, as if she disowned the craven memory of the night, but it afforded Aggie an obscure consolation to think of it. Elaine had had those "turns" (as Aggie called them to herself) ever since her early teens, and at first Aggie had been very much worried by them, suspecting some real cause, but now she accepted them as part of the ordinary routine of life. It was as if Elaine, so hard and efficient and fearless on the surface, had repressed some secret timid self that could only find outlet at the dead of night and that had to flee to Aggie for solace.

She went to the window and moved the curtains aside so that she could look out. The road was called Beech Avenue—a title barely justified by two plane trees both on the same side of the road. There was her next-door neighbour, Mr. Bolton, wheeling his mother in her bath-chair. He was a neat, solid little man, rather like a robin redbreast, and he had lived with his mother all his life. She was a querulous, exacting, bad-tempered old lady who snapped at him and grumbled at him and kept him running about for her all day long, and he was as proud and devoted as if he had been a young mother and the old woman her first baby. The two of them lived alone, and the son did all the cooking and housework as well as looking after her. He was busy, cheerful, and supremely happy, bustling about his kitchen among the pots and pans, and humouring and nursing the old lady.

He looked up at the window as he passed and smiled at Aggie. Aggie smiled back and went down to the gate. Elaine, of course, disapproved of her standing at the gate in her overall gossiping with the neighbours, but Elaine wasn't here, so it didn't matter.

"Well, Mrs. Bolton," she said, "how are you today?"

Mrs. Bolton stared at her malevolently and said nothing. Mr. Bolton beamed all over his rosy face.

"Not too bad, not too bad at all," he said. "She didn't have a very good night, but I got her to sleep about half-past one by reading to her. The night before she hardly slept at all, and I was up with her all night, but last night was much better, much better. Just off to do the shopping now. ..."

For Mr. Bolton went down to the shops every morning with the other young mothers, put his parcels in the bath-chair (as they put theirs in their prams), and hurried back to cook the lunch.

"She's really looking wonderful, isn't she?" he went on with a sort of deprecating pride. "She'll be eighty next month, you know."

"How much longer are you going to stand gossiping here, Reginald?" snapped the old lady suddenly.

Mr. Bolton smiled at Aggie, as a mother might smile at her child's quaintness. "We're just going on, darling," he said reassuringly. "Say 'goodbye' to Mrs. Lessington."

"Hurry up, then," snapped the old lady, "and don't keep me hanging about here all morning."

Aggie stood at her gate and watched them disappear round the corner. He had long thin legs and a small plump back. He really was very like a robin redbreast.

Mrs. Parmenter, her neighbour on the other side, followed by her little girl, Queenie, was now coming down the road, carrying a shopping basket, and Aggie stayed at the gate for a word with her. Aggie always enjoyed a word with a neighbour over the gate when Elaine wasn't there to scold her for it.

"*Do* keep up, Queenie," Mrs. Parmenter was saying in her high-pitched complaining voice.

Mrs. Parmenter spent a good deal of time trying to "make the best" of herself, in accordance with the advice of the cheap women's weeklies that were her sole reading, but her figure was the wrong shape for the free patterns, and her hair didn't lend itself to the latest fashions nor her face to the home-beauty treatments, so that the result was not altogether successful.

Queenie was a fat precocious child of ten, treated by her parents sometimes as a contemporary and sometimes as an infant in arms. Often in the evening the Parmenters would have colossal rows, which could be heard quite plainly through the thin wall. Aggie would listen, entranced (Mr. Parmenter's angry roar, Mrs. Parmenter's shrill whine, and Queenie's childish pipe, for Queenie always joined in, supporting one or the other), and imagine some rich human tragedy at the core of it, but tactful enquiries the next morning would generally elicit the fact that the subject of the dispute had been whether they should go to Clacton or Southend for their holiday, or whether Queenie should take Dancing or Drawing as an extra, or who had left the bathroom tap running. The Parmenters seemed to have brought the art of quarrelling for quarrelling's sake to a fine pitch of perfection. All three had the technique at their fingers' ends. Even Queenie unaided could start a row about nothing at all. They had had another one last night, and Aggie was longing to know what it had been about, but Mrs. Parmenter had read, in that morning's issue of her women's paper, directions for making a handbag out of old silk stockings and was anxious to begin on it. She returned Aggie's greeting shortly, said "Come on, Queenie, do, for goodness' sake," and went indoors. Aggie stood at the gate for a few minutes longer, and a Stop Me and Buy One man, who was passing the end of the road, saw her and pedalled quickly up to her before she could escape.

"I don't *really* want one," said Aggie "I've only just had a cup of tea. . . ."

She bought a twopenny carton and took it into the house with her. Passing the mirror in the hall, she caught sight of the hole in her overall and said, "Dear me, I really must mend that."

Chapter Seven

THE chart on the wall seemed to gaze down on Monica disapprovingly. She had meant to do six hours of work a day throughout the vacation, and she'd only done five yesterday and four the day before. She wouldn't be able to do much today, either, with that wretched tea-party at Aunt Doreen's. She wished she needn't go to it. . . . She wished that one could remain comfortably inside one's own world instead of having to tear oneself away from it so often, wasting time and energy on things that didn't matter. She'd suggested staying at home, but Mother had said, "Oh, you'd better come, dear. Aunt Doreen would be annoyed if you didn't. Besides, Aunt Viola and Uncle Humphrey might be there, and, considering all they do for us, you ought to be polite to them."

That was silly, because Uncle Humphrey and Aunt Viola hated being made a fuss of. Aunt Viola had offended quite a lot of people in Reddington by not responding with sufficient enthusiasm to their overtures of friendship.

Monica had always liked Aunt Viola. She didn't pretend to be interested in you when she wasn't, or think (as Aunt Doreen did) that family relationship implied a right to make personal remarks and ask leading questions. Even before she got to know Hilary, Monica had liked Aunt Viola. Hilary . . . Again the feeling of guilt swept over her, and she cast another deprecating glance at the chart over her desk. The time marked on it represented more than the actual work she had done, because, though she'd tried hard not to, she'd spent part of almost every hour thinking of Hilary. She jerked her mind away determinedly every time it strayed, but it always crept back as soon as she stopped watching it. She didn't want to think of Hilary. She rebelled against this new complication in her calm ordered life, this obstacle in her clear self-appointed path. And yet the thought, when she yielded to it, brought with it a strange deep delight that she had never felt or even imagined before.

Hilary seldom spent his vacations in Reddington (on the rare occasions when he did so, he treated the Lessingtons as though they did not exist) and Monica knew that, when he met her suddenly face to face at Oxford in High Street at the beginning of the term, his first impulse had been to cut her. He had thought better of it, however, had stood talking to her for a few minutes, and then, as if to disown altogether the craven impulse, had asked her to have tea with him at Kemp Hall.

After that they had met frequently, and a shy tentative friendship had sprung up between them. It was very shy and tentative, for both were reserved, and Hilary was in addition highly strung and over-sensitive. On the surface he was self-assured, rather haughty in manner, with a quick caustic wit, but beneath the surface he was uncertain of himself and lived in a world of heightened emotions and exaggerated values in which the most casual contact assumed an importance wholly out of proportion with reality. He was as ready to imagine slights and rebuffs where none existed as to magnify a superficial acquaintanceship into a lifelong friendship. His gifts and good looks attracted attention wherever he went, but Monica alone, as it seemed to her, saw the something lonely and bewildered in him, the child walking in the dark and secretly afraid.

Leaning back in her chair, gazing dreamily in front of her, she tried to recall his features. She had seen him only a week ago—the day before she left Oxford—but she always found it difficult to remember exactly what he looked like. . . . Suddenly the picture of him became clear—dark and rather girlish-looking, with finely moulded features and long mobile lips. It was odd how his appearance remained, as it were, a stranger to her. Apart from him, she felt near to him, bound by a tie of close intimacy, despite the fact that they had met so seldom. She knew him, loved him; he turned to her instinctively for help and reassurance; yet, when they met, his good looks and elegance (he was very particular about his clothes and always had the latest in shirts and socks) abashed her, making her feel shy and diffident. What had she—plain, drab, ordinary—in common with this glamorous youth? It was in their absence from each other rather than in their meetings that the friendship seemed to grow. She had not told her family about it, and they took for granted that she knew Hilary as little as they did themselves.

She gave her head a jerk, as if to shake the thought of Hilary out of it. It was dreadful not to be able to keep her mind on her work. Always before she had prided herself on her power of concentration. She returned to the Agamemnon, which she had begun last night:

τὸν φρονεῖν βροτοὺς ὁδώ-
σαντα, τὸν πάθει μάθος
θέντα κυρίως ἔχειν.
στάζει δ' ἀνθ' ὕπνου πρὸ καρδίας
μνησιπήμων πόνος· καὶ παρ' ἄ-
κοντας ἦλθε σωφρονεῖν.

She looked up the notes and her lips moved silently as she translated the lines to herself. "Zeus . . . who has appointed wisdom by suffering as a sure law. The memory of ills trickles in sleep upon the heart and wisdom comes to men in their despite."

Was it true that you couldn't have wisdom— real wisdom—except by suffering? It was a terrible idea, but it was beautiful, too. Why did things sound more beautiful in Greek than in any other language? Sometimes she had a queer feeling of nostalgia for the Athens of Pericles, "violet-crowned, queen of cities," like the longing of an exile for his home, a strange almost bitter envy of those whose lot had been cast there. She had felt like that much less frequently since she had known Hilary. Anyway, she thought, as she turned the pages of her Liddle and Scott, even if I had lived then, I'd probably have been a slave or something dull like that. I'm too ordinary to have been anything else.

ἔμπαιος, bursting in, sudden.

Yielding to sudden fate.

But I'd have been there, anyway, even if I'd only been a slave.

κεναγγής, emptying vessels; hence, breeding famine.

When the Achaeans were unable to sail and distressed by famine.

I'd have passed Socrates and Alcibiades talking together in the market-place. I'd have watched the Panathenaic procession making its way to the Acropolis. I'd have seen the triremes sail into Phaleron Bay and the sun set over Hymettos. . . .

βροτῶν ἄλαι, wandering of mortals, drifting men away.

Not many words one didn't know, but difficult to translate all the same.

The door opened and her mother came in with a cup of tea.

"I'm sorry to interrupt you, dear," she said, "but I thought you'd like a cup of tea."

"Thank you, Mummy," said Monica. "How nice of you!"

Monica was fond of Aggie in a matter-of-fact, impersonal way. When Aggie had gone she took a sip of the tea, then put her cup down with a grimace. It was strong and stewed. The interruption had disturbed her train of thought, and her mind turned to Hilary again. He was given to sentimental friendships, and that sometimes worried her a little. Fordwick. . . . She hated Fordwick, a thickset giant of a man with a Mussolini-like face and a never-far-absent sneer. He was jealous of Hilary's other friends and made scenes. Once Hilary had come to her after a scene with him in which Fordwick had said he never wanted to see him again, and, telling her about it, had suddenly broken down and cried. She had comforted him, and he had seemed nearer to her than he had ever been before, but the next day he had met her in the Broad and had been barely civil. She had not minded, because she understood how he hated to lower his defences, how the memory of his confidences to her must have irked his pride. Besides, Fordwick had been to see him the night before and they had made up their quarrel.

She tried the tea again. It was quite undrinkable. She pushed it away and turned the pages of the dictionary again.

παλιμμήκης, as long again.

And the winds that blew from Strymon, bringing idleness, famine, bad harbourage, drifting men away, careless of ships and cables, making the time as long again, wasted the flower of Argos.

She glanced at the tea-cup. Mother might be hurt if she left it there untouched. She took up the cup, went along the passage to the lavatory, emptied it, and returned to her desk.

But when the prophet, pleading the wrath of Artemis, told of another cure for the bitter tempest, heavier for the chiefs ...

It was strange to think that Hilary was Aunt Viola's son. They seemed so detached from each other. And yet there was something alike in them—a sensitiveness and fastidiousness, balanced and sane in Aunt Viola, unbalanced and neurotic in Hilary. He had always refused to have more to do with Uncle Humphrey than was necessary, but he had spent part of his last vacation at home, and during the term he had once said casually to Monica, "He's not a bad sort, you know, old Humphrey." Monica had been conscious of a sudden rush of relief. Uncle Humphrey—so safe and kind and good. She had felt much less anxious about Hilary since he had said that to her. ...

She heard her mother's voice in the road outside ... then Mrs. Bolton's ... then Mrs. Parmenter's, "Do keep up, Queenie. ..."

She glanced guiltily at the clock. She'd done practically no work at all this morning. She really must try harder to concentrate. ...

Chapter Eight

ELAINE handed the last letter to Mr. Randolph for his signature. She looked smart and extremely pretty in a well-fitting black suit with a white waistcoat. He glanced at her sideways as he took the letter from her. Never before had he met a girl of her age so cool and composed and impervious to flattery. He had fallen in love with her in the casual fashion in which he generally fell in love with pretty employees and had expected an immediate response, for he was good-looking, fiftyish, and comparatively wealthy. Such affairs, in his experience (and it was a wide one), generally ran smoothly and tractably to their appointed ends. He had an invalid wife with conveniently strict views on divorce, and any complication that arose could usually be settled by money. But this child had kept him at arm's length ever since she came into the office, ignoring all his overtures without the slightest sign of emotion. She would go out to dinner with him or for a drive in his car, but so far she had effectively repulsed his every attempt at love-making. Sometimes he wondered where on earth the little devil had learnt her technique. She was barely out of her teens and had come to him straight from school. It was incredible. He found himself, for the first time in his life, uncertain of his ground. He was anxious to propitiate, afraid of offending, an inexperienced chit of a girl out of a Midland back street. The situation galled and intrigued him. Despite her youth there was nothing of the schoolgirl about her. She knew exactly what he wanted, accepted without offence the fact that he wanted it, and dismissed the idea with complete indifference. He had tried several times to give the whole thing up, but she had gone to his head and he couldn't get her out of it.

Moreover, she was amazingly efficient in the office. She had picked up the system of it with no difficulty at all and when they were short-handed could do two people's work as easily as she did one. The assurance with which she interviewed clients astonished him. In his experience capable women were plain and unattractive and middle-aged. He had never before come across a girl as young and pretty as Elaine, who was also so outstandingly capable. The combination was irresistible. It held him against his will. Moreover, she was a perpetual challenge to his complacency. He was accustomed to excite admiration in his girl employees, to accept it as a matter of course, and to bestow his favours where he chose. Never before had his undeniably handsome person made so little apparent impression upon anyone. Apparent—for he still hoped that, beneath her exasperating shell of self-possession, Elaine was more interested in him than she allowed to appear.

His hopes had revived since it had been arranged that he should change places with his brother and take charge of the London end of the business.

"Have you thought over what I said about coming to London?" he said.

He had offered her the post of secretary to him at the London office last week and had made the implication quite clear. She had shown no emotion at the suggestion, merely replying that she could not leave Reddington.

"Why not?" he had asked bluntly.

She had shrugged.

"My home's here," she had said, "and I don't want to leave it."

She watched him make his rather ornate signature after the "Yours truly," noticing dispassionately the creases in the neck above the starched white collar. He was handsome enough still, but just beginning to run to seed. He'd be flabby in a few years' time. . . .

"Think it over," he said, as he described the final flourish that encircled the whole name.

"There's nothing to think over."

"I'd be very good to you," he said.

He looked at her meaningly as he spoke. He had slightly protruding eyes—not marked enough to spoil his good looks.

"I'm sure you would," she returned casually.

She met his gaze without flinching and his eyes slid away from her. Damn the girl, he thought resentfully. He would have minded less had there been outraged virtue in her expression, but there was merely indifference.

He tried another tack.

"Doing anything this afternoon?"

She considered. She liked going out with him. He took her to expensive luxurious places, and she liked expensive luxurious places. Besides, she had him well in hand. He hardly dared attempt so much as to slip an arm around her now. She had always hated being touched unnecessarily. Even when she was a child, she had refused to sleep in the same bed as Monica and would struggle fiercely out of Aggie's maternal embraces. Kissing gave her no pleasure. It seemed messy and stupid. . . . As long as he didn't maul her about (as she put it to herself) she enjoyed going out with him, and it was quite easy to prevent his mauling her about. She didn't shrink from him or make a scene. There was no need to. Her physical inviolateness protected her—aloof, unruffled, faintly contemptuous. It made him feel silly and undignified.

" 'Fraid so," she said. "Got a family tea-fight on and heaven knows when it will end."

"Tomorrow then? What about a drive?"

"Yes, I think tomorrow would be all right."

"Good. I'll call for you. About three?"

"Thanks. Well, I'll be going now, shall I?"

"I suppose so." He looked at her wistfully. He would have liked to employ his usual formula of "Got a kiss for me, little girl?" but he knew by experience that she would ignore it if he did.

"Good-morning, then," she said briskly and went to the little cloakroom at the end of the passage to put on her hat. She did up her face with frowning concentration—rouge, powder, lipstick—gave a few deft touches to the massed curls, then perched the small black hat at a careful angle. She took immense pains over her appearance, but with as little vanity as if it had belonged to someone else. She studied her good points and enhanced them, so that she looked prettier than she really was. She could not have told why she did this. It was certainly not in order to attract men. Its aim was perhaps to increase her value in her own eyes, to assist her poise and self-confidence. Life was a fight in which every advantage must be carefully utilised and cultivated. Her salary was small and she made most of her clothes herself, but she always looked expensively turned out, and that in itself was a triumph.

She went through the room in which the typists and clerks worked. She knew that they thought she was Mr. Randolph's mistress, but she didn't care. She hadn't even considered his proposal that she should go to London with him. If his successor didn't want her, she must find another job. That wouldn't be difficult. There were plenty going.

As she walked away from the office a feeling of exaltation seized her—so strong and buoyant that it seemed as if it must lift her right off the pavement. She had to steady herself against its onset. It was a feeling difficult to analyse—a sudden sense of power, an intoxicating certainty of success. Consciously or unconsciously she was always aware of it, though it was sometimes so faint as to be little more than a vague background to her thoughts. It would uphold her in moments of depression or disappointment. It would sometimes flood her soul as it did now, taking her by surprise, snatching her up with it. It was what inspiration is to an artist, what, perhaps, the thought of a love affair is to a different type of woman. Gradually it subsided and she fell to her usual occupation of re-dressing the women who passed her in the street. That skirt should be shorter ... that jumper should be ash-pink not yellow (or else the woman should rouge more) ... take off that hideous collar and make the dress come right up to the neck ... hat brim far too large. ... Swiftly, competently, she re-clothed each figure as it passed her, altering shape, colour, fit, costume. She did it instinctively, almost unconsciously. She had done it ever since she could remember. A dreadful beige outfit. ... The woman was enormous, too. ... Helplessly, Elaine let her go. She seldom admitted defeat, but she couldn't do anything with that particular woman. Ah, this was better. Young, pretty, slender . . . just a touch here and there . . . hat at a different angle . . . take off that sloppy cape effect. . . .

The glance she threw at each was so impersonal that the passers-by would hardly have known she had noticed them.

She stopped at a little hat-shop and examined the row of hats with frowning critical gaze. They were chic and French-looking, and she could find no fault with any of them. About a month ago Aunt Viola, who was coming in to Burchester for some shopping, had asked her to meet her for lunch, and afterwards they had gone to this shop because Aunt Viola wanted a new hat. The shop was kept by a middle-aged Frenchwoman called Madame Bertier, anxious and harassed and ill-at-ease with her unaccommodating Midland customers. She liked Aunt Viola, who was pleasant and friendly and talked French to her, but on that particular day could find nothing to suit her. Elaine, however, had suggested a slight alteration in the hat that seemed to suit her least of all, and the little Frenchwoman had been delighted. It had made all the difference. It was now Madame's hat, Madame's hat *absolument*. She had treated Elaine ever since as if they were two civilised beings shipwrecked on a desert island. Mademoiselle understood. She had chic and taste. She was different. Looking through the curtains now, a small compact study in black and white—black dyed hair, white face, black dress, white lace jabot —and seeing Elaine outside, she smiled and beckoned. She had some new hats she would like to show to Mademoiselle—not as a customer, no, but as a fellow artist. Elaine examined them critically, and Madame nodded her head in approval at each comment. This girl with the innocence of a child and the composure and taste of a woman of the world, so hard and competent, so honest and uncompromising, who could dress herself so exquisitely on so small a sum (for Elaine had told her all about that), whose clever fingers could cut and sew as though she were a mistress of her art, who knew, *knew* by divine instinct, what others took a lifetime to learn. . . . Madame felt to her almost as she might have felt to her own daughter, if she had had one.

Elaine tore herself away at last and went out, still with that faint critical frown between her brows. What a muddle the place was in! Madame was an artist, but she was impractical and un-businesslike. She was too frightened of her customers, too timid, too diffident. She would never make the little shop pay. Customers wanted managing. They even enjoyed being bullied just a little. One ought to *make* them have the right things, whether they wanted them or not.

She stopped at a book-shop outside which was displayed, among other magazines, the latest number of *Vogue*. She did a hasty sum in her head, still frowning abstractedly. Yes, she could afford it if she lunched on coffee and a bun for a few days. Every penny of Elaine's salary was budgeted. So much for fares, so much for clothes, so much for her lunches, so much to Aggie for her keep at home, so much for amusements. Aggie's feckless muddling with money infuriated her.

"But what have you *spent* it on?" she would demand impatiently.

"I really don't know, dear," Aggie would reply apologetically. "It just seems to have gone. It always does."

She went into an A.B.C. near the station and had her coffee and bun, reading *Vogue* as she ate, lost to everything around her. Then she ran to catch her train and settled down in a corner seat, still reading the magazine.

Two young men opposite tried to attract her attention by a series of elaborate manœuvres, but she was quite accustomed to this and it affected her as little as the buzzing of a fly.

At Reddington station she rose and gave each of them a cool quelling glance before she got out of the train. Then she walked to the Market Square and stood there waiting for the tram. As long as anyone remembered, Reddington market had been held in a large covered building off Cobden Street, but the open space in the centre of the town had always been called the Market Square. In the middle stood an imposing statue of Robert Peel, wearing a Roman toga and wielding a roll of paper, intended, presumably, to represent the Repeal of the Corn Laws, in gratitude for which the statue had been erected by the Reddington citizens of 1846. Occasionally local wags climbed it by night to put incongruous or indecent headgear upon the statesman's bare head. On one side of the square was a dingy building whose blank fly-blown windows announced it to be a "Co ee House" (the two *f*'s had been missing for the last two years), and on the other stood Reddington's largest hotel, which had been the latest thing of its kind in 1870 and had. rested on its laurels ever since. The square, which was the general rendezvous of the town, was already seething with people. By evening it would be a tightly packed mass of humanity through which cars would have to make their way at crawling pace, hooting incessantly. The tram that Elaine was waiting for clanged to a stop, but was at once boarded by a rough good-natured crowd of mill operatives, who had gone home from work, had their dinners, washed and changed, and were now on their way to the football field for a local fixture. They shouted greetings and jostled each other, surging on to the steps four or five abreast. Elaine drew back and waited, but the conductor, calling "Full up," pushed half the would-be passengers on to the pavement, and the tram set off again slowly through the Saturday afternoon throng.

Elaine decided not to wait for the next. The crowd was larger than ever and she had little chance of getting on to it. Besides, she felt that she would rather walk. Something of the sense of exaltation remained with her and walking would afford an outlet to it. She set off along Peel Street, where most of the shops were. They began well with Lessington's at the corner of the square and gradually tailed off to small sweet-shops and drapers that suggested cottages rather than shops. Then came rows of houses—middle-class houses with steps up to the front door and a window on either side of it displaying Nottingham lace curtains and a little table holding a plant or a vase of flowers. Then down a turning on the right into Beech Avenue.

As Elaine entered it a familiar dragging feeling of depression came over her spirit. But she fought it off determinedly. She'd get away from all this . . . from the drab monotonous little houses, the small provincial interests and cliques and jealousies. She didn't know how she'd get away from it all, but she knew quite confidently that she would. Her lip curled contemptuously as she thought of Aunt Doreen's petty social manœuvres—Aunt Doreen, to whom acquaintance with local tin gods like the Hamwells represented the summit of earthly success. And Bridget. ... One couldn't dislike Bridget—she was so amiable and good-natured—but Elaine despised her, just as she despised everyone in Reddington. Even Aunt Viola. Aunt Viola didn't belong here and was a fool ever to have come here. She needn't have done. She'd come, of course, because she'd fallen in love with Uncle Humphrey. Women were fools to fall in love.

As she drew near Number 4, her frown deepened. The curtains were hanging unevenly at the window—one pulled right back and looped over a chair. Mother had been looking out, of course. It was dreadful the way Mother stood at the window, generally in that horrible overall, with her hair coming down or a smudge of blacking on her face, to watch the passers-by. It never seemed to occur to her that they could see her as plainly as she could see them. She entered the little hall and stood there for a moment looking round. It was dark and airless, and the faintly musty smell that hung over the whole house seemed somehow to be concentrated there. The linoleum was dusty, the little hat-stand overladen with coats and raincoats and hats (Aggie seemed to keep most of her wardrobe on the hat-stand). The panes of cheap coloured glass in the door that used to fascinate her when she was a child, turning the world blue and red and yellow, she now loathed with a peculiar intensity. The door of the sitting-room was open, and through it she could see the many deficiencies of Aggie's hasty tidying-up—the shopping-basket on the settee, the dustpan on the hearthrug, the empty ice-cream carton on the mantelpiece. She shut her eyes for a moment and summoned a vision of large cool rooms ... subdued colourings ... spaciousness ... soft carpets. ... That was where she belonged, where some day she would attain. She had no doubt at all that some day she would attain to it. Meantime she must fight this atmosphere, fight it with every ounce of her strength, so as to prevent its engulfing her spirit. She whipped up her hatred of it, feeling that her very hatred was her safeguard against it.

Aggie came out of the kitchen. Her face wore a propitiatory and slightly apologetic smile. She never knew what sort of a mood Elaine would come home in. She'd changed ready for going to Doreen's, so that at any rate Elaine couldn't scold her for keeping them waiting.

"Hello, darling," she said, smiling brightly. "I'm all ready for going to Aunt Doreen's. Had a tiring morning?"

"No, thank you," said Elaine rather shortly. Her quick glance flashed over Aggie. "Mother, you *can't* go to Aunt Doreen's in those stockings."

"Can't I, dear?" said Aggie mildly, looking down at the heavy lisle stockings that rucked about her ankles. "There aren't any holes in them."

"You must put some silk ones on," said Elaine, trying to speak patiently.

"I thought it didn't matter just for the family," said Aggie.

"Of course it does," said Elaine. "It matters for everyone. It ought to matter just for yourself. Have you done your hair since this morning?"

"Well, not actually *done* it, dear," admitted Aggie, "but I've sort of tidied it up."

"I'll come up and do it for you," said Elaine.

She tried to speak kindly, because right down at the bottom of her heart she loved Aggie—loved her for her kindliness and generosity, her quickness to forgive insult and rebuff, for the warm motherliness of her encircling arms in those nightmare times when terror and despair fell suddenly upon her in the darkness. But she tightened her lips as a picture of the mother she had always longed for arose unsummoned before her—a tall beautiful aristocratic woman, exquisitely dressed. She had first imagined that mother when she was quite a child, and she could see her as plainly as if she had been a real person. Aggie's apologetic expression intensified as they entered her bedroom. She had changed hurriedly when she realised that it was almost time for Elaine to come home, and the clothes she had taken off lay here and there on the floor and over the chairs. The wardrobe door and several of the drawers were open, and Nero lay curled up on the eiderdown. Elaine took Nero by the scruff of his neck, carried him at arm's length to the door, and dropped him on to the landing. Then she returned to the room and moved about it, tidying up the disorder, while Aggie made ineffectual attempts to help her, murmuring guiltily, "I was a bit pushed for time, dear. . . ."

"Now," said Elaine, at last, in a business-like manner, "I'll do your hair."

Aggie sat down on the chair in front of the dressing-table, and let Elaine take down her hair and brush it out.

"Mr. Randolph quite all right, dear?" she said, with an elaborate affectation of indifference.

Aggie, who knew that Elaine often went out with Mr. Randolph and took for granted that he was an eligible bachelor, had built many secret romantic dreams on the friendship. Her favourite reading was the paper-backed novelette in which the secretary invariably marries the rich employer.

But Elaine's "Yes, he seems so" was so curt that she dared not pursue the theme. She thought wistfully how nice it would be if Elaine would confide in her as she used to confide in her mother. Elaine was very pretty, and several young men in Reddington were obviously interested in her, but she would never talk about them. Aggie and her mother used to sit up half the night talking about Aggie's young men (for Aggie had been pretty too), and she would tell her mother just what they had said to her and what she had said to them, and the two would grow as confidential as a couple of young girls. . . . And here were she and Elaine together in her bedroom, Elaine brushing her hair—a situation that should inspire confidences if any could—and she hardly dared ask her anything. Aggie had always longed to be a "pal" to her daughters, and was often depressed by their uncompromising rejection of her efforts in that direction.

"I saw Tom Redfern in the town this morning," she said coyly. "He was asking about you."

Tom Redfern was a shy awkward youth who lived in the last house of the Avenue and had admired Elaine since she was a little girl.

"Was he?" said Elaine, with a curl of her lip.

Aggie sighed again. It wasn't any use. The daughter she sometimes imagined for herself (with a dreadful sense of disloyalty towards Monica and Elaine) would have been pouring out all her hopes and fears about Tom Redfern or Mr. Randolph or some other eligible male. She wished that Monica and Elaine were more interested in men. It would be so lovely to have weddings and grandchildren in the family. ...

Elaine had finished her hair (she'd done it in a very severe style that Aggie secretly disliked) and was now taking off the lace collar that Aggie had pinned on to her dress in a last-minute attempt to brighten it up. The pins showed and the collar was grubby, but Aggie knew that in any case Elaine wouldn't have approved of it.

"I can't think why you always put on those dreadful collars," she was saying severely.

"Well, dear, it's just an accessory," said Aggie, trying to defend herself. "Fashion articles are always talking about accessories."

"Accessories!" repeated Elaine scornfully, but her eyes were approving now. Mother really looked quite nice when one had done her hair the right way and taken off those unspeakable things she pinned all over herself.

"*Now* you look better," she said.

"That's all right then, dear," said Aggie. "Thank you."

She could never make up her mind whether to be irritated or gratified by Elaine's attentions. It was nice to think that Elaine cared how she looked, but it was dreadful never to be allowed to wear anything dressy.

"I needn't put on my hat yet, need I?" went on Aggie.

"*I'll* put your hat on for you," said Elaine. "You'll have it right at the back on one side if I don't. And you'll change your stockings now, won't you?"

"Yes, dear," sighed Aggie.

Elaine went along the landing to Monica's room and knocked at the door.

"Come in."

Monica turned round from her desk.

"Hello," she said, glancing at her watch. "You back already?"

Elaine sank down into the small arm-chair and looked round the neat, austere little room. The sisters' interests were so different that they had always got on together excellently.

"Things are in an awful mess downstairs," she said.

"Are they?" said Monica vaguely.

Elaine wished that she could feel as detached from everything as Monica did. It wasn't that Monica liked things messy. It was that she simply didn't see the things that exasperated Elaine so. She kept herself and her immediate belongings immaculate and noticed nothing beyond them.

"You'll end up as a don in a women's college, you know," said Elaine suddenly.

Monica thought of Hilary, then tried not to think of him.

"I'd like that," she said. Hilary's wife would be someone elegant and beautiful with a background of luxury and culture. "I'd like that very much indeed," she added emphatically.

"I expect you would," said Elaine. "You run terribly true to type."

"Do I?" said Monica anxiously. "I suppose I do." She saw someone prim and stooping and scholastic-looking in spectacles, then comforted herself by the reflection that at any rate she didn't yet stoop or wear spectacles.

There was a silence. Elaine made fun of this bed-sitting-room of Monica's (with its suggestion, she said, of a "highbrow nun"), but she found its atmosphere curiously restful. Her own bedroom was as it had been since her childhood. To compromise would be to surrender. Some day she would have the bedroom of her dreams. Till then she didn't care what it was like.

Monica turned over the pages of her dictionary and wrote something down in a little note-book. Then she glanced at her watch.

"Isn't it awful the way time goes on and on and on?" she said. "I've simply done no work today."

"I'm sure you needn't," said Elaine. "I'm sure you know everything by now."

Monica smiled, then said rather guiltily, "I find it awfully difficult to concentrate."

She wondered suddenly if Elaine were in love with anyone. . . . She wouldn't tell her if she were. They had never confided in each other.

"I've just been doing Mother's hair," said Elaine. "It was an awful sight."

Monica looked up another word in the dictionary then said, "Listen, Elaine, isn't this beautiful? It's a description of Iphegenia being sacrificed by Agamemnon at Aulis. Agamemnon was her father, you know, and they were sacrificing her because the prophet said that the wind wouldn't blow in the right direction unless they did. 'And her prayer and her maiden prime they set at nought, the cruel judges. And her father, having prayed, told the attendants boldly to lift her like a goat upon the altar, her robes flowing about her, her spirit fainting, and with the curb to stifle her sweet lips' cry fraught with curses to her house. Then, dropping on the ground her saffron robe, she smote each one of her murderers with a piteous shaft from her eye, plain as a picture, fain to speak, as ofttimes in her father's hospitable halls she had sung. ...' " She stopped and added apologetically, "It sounds rotten translated, of course. . . ."

"It sounds all right," said Elaine kindly, "but it just doesn't thrill me. I suppose different things thrill different people."

Monica wrote down another word in her little note-book, then said:

"What were you doing Mother's hair for?"

"Going to tea to Aunt Doreen's."

"Good Lord, I forgot. ... Am I going?"

"Course you are. We're all going."

"I ought to get ready, then."

"It only means putting a coat on as far as you're concerned, I suppose."

Monica looked apologetic again. "It does so simplify life."

Elaine glanced at Monica's neat roll of hair, thin cashmere jumper, and tweed skirt.

"Oh, I don't mind. You're definitely the coat-and-skirt type, so you may as well stick to it. At least I don't have to claw lace collars off you."

Monica laughed.

"Poor Mummy! I wish I didn't have to go to the beastly party. I've such a lot to do and it's such a waste of time."

But she couldn't help hoping that by a miracle Hilary would be there. He'd said he wasn't coming home this vacation, but he just might have come, after all. He might be there with Aunt Viola or call to take her home at the end. Her heart beat unevenly at the thought.

"I suppose Aunt Viola will be there?" she said carelessly.

"The whole boiling of them will be there," said Elaine with a grimace.

There was a silence, then Monica said, "Somehow it's funny to think of her being Uncle Humphrey's wife. Don't you think so?"

"I don't know," said Elaine indifferently. To her Aunt Viola and Uncle Humphrey were just an aunt and an uncle, with only the most nebulous of personalities.

Monica gazed dreamily into space.

"She's—different somehow, isn't she? But they get on awfully well."

"Uncle Humphrey would get on with anyone," said Elaine. "He's stodgy and uninteresting, but terribly reliable. I think men like that make the best sort of husbands."

"Perhaps," said Monica doubtfully, again trying not to think of Hilary.

"You'd be certain of them always," said Elaine. "They'd stick by you through everything. Even if they bored you, they'd never let you down."

"I suppose not," agreed Monica, telling herself triumphantly that she wasn't thinking of Hilary, "but I don't think I want a husband like that."

"I don't want one at all," said Elaine very firmly.

Chapter Nine

BRIDGET turned slowly away from the front door after seeing off the last of the guests, Aunt Harriet and Aunt Hester. It had been quite a nice party, but she was disappointed that neither Aunt Viola nor Uncle Humphrey had come. Family gatherings always seemed rather flat to Bridget without them. Generally Uncle Humphrey called for Aunt Viola at the end, and just to watch them as he helped her into her coat sent a warm happy glow through Bridget's heart.

In the drawing-room Doreen was moving the chairs back into their places and piling on to one plate the sandwiches that had been left. Then she went into the kitchen and Bridget heard her say, "That will do for your supper, Annie."

She came back into the drawing-room with a faint triumphant smile on her lips.

"I wasn't going to have her eating up everything left over from tea and then wanting an enormous supper on top of it."

She looked at Bridget, and the smile faded as she remembered how much smarter and more sophisticated Elaine had looked.

"You'd better go and take off that dress," she said. "It's no good getting it all messed up. It'll do to wear at the Hamwells' on Friday if you press the creases out."

That thought comforted her. Elaine would never get invited to the Hamwells' for all her poise and elegance.

Bridget's spirits sank. The Hamwells' ... where Mother would expect her to be a "success" —bright and popular and entertaining—and where she would, as usual, be paralysed by shyness and misery. She wished that she needn't try to be a "success," try to make people like her when she didn't really care whether they liked her or not.

She had a sudden vision of herself as mistress of a little house, cleaning, dusting, cooking. Towards evening she would put the dinner in the oven and run upstairs to change her dress. The little drawing-room would be bright and cosy. She'd go into the hall as soon as she heard her husband's key in the lock. They couldn't afford a maid. She did all the work herself. They didn't go out much or know many people. They preferred to sit by the fire in the evenings, reading or listening to the wireless, or, in summer, pottering about the little garden. It wasn't wrong, surely, to imagine that one was married as long as one didn't think of any particular man. The trouble was that she couldn't help thinking of Terry, though she tried not to. Somehow that brought her thoughts back to Aunt Viola.

"Aunt Viola didn't come, after all," she said regretfully.

"No, I told you she had a headache," said Doreen impatiently.

It had been absurd of Viola to ask her not to tell Bridget about the trouble with Humphrey, but she'd promised not to, and she prided herself on being a woman of her word.

Bridget turned to go upstairs. Something had happened at the tea-party, she didn't know what. She'd suspected it at the time, and the way Mother spoke now made her quite sure. She had taken Monica into the garden after tea to get some parsley for Aunt Aggie, and when they came back into the drawing-room everyone stopped talking suddenly, then after a short constrained silence began to talk about the weather.

It was something to do with Aunt Viola. She knew that, because when she happened to mention Aunt Viola a few minutes later they all looked at each other meaningly and said nothing. It was something worrying, of course. If it hadn't been they would have told her. It was only worrying things that were kept secret. And at once her mind leaped to the explanation. Aunt Viola was going to have an operation. It must be that. Peggy Martin's mother had had an operation last month and they hadn't told Peggy till it was all over. And it would be like Aunt Viola to want it kept secret.

She was so proud and reserved. She'd hate the thought of people discussing it, being sorry for her. But it was Uncle Humphrey to whom Bridget's thoughts went out in a rush of love and pity. How anxious and unhappy he would be! How dreadful it must be for him to have to face the possibility, however faint, of life without her! They loved each other so much that they were almost the same person. You couldn't imagine one without the other. And yet sooner or later one would be left without the other. In every marriage that must happen eventually. She wondered how people who were in love with each other could bear it—to know that. Her pity for Uncle Humphrey became a heavy aching pity for the whole world.

She took off her crêpe-de-chine dress and put on a plain blue linen, fastening the big white buttons mechanically. Her thoughts had turned for comfort to Terry. There was something safe and solid in the thought of Terry. He'd have come home from the office now. Suddenly she decided to go round to Lucy's and see him. She couldn't just stay indoors with this dreadful anxiety about Aunt Viola weighing on her heart. She stood hesitating a moment. If she told Mother that she was going to the Wheelers' she would be sure to find some way of stopping her. She was always trying to make Bridget drop them. Bridget decided to say that she was going to the Free Library to change her book and to call at Lucy's on the way back. It wasn't really deceitful—at least not very—because she did want to change her Library book. One couldn't help being just a tiny bit deceitful with Mother. . . .

She went down again to the drawing-room, where Doreen was sitting by the window reading the newspaper.

"I've hardly had a minute to look at it till now," she said. "It's so important to keep up with the news. . . . Where are you off to?"

She spoke genially. She was still feeling pleased about Viola and Humphrey, though she wouldn't have admitted it even to herself. Her mind was dwelling on Viola's humiliation (and, after all, it *was* humiliating not to be able to keep a man) in the town where she had held her head so high. Thinking such a lot of herself, giving herself such airs. . . . No wonder poor old Humphrey had got tired of her. The wonder was it hadn't happened years ago. She, Doreen, mightn't be a baronet's granddaughter, but at least she'd been able to keep her husband.

"I'm just going down to the Library," said Bridget, taking a book from the shelves.

Doreen looked at her critically.

"I think you'd better have a new hat for Friday," she said. "You can come into the town with me one morning next week and we'll get one."

Bridget braced her courage for the ordeal. Doreen prided herself on being a good shopper. Over the smallest purchase she would demand, "Is that the least you'll take for it?" or "Is there no discount for cash?" Sometimes she would refuse to believe the assistant and demand to see the manager, and Bridget would stand by, hot and miserable, trying not to notice the smiles that were exchanged on all sides. But as she set off down the road her heart was too full of anxiety about Aunt Viola to have room for anything else.

It must be a serious operation or they wouldn't be keeping it a secret. Elaine had been there when they were talking, but somehow Elaine had always counted as a grown-up. She was passing St. James's Church, and on an impulse she entered it and walked up to the front pew. There she knelt down and prayed silently. . . . "Please, God, don't let Aunt Viola die. Uncle Humphrey wouldn't be able to live without her. He loves her so terribly. . . ." She stopped. Of course she needn't explain to God. He understood everything. . . . "Please don't let her die," she said again. She stayed there for a few minutes, then went out into the street again, feeling comforted. It would be all right. She was sure it would be all right. Hundreds of people had serious operations and got well again.

She went through the Market Square to the Free Library and changed *The Mill on the Floss* for *Pride and Prejudice*. She felt sorry to say goodbye to Tom and Maggie and Aunts Pullet, Deane, and Glegg, but there would be Mr. Bennet and Mr. Collins and Lady Catherine de Bourgh.

Monica laughed at her for reading the same books over and over again, and hardly ever reading anything modern, but the people in them were like old friends, and she had to keep going to see them.

As she approached the Wheelers' house she slackened her pace. It was too much to hope that Aunt Agatha wouldn't be there. She'd be there, as usual, sitting in the little sitting-room at work on her interminable embroidery. Bridget would have felt less nervous in her presence if Lucy were not continually impressing on her how important it was not to offend her.

"For heaven's sake," she would say, when Bridget was going to tea, "make a fuss of Aunt Agatha or she'll give us all hell, and I'll never be able to ask you again!"

Bridget was far too nervous to do more than answer Aunt Agatha's questions, but she was also too nervous to talk much to Lucy or Lucy's mother in her presence, so, as the one thing Aunt Agatha could not endure was to be "passed over," no great harm was done.

Lucy's father had died when she and Terry were hardly more than babies, leaving his affairs in hopeless confusion, and Aunt Agatha had given them and their mother a home ever since. She was a widow and quite well off, but with a firm belief in the proverb that "He who pays the piper calls the tune."

Glancing at the sitting-room window out of the corner of her eye, Bridget could see the greyish black head bent over the protruding bosom.

She knocked at the door, and in a few moments Lucy opened it. Lucy was small and dark, with a trim neat figure, trim neat features, and bright restless eyes.

"Hello, Bridget," she said. "Come in."

"I was just passing," murmured Bridget in explanation.

"Come and be nice to Aunt Agatha a minute," whispered Lucy in a conspiratorial fashion, "then we'll go upstairs and have a talk. ... Here's Bridget come to see you, darling," she went on affectionately, as she threw open the sitting-room door.

Lucy's affectionate manner to Aunt Agatha surprised Bridget every time she witnessed it. It was such a convincing performance. One could hardly believe that behind her back she mimicked her affectations and referred to her as "the old hag." In return for the affectionate manner Aunt Agatha gave Lucy frequent presents of clothes and money. She never gave anything to Terry, because he had never made any secret of his dislike of her.

"Well, dear, how are you?" said Aunt Agatha in the little wheezy voice that seemed to find its way with such difficulty through the round pigeon chest.

Her face was too plump and distended actually to smile, but her features would flicker in a vaguely reassuring fashion when she was pleased.

Lucy sat on the arm of her chair and dropped a kiss on the patchy lifeless hair.

"Isn't that embroidery lovely, Bridget?" she said.

Bridget watched the little balloon-like hand that drew the thread deftly in and out.

"It's quite ordinary," murmured Aunt Agatha modestly.

Lucy winked at Bridget over Aunt Agatha's head.

"It's the colouring that's so lovely," she said. "You've got a marvellous eye for colour, darling."

The convulsive spasm that represented a smile passed over Aunt Agatha's features.

"Well, I've always had good taste." She looked at Bridget. "And the naughty girl's going to run off and leave me."

"Only for a week's holiday," said Lucy, "and you know I hate leaving you, but, after all, you're really sending me away because you're paying for it. . . . Isn't she sweet, Bridget? The Bordens asked me to go to Belgium with them for a week. She's paying all my expenses."

Aunt Agatha heaved a deep sigh that made her shiver and go on shivering for some moments in a manner suggestive of a carelessly handled jelly. Probably the only real emotion in Aunt Agatha's life was her love for Lucy. She had adored her ever, since she was a pretty, clever little girl, and had been desperately jealous of her mother's claims on her. Terry, the dull, heavy, stupid little boy, she had disliked proportionately. She loved to give Lucy presents, to deck her out in nice clothes and see that she had a "good time," and she firmly believed that Lucy returned her affection.

92

"I really think you do care just a little for your old Auntie," she would wheeze coyly.

She turned her small eyes to Bridget.

"All quite well at home, dear?"

"Yes, thank you," replied Bridget nervously.

Then the door opened and Mrs. Wheeler came in. Mrs. Wheeler was vaguely understood to be an invalid. When asked how she was, she would reply, "A little better," or "Not quite so well today." She never got up till the afternoon, and took medicine of some sort or other every few hours. She suffered from a mysterious complication of diseases that no one seemed quite to understand. "The trouble is," she would say darkly, "that what's good for one isn't good for another."

When first she went with her two small children to live with her sister-in-law there had been a succession of angry scenes between them. Over Lucy in particular (who even in those days had a secret contempt for both), a bitter unremitting struggle had been waged for years. But Mrs. Wheeler was lazy and fond of the good things of life and well aware on which side her bread was buttered, and in the end she had surrendered, taking refuge in the fastness of ill-health. There, at any rate, she could reign supreme. And Agatha was very good to her as an invalid, asking her solicitously how she felt at regular intervals throughout the day, urging her to rest and stay in bed, and ordering appetising little dainties for her meals. As a compromise the arrangement worked admirably. There were still occasional slight frictions, but Agatha had only to hint that she was beginning to think that the care of a house was too much for her and that she ought to go and live in a boarding-house, for her sister-in-law to cave in completely. Agatha, w hen given her own way, was very generous, and Mrs. Wheeler was quite willing to pay the price of dependence. She was a grey, colourless little woman, with the smooth expressionless face of the professional hypochondriac.

She settled herself down in the other arm-chair, threw an indeterminate smile in Bridget's direction, then took a bottle of pills from her bag and put two in her mouth, explaining that her heart was better, but that her rheumatism had come on again, and that she thought her blood pressure was about the same.

"Come upstairs to my room, Bridget," said Lucy. "I want to show you the perfectly lovely dress that Aunt Agatha's given me."

The slightly sulky look that had come over Aunt Agatha's face at the thought of the two girls' leaving her and going upstairs together, was dispelled by the latter part of the sentence.

"Try it on, darling," she said to Lucy, "and let Bridget see how nice you look in it."

A tiny pang of jealousy shot through Mrs. Wheeler's heart at Agatha's possessive tone, but it was only a faint distant echo of the tempests that used to rage there.

Lucy's bedroom had been done up by Aunt Agatha in the spring, with cream walls, deep blue curtains, blue carpet, and blue bed-cover. There was a desk against the wall and on it a pile of school text-books. Lucy had intended to study for a Frœbel degree on leaving school, but Aunt Agatha had cried and begged her not to, because she'd miss her so if she took a post, and in the end Lucy had given up the idea. She didn't regret it. It would have been, she said, an awful grind, and Aunt Agatha's generosity compensated amply for the sacrifice.

Bridget sat down on the bed.

"Let's see the dress," she said.

Lucy laughed.

"Oh no. I only said it to escape from the old devil. I have to dance attendance on her all day and every day, and I can tell you I need a change sometimes."

"She's awfully fond of you. ..."

Lucy shrugged.

"Oh, I get all I can out of her and I don't do too badly, but she's so damnably touchy, and she does love scenes. She shut herself up in her room all Monday afternoon and cried, because I forgot she'd said she was going to take me to the pictures and went to tea to the Favershams. I had the hell of a time getting her sane again. She's absolutely repulsive when she cries."

"It must be dreadful," said Bridget sympathetically.

Again Lucy shrugged.

"Oh well, if it weren't for her we'd be pigging it in some awful little place on nothing at all and I'd have to sweat at a job. ... I think Terry's a fool."

"Why?"

"He won't kow-tow to her, and she takes it out of him. She wouldn't even have his bedroom done up when she did up the rest of the house. The paper's hanging from the wall in ribbons. He'd only got to ask her and make a bit of a fuss of her, but he wouldn't. He never will. It's so stupid of him. The result is that she hates him. It's so easy to keep the poor old thing in a good temper if you set about it the right way. He just won't try."

Bridget looked at Lucy's small pretty face, with the tiny pursed mouth and sharp dark eyes. It was Lucy who made it quite clear that Aunt Agatha must once have been pretty. Aunt Agatha was like a grotesque caricature of Lucy—the same small delicate features buried deep in the puffy fleshiness that still suggested someone who had once been slender and dainty.

Bridget's mind travelled back over their friendship. Lucy had been in the form just above hers at school—pretty, popular, outstandingly good at games. Bridget had admired her from a distance for some time, and could hardly believe her good fortune when Lucy singled her out for her friendship. They had been inseparable till Bridget went to boarding-school, and then they had written to each other every week and met frequently in the holidays.

The friendship had become a habit, and Bridget sometimes wondered, with a guilty sense of disloyalty, whether she would have chosen Lucy for a friend if she had met her now for the first time. And suddenly another disturbing thought struck her. Was she clinging to the worn-out friendship because it was the only link with Terry, because as long as she went to see Lucy she would always have a chance of meeting him?

"I hear that Roy Hamwell's keen on you," said Lucy bluntly.

"Oh ..." said Bridget, disconcerted. "I've just met him a few times."

"Rot! It's much more than that. My goodness! I wish I'd got a chance of marrying him."

"But ... surely not if you didn't love him," said Bridget.

Lucy laughed shortly.

"Love! Look at all the people round one. Sooner or later it always goes." She sat on the bed by Bridget and gazed frowningly into space. "I think that one should marry where one will be most comfortable when it's gone. That's what I'm going to do, anyway."

"But it doesn't always go, Lucy," protested Bridget. "Look at Aunt Viola and Uncle Humphrey. They adore each other. They always have done. And they've been married for about fifteen years. It'll never go with them."

"They're the exception that proves the rule, then," said Lucy. "Anyway, that's what I'll do if I get the chance. I'll marry someone who can make me comfortable when the soppy stuff goes."

Bridget smiled a gentle smile of superior knowledge.

"You won't feel like that when it happens," she said.

Lucy looked at her sharply.

"Why? Has it happened to you?"

Bridget blushed.

"No, I didn't mean that. ... I was thinking of Aunt Viola and Uncle Humphrey. ..."

They heard Aunt Agatha's voice in the hall calling, "Lucy! Lucy, dear!"

"Oh, blast her!" groaned Lucy. "She can't bear to hear me talking to anyone else. It gets her all on edge. She's afraid I'm telling them things I haven't told her, or that I'm running her down. ... Come on. We must go or she'll sulk all night." She threw open the wardrobe door. "You'd better see the dress. Be an angel and rave about it a bit. We'll pretend I've been trying it on."

"Is Terry in?" said Bridget, as they went downstairs.

"I don't know. He's probably in his shed, if he is."

"I'll just go out and see."

There had never been much sympathy between brother and sister. Lucy had always been irritated by his slowness, and he by her quickness. When they were children Lucy had taken a perverse delight in goading him, with apparent innocence, into blundering rages for which he was punished. They did not quarrel openly now, but there was still a deep-seated antagonism between them. Lucy resented his not being the handsome charming brother who would have been so useful to her, and Terry on his side resented the barbed stings that she could still cleverly introduce into any casual conversation with him. He was fond of his mother, but Mrs. Wheeler, who was a stupid sheep-like woman, copied her sister-in-law and daughter in despising him, and poured out what maternal love she had upon Lucy, entering into a competition for her affection with Aunt Agatha, in which she was perpetually being worsted.

From childhood Terry had perforce lived a self-contained life. Secretly he believed himself to be as stupid and unattractive as Lucy said he was, and that had made him shrink from forming friendships. Only with Bridget did he feel at his ease. She was so kind and simple that, with her, cleverness and stupidity didn't seem to matter. He could talk to her as he could talk to no one else.

He still pursued the hobbies of his solitary boyhood, spending most of his time in a shed at the bottom of the garden, which he had gradually furnished as best he could. In it were his carpentering bench and tools, the glass-topped case in which he kept his insects, his stamp-album, the accordion on which he practised when he was sure that Lucy was away from home, and a couple of canaries. On the floor was a tattered rug that had been turned out of the kitchen as past repair, and an old card-table by the window supported an oil-lamp and a little pile of penny exercise-books, in which he made notes after his country walks. He was passionately interested in birds and insects, and would spend long hours on the moors or in the woods of the surrounding countryside watching them. In front of the card-table was a wooden chair, and against the wall a deck-chair in which he sometimes took his ease on Sunday afternoons. This was his world—right outside the queer emotional triangle that the other three formed.

He was sitting at the card-table reading a volume of Morris's *British Birds*, which he had borrowed from the Free Library, when Bridget appeared in the doorway.

"Hello, Terry. . . . May I come in?"

He leapt to his feet.

"Of course." He was furious with himself for blushing. "Do, please. . . ."

He looked round wildly for something to offer her, but all he could see was a rather grubby screw of bull's-eyes on the card-table. You couldn't offer anyone as wonderful as Bridget bull's-eyes—or, at any rate, not the twopence a quarter kind.

He took the deck-chair from against the wall and set it up with awkward bungling movements. The little room of which he had been so proud seemed of a sudden terribly makeshift and inadequate.

"Won't you sit down?" he stammered.

She looked at him, noticing how plain and shabby he was, with his sandy hair, pale face, crooked mouth, and worn suit; thinking how odd it was that she wouldn't have loved him so much if he'd been handsome and well dressed.

"I—I can't stay. I only just called round to see Lucy. I must get back or Mother'll be wondering what's become of me."

"Let me come with you," he said.

His pale face flushed as he spoke. He looked as if he were afraid of being snubbed. (He's used to being snubbed, of course, thought Bridget compassionately. Lucy snubs him whenever she gets the chance.)

It gave her a secret delight to think that Aunt Viola must once have felt like this about Uncle Humphrey, must have yearned over him in her heart because he was clumsy and plain like Terry. She summoned the picture of Roy with a kind of fierce exultation—Roy, so well turned-out, so good-looking, so charming and prosperous and rich. The contrast only made Terry more lovable and beloved.

"Yes, do," she assented.

They set off together through the side gate and along the road. A deep serenity of happiness descended upon her. It was curious to think how little she had really seen of Terry. She hadn't been alone with him more than half a dozen times ever since she could remember. And yet—she'd always had the feeling of belonging to him, of having known him for hundreds of years. Just to think of him gave her this warm happy sensation of home-coming. Perhaps that was what love really was, she thought dreamily, the feeling of belonging to people, of coming home when you were with them. Not the exalted emotions that you read so much about in books.

Perhaps once Aunt Viola and Uncle Humphrey had walked along the streets together like this, rather shy, and not quite knowing what to say to each other, but knowing secretly that they belonged to each other for all their lives. She didn't know why her thoughts kept turning so much to Aunt Viola and Uncle Humphrey. Perhaps it was the worry about Aunt Viola. She wasn't lovely and charming as Aunt Viola was, but once, surely, Aunt Viola had felt just like this. She wondered what it would be like to be kissed by Terry. Would it be something shattering, ecstatic, or just a deepening of the happiness it gave her to be with him? Just a deepening of the happiness, she thought. She and Terry were like that—slow and shy and ordinary, not made for ecstasy and rapture. Aunt Viola and Uncle Humphrey, she thought, had been like that, too. . . .

"I—I—don't know if you'd care to have a book-case," Terry was saying earnestly. "I'd love to make you one, if you would. I'd give you the one I made for myself, but I spilt ink on it, and I'd like you to have more fret-work on yours."

"I'd love it," she said happily.

"I'll get the wood and start on it tomorrow," he promised.

Into his mind had flashed an exact replica of the picture that had been in Bridget's a short time before—a little house, with Bridget bustling about in it, welcoming him home in the evening, sitting in a deck-chair in the garden while he mowed the lawn. But one couldn't propose to a girl like Bridget on two pounds a week. Besides, she probably wouldn't even look at him, anyway. . . . Not a girl like Bridget. He wasn't good enough. And yet, though he told himself this, part of him kept saying triumphantly, "She does care. I know she does, I'm sure she does. . . ."

They had reached the gate of her home now, and stood there, silent but not embarrassed, trying to postpone the moment when they must part.

"Well ..." said Terry, at last, with his grave smile. "I suppose ..."

It struck Bridget suddenly that she had never seen him without that troubled uncertain look on his face. He wasn't used to sympathy or understanding. But he will be, she said to herself exultantly.

Suddenly the door opened and Doreen appeared there. All Bridget's newly found serenity fell from her and she looked guilty and embarrassed. She realised that she only felt quite sure of herself when she was with Terry—or with Uncle Humphrey, of course.

She glanced nervously at Doreen and was surprised to find her smiling quite pleasantly.

Terry had begun to scowl—the sullen aggressive scowl that was his defence against the world—but the scowl faded as Doreen came slowly down to the gate, still smiling, and he watched her, wary and on his guard, like a shy animal ready to take to flight.

"There you are, darling," said Doreen affectionately to Bridget. "I was beginning to feel quite lonely without you. ... How nice to see you, Terry! You're quite a stranger. Do come in, won't you?"

Terry hesitated.

"I want to consult Terry about that fire-screen in the drawing-room," Doreen went on, turning to Bridget. "I think it's too high. You're quite a carpenter, aren't you, Terry? You'll be able to advise me about it."

She put a hand through the arm of each and drew them, one on either side of her, towards the door, Bridget felt bewildered. Could it possibly be that Mother was going to be nice about Terry? It seemed too wonderful to be true, but wonderful things did happen sometimes. That was what made life so exciting. ...

"Now, darling," said Doreen, as soon as they were in the little hall, "while Terry's looking at the fire-screen I want you to be an angel and run upstairs and get me my little coat. The brocade one. I think it's hanging in my wardrobe. It's really getting quite chilly."

Bridget ran happily upstairs. It *was* going to be all right, after all. She was sure it was. Mother had never been nice to Terry like this before. The fire-screen must have been just an excuse, because she'd never mentioned its being too high till now.

Downstairs Doreen was showing the fire-screen to Terry.

"Don't you see, Terry?" she was saying. "Is it just about two inches too high—or isn't it?"

Terry felt dizzy with relief and gratitude. He was too young not to respond instinctively to kindness whenever and wherever he met it, and the prospect of kindness from Doreen's mother, hitherto so frigid, was a breath-taking one. He couldn't help trusting life when it suddenly showed itself so friendly. Like Bridget, he thought that, after all, wonderful things *did* happen.

"No. I mean, yes," he stammered. "I—I don't know. ... But"—he was flushed and tense with eagerness—"I could easily take two inches off the stand. I'd finish it off quite neatly."

"I'm sure you would," said Doreen smoothly. "I think you're very clever, Terry. And such a healthy hobby, carpentering." A note of severity crept into her voice. "That's what I say to Bridget. I say, 'It's easy enough to make fun of other people's hobbies, my dear, but it's a pity you haven't a useful hobby yourself.' "

The new warmth at Terry's heart yielded to an icy chill. "It's easy enough to make fun of other people's hobbies." So Bridget made fun of his hobbies, just as Lucy did. ... Bridget, who had seemed so kind and understanding.

"Have a cigarette, Terry?" Doreen was saying.

"No, thank you."

He was hot and miserable, only prevented by his lack of social address from making his escape at once, before Bridget should come downstairs.

"Bridget called at your house, I hope?" went on Doreen.

"Y-yes," he stammered.

She nodded as if satisfied.

"That's right. I had a talk with her last night, and told her that she oughtn't to drop her old friends just because she'd found new and more exciting ones."

He almost staggered under this fresh blow. ... Bridget, sent by her mother against her will to pay a duty call, so that her old friends should not think themselves neglected. "New and more exciting friends." What a fool he'd been to think that he could ever be anything to her but a laughing-stock!

Doreen sighed.

"I'm going to miss my little girl terribly, you know, Terry."

He found his tongue at that.

"Miss her?" he echoed dazedly.

"Yes. . . . Of course, they aren't officially engaged yet, but it's an open secret. Fortunately Roy and I get on together splendidly." She smiled her bright hard smile. "I don't think I shall be a very formidable mother-in-law, do you?"

He stared at her dumbly, his heart cold and heavy with anguish. She continued to smile at him. What a booby the boy is, she was saying to herself. Plain and stupid and common. The child must be mad even to think of him. She'll thank me for this when she's older and has a little more sense. When she's Roy Hamwell's wife. . . .

"You'd better not mention it to anyone, just yet," she went on. "Bridget doesn't want anyone to know till it's really official. I'm afraid the little monkey's a bit of a flirt—such a demure baby she looks, too, doesn't she? She kept poor Roy hanging about for——"

He couldn't stand any more. With a muttered unintelligible excuse he jerked himself up from his seat and went into the hall. Bridget was just coming downstairs with the little coat. Doreen frowned. A pity they had to meet. The coat had been in the bottom drawer of her chest of drawers, and she had thought that it would take Bridget longer to find it.

Bridget stood half-way down the stairs and gazed in surprise at Terry's flushed unhappy face.

"Terry . . ." she said.

He didn't look at her or answer, but plunged clumsily at the front door, pushed it open, and vanished.

"Bridget, dear!" called Doreen from the drawing-room, but Bridget didn't even hear. She threw the coat on to the hall chest and ran down the short walk after him, catching him up at the gate.

"Terry . . ." she said again, laying her hand on his arm. "What's the matter?"

Her eyes were fixed on him in loving concern, but he wouldn't meet them. He was on fire with shame and misery. She laughed at him with Lucy, she looked on her friendship with him as a disagreeable duty. It was the thought of her laughing at him that hurt most. He didn't doubt Doreen for a moment. So deep-rooted was his self-distrust that he believed her implicitly. He didn't even feel resentment. He only felt desperately hurt. He shook off her hand.

"Nothing . . ." he muttered, and set off, almost running down the road.

Bridget turned slowly back to the house. She wasn't annoyed by Terry's brusqueness. She was so much part of him that she could feel his unhappiness as though it were her own. She went into the drawing-room, where Doreen stood smiling to herself.

"Mother," said Bridget slowly, "what have you been saying to Terry?"

Doreen looked at her in guarded surprise. There was a hint of maturity about the child that had not been there before. She realised that the danger was not over yet. She would have to go very carefully.

"Nothing, darling," she said, opening her eyes wide. "Why?"

"He seemed——"

Bridget stopped. The new-found assurance, the angry courage that would have forced an explanation from her mother, was fading, leaving her uncertain, vaguely unhappy, and apprehensive. That amused smile of Doreen's always made her feel young and foolish and clumsy.

"We just talked about the fire-screen, darling. He agrees that it's a bit too high. . . . He was very rude to you, wasn't he? One didn't expect *quite* such bad manners, even from him."

"He hasn't got bad manners," flashed Bridget.

"Then why did he behave like that?"

"I don't know," said Bridget.

The ingenuousness of Doreen's expression, the clear candid gaze of her eyes, dispelled the suspicion that she might have deliberately snubbed or teased him.

"It's just that he's . . ." Again she stopped. One couldn't explain Terry to Mother, not while she was looking at one like that.

"Come here, darling," said Doreen, and the amused smile melted into a warm loving one. "Come and sit down by me. I want to talk to you."

Bridget sat down on the settee—rigid, unhappy.

"Darling," went on Doreen, "I don't think it's good for you to see too much of people like the Wheelers. They're common and ——"

"They're not common," interrupted Bridget. "You mean that they're poor. They *are* poor, of course."

Doreen shrugged.

"I mean just what I say," she said. "They won't do you any good at all, and they may do you definite harm. The girl's all right, but the boy's an ill-mannered boor, and——"

Anger blazed suddenly and uncontrollably in Bridget. "I love Terry," she said unsteadily. "I'd marry him tomorrow, if he asked me to."

Doreen gathered her forces. It was worse than she had thought. To oppose the marriage generally on the score of Bridget's youth would be unwise, considering that she hoped to have her engaged to Roy Hanwell within the next few weeks. She must be very careful.

"Oh, my dear!" she said, smiling tenderly. "What nonsense! You'd never be happy with Terry."

"Why not?" said Bridget defiantly.

"For one thing, his people aren't our class."

"That's nonsense," said Bridget. "We're only shopkeepers, anyway. But even if what you said were true, it makes no difference."

"No difference, darling?" expostulated Doreen. "You know very little of the world," she went on sententiously, "if you think that a woman who marries beneath her is ever happy."

Bridget looked at her, her heart thrilling with sudden happy conviction.

"That's not true," she said. "Look at Aunt Viola and Uncle Humphrey."

Doreen considered. Viola had said, "Don't let her know till she has to." That time had surely arrived.

"Listen, darling," she said, still with a note of loving reasonableness in her voice, "I have something to tell you about your Aunt Viola and Uncle Humphrey."

Chapter Ten

HUMPHREY walked slowly down Oxford Street towards Frascati's. He had been surprised and rather troubled by Hilary's note: "Dear Humphrey, I believe you're up in town just now. I'm passing through on my way home on Monday, so shall we lunch together?—Hilary."

In that last interview with Viola at Reddington she had said, "I don't want Hilary to know about it till he comes home. I'll tell him myself then."

And now he would have to meet the boy as if nothing had happened and talk trivialities with him, knowing all the time that he was going straight back to Reddington to hear the whole story from Viola. The alternative—to tell him the truth—was impossible. Viola had said that he must hear it from her, and of course she was right.

He might have avoided the meeting by pretending to have another engagement, but that was too much like shirking. So he had decided to go through with it, even though Hilary hated him for it ever afterwards (as he probably would), and had written suggesting lunch at Frascati's.

Though Humphrey had acquiesced in Hilary's attitude of armed neutrality, he had never been able to rid himself of a certain feeling of responsibility for the boy. There was a neurotic element in him that, Humphrey had always felt, might easily land him in difficulties if someone were not at hand to help. Unobtrusively, and as far as he could in the circumstances, he had kept an eye on him, watching with particular interest the friends whom he occasionally brought over to Reddington. One of them he disliked intensely, a bull-like surly youth called Fordwick. Perhaps Hilary was in some sort of a mess now, and that was why he had written to arrange the meeting. The overture was quite unprecedented. Well—the feeling of compunction grew heavier at his heart—he wouldn't be able to help him. He'd have to let him down—with a good many other people. Probably, though, Hilary would be delighted to hear the news. He'd be able to take Viola away from Reddington and shake off the whole Lessington connection, which he had always hated. Perhaps it was fancy that had made Humphrey imagine that of late he had been showing himself more willing to accept the friendship that Humphrey had always been ready to give. At any rate, he wouldn't be letting him down as he'd be letting Bridget down. He had loved Bridget from her babyhood and done his best to protect her from Doreen's worldliness, and the knowledge that it was he who was bringing the first direct contact of evil into her life was not a pleasant one. It would not affect the others much. The aunts would be shocked, of course, but it would not disturb the even tenor of their lives. He saw them—prim, remote, absurdly alike—Aunt Harriet, who could talk of nothing but tradesmen and recipes, and Aunt Hester, who was always embarrassing him by mysterious references to some visit he had evidently once paid her as a child but which he had completely forgotten. The others—Doreen, Aggie, Elaine, Monica, Joey—it would not affect at all.

His thoughts went back over the affair, whose course still seemed to him fantastic and unreal. He remembered that evening at Hampstead when he first met Lily. A business friend had asked him home to supper, and Lily had been there—small and soft and pink and white and golden. He had seen her home to a rather dingy flat in St. John's Wood and she had asked him in. They had arranged to meet the next evening.

She was the opposite of Viola in every way, expansive and exuberant, and, beneath a thin veneer of unconvincing refinement, frankly common. She made no secret of the fact that she had fallen in love with him, and accepted his response as natural and inevitable. Affectionate, light-hearted, pagan in her zest for living and lack of restraint, she was something quite new in his life. It was his first infidelity, and never, even in his most rapturous moments, did he look on it as other than a sin, but he deliberately surrendered to it. Everything about her, even her slovenliness and the atmosphere of picnicking that was the normal *ménage* of her flat, enchanted him.

Viola had always been somewhat prudish, shrinking from physical love after the first few years of marriage; Lily delighted in it unashamedly. Viola was fastidious and exquisite in her person, almost schoolgirlish in her modesty; Lily sprawled about the flat naked or half naked, in entire unself-consciousness. Viola was fond of him but looked down on him from superior heights of breeding, education, and intellect. The knowledge that she had sacrificed herself in marrying him had always been there between them. Lily, on the other hand, looked up to him as to a being from another world. She seemed to feel towards him something as he had felt towards Viola. His response was as instinctive and uncontrollable as a starved man's snatching at food. And there was nothing of the gold-digger about her. She hated him to spend money on her unnecessarily or to buy her expensive presents. She would rather picnic *en déshabillé* in her frowsty little fiat with him than dress up and go out to a smart restaurant. She made no secret of the fact that she had had lovers before—boys of her own age, mostly—but she gave him to understand that she had not loved any of them as she loved him.

Her childishness and lack of sophistication stirred his sense of chivalry. She needed him as Viola had never needed him. Yet he had not contemplated marriage with her till he received her letter telling him that she was to have a child. Even then he would not have realised how inevitable that made their marriage had not Viola herself pointed it out—Viola, coldly remote in her fortress of fastidiousness, treating the whole affair as one would treat something noxious but not altogether unexpected. She seemed to hold it from her with delicate white fingers, turning her head away and grimacing faintly in disgust. Looking at her, he had had a vivid picture of Lily's round childlike dimpled face, "cupid's bow" mouth, and peroxided hair (Lily had no toilet secrets. She shook the peroxide bottle over her hair openly at the mirror, giggling, "Coo! Aren't I making a mess of it!"), and was conscious of a sudden rush of tenderness, a desire to shield her from the disdainful light in Viola's eyes. Viola had asked no questions about Lily, but he felt that in imagination she saw her exactly as she was—or rather as she would Have appeared to Viola—with her flashy clothes, obtrusive make-up, and slightly cockney accent.

"You'll marry her, of course?" Viola had said. "I'll divorce you as soon as it can be arranged."

The memory sent an icy chill through his heart, and he turned from it to the memory of Lily's soft lips and warm caressing arms. It was strange how little he thought of the child, considering how sorely he had once longed for one. But then it was too late and—it wouldn't be Viola's.

He must write to Viola when he returned to his club and explain why he wasn't able to let her have the evidence at once. There had been an unexpected hitch. He would have felt worried by it had it not been so exactly typical of Lily.

Lily was by profession a music-hall artiste. She did little song and dance acts—not very successfully, he gathered, as her engagements were few and far between. She used to do them with a man called Tony Wilson, but their connection had been broken off before Humphrey met her, and she was now trying to get engagements on her own and finding it rather difficult. Lily, however, took her profession seriously and refused to abandon her search for work.

"But why on earth should you work?" Humphrey had said. "I'd much rather you didn't."

"But I must," Lily had replied. "Honestly I must, duckie. I'm happier when I'm working. It's ever so much better for me."

There was a strain of independence in her that made her dislike living entirely on his money. He gathered that her people were respectable chapel-going working-class people in the North, and that she had run away from home soon after she left school. There was, beneath her surface lightness, a secret unformulated craving for respectability, and that, he guessed, was partly what had attracted her to him. He represented security, solidity. He wasn't like the men who, before, had taken her and left her so lightly. . . . They had had an argument last week about a job in a cabaret in Paris that her agent had mentioned to her.

"Paris!" Humphrey had grumbled. "Why must you run off to Paris, now of all times?"

But she had been desperately eager to get the job.

"I must," she had said. "It'll help me ever so much to get a job like that. My career, I mean."

Her longing for a "career" struck Humphrey as pathetic. She had a thin little voice, and her dancing was only mediocre.

"Don't worry about a job," he kept saying. "I'll look after you."

A few days later he received the letter that had sent him to Viola.

"I didn't tell you before," Lily wrote, "because I wasn't really sure till I saw the doctor last night."

But when he went to the flat to tell her that Viola was going to divorce him he found that she had gone away. The caretaker handed him a hastily written note:

"I've landed that job in Paris, darling, but I've got to go over at once. Isn't it lovely? I'll write you from Paris. Don't worry about what I told you the other day. It'll be all right. . . ."

That was like her, too, with her recklessness, her generosity, her light-hearted optimism. Why worry about anything before one need? It'll be all right. She didn't even give him an address in Paris. Oh well, it would only postpone the thing for a few weeks. The Paris engagement was for a month, he believed. . . .

He had reached Frascati's now. He entered and glanced about the foyer. Hilary wouldn't be there, of course. Hilary never was on time, anywhere.

Hilary was at that moment emerging from the Oxford Circus Underground and making his way automatically through the crowds, not noticing anything or anyone around him. He was thinking of Monica, and of how her grave little face would lighten suddenly when she smiled. It was like a lamp appearing in a dark room. Her eyes and mouth crinkled up, and her whole face smiled—not just her lips. Its charm lay in the contrast between that and the gravity of her natural expression. He was exuberantly happy, hilarious from sheer relief. For weeks he had been fighting against his love for Monica, and now suddenly he had given in to it. It would have been incredible a few months ago. Then she had not existed for him except as one of the despised and hated Lessingtons. He had been furious when he heard that she was coming to Oxford, and had decided to cut her if ever he should meet her there. He had still meant to do so when he actually met her in High Street, at the beginning of the term. He had seen quick recognition of him flash into her face, then hesitation, then the summoning of all her resources to meet his rebuff. And he couldn't do it. He had stopped to speak to her, aware that in his sudden reaction he was being more friendly than he really meant to be. He had even taken her to tea at Kemp Hall.

"I've shown her that I'm not quite such a cad as she thought I was," he had said to himself. "I needn't bother with her again after this."

But when they had finished tea he had arranged to meet her again the next week. And so the friendship had run its slow tortuous course. He hadn't wanted to be friends with her, and he had fought hard against the friendship, but it was always he who made the next overture after a meeting. He sometimes waited for her to do it, but she never did. He rather resented this, for he liked to be the one whose friendship was sought, and it piqued his vanity to have to do the seeking. He didn't know why he did it. He often told himself that he wouldn't. . . . But sooner or later his need of her gentle serenity would drive him to approach her again.

They had much in common apart from the joint interests of University life. They enjoyed the same kind of books, were interested in the more modern forms of music and poetry, but he had those things in common with innumerable other friends. It wasn't that that had drawn him to her so irresistibly. He had always been aware of a secret strain of weakness that betrayed him into doing things he didn't want to do and involved him in emotions of which he was ashamed, and it was this part of him that seemed to reach out, as for salvation, to Monica's wholesomeness and strength. He wouldn't recognise it, of course, for some time. It was an outrage to his pride that he should come to depend even ever so little upon a niece of his stepfather's. But, once he had surrendered to it, it seemed to enter his whole being, taking the sting from all his secret fears. It was a light shining into the dark places of his mind. And in one of the dark places was his mother's marriage to Humphrey Lessington.

As a child he had adored his mother with a possessive unchildlike passion. The news of her re-marriage had come to him when he was at his preparatory school at the same time as a schoolfellow had enlightened him, with unnecessary coarseness, into what are generally known as the facts of life. He had been a highly-strung, over-fastidious child, and he had conceived a sick hatred of Humphrey and a secret revulsion from Viola that had never really left him. He was, moreover, as are most small boys, something of a snob, and he had, with secret gratification, labelled Humphrey "second rate" as soon as he met him. The Ellisons and his father's people had encouraged his attitude, and the small boy—outraged and disgusted by the news of his mother's marriage, fiercely resentful of both her and Humphrey—still lurked within him. His shrinking from the idea of physical intercourse between man and woman dated from that time.

And into that dark corner Monica's saneness had shone, exorcising the ghosts, dispelling the horror, making everything normal and clean and happy. His dislike of Humphrey faded away. He even felt grateful to him for his devotion to Viola, deciding that he would show the same devotion to Monica when she was his wife, for he meant to propose to her during this vacation. He was not yet in a position to marry, but he was sure that Monica would not mind waiting. And he was sure that she would accept him. He belonged to her. She couldn't throw off the responsibility that had always been implicit in their relationship. He had written to her that morning, a letter that plainly showed his feelings for her, that burnt his boats behind him. He had refused curtly and without excuse Fordwick's invitation to spend the vacation touring with him in his new car. Fordwick had been furious, and he hadn't cared. It had been exhilarating to find that he didn't care, that Fordwick's anger no longer had power to hurt. He had heard that Humphrey was in London, and in his new exuberant happiness he had written to him asking him to have lunch with him before he went up to Reddington. He belonged to the same world as Humphrey now—the world of sane normal human beings.

He had reached Frascati's, and there was Humphrey—his solid thick-set figure planted firmly in the middle of the foyer. His kindly rough-hewn face wore a worried frown. He did not see Hilary at first, and Hilary stood for a moment watching him in affectionate amusement. Poor old Humphrey! Weighing up the rival merits of two different makes of cash registers, probably. . . . Then Humphrey saw him and came to him with a welcoming smile, his hand held out. Hilary took it in a long firm clasp.

Chapter Eleven

VIOLA entered the dining-room, where breakfast for two was laid on the small oval mahogany table. The cheerful smell of freshly made coffee mingled with the scent of the roses that stood in a low bowl in the centre of the table. Bright morning sunshine flooded the room, dancing on the cutlery and on the polished surface of the furniture.

She stood for a moment at the window, gazing out unseeingly at the silver filigree of cobwebs on the lawn. Her heart was heavy with anxiety and disappointment. She couldn't understand what had happened last night. Had it been her fault? Had she broken the news too abruptly, struck a jarring note? Thinking over the interview, she couldn't see where she had gone wrong. It would have been natural, of course, for him to be angry at Humphrey's desertion of her, but somehow it hadn't been that. . . .

She had looked forward so eagerly to his return, assuring herself over and over again that his devotion would compensate for all she had lost in Humphrey. And when he came he had been his happiest self. The moodiness and nerviness that so often hung about him seemed to have vanished. His manner to her—affectionate, light-hearted—reminded her of the little boy who had adored her so before Humphrey came into her life. He had lunched with Humphrey in London, and at first she thought that, despite her request, Humphrey must have told him about the divorce. He was young enough to forget her possible sorrow in his own relief at the thought of freeing himself for ever of Reddington and all it stood for. It soon became clear, however, that he knew nothing, so she told him slowly and deliberately—trying to confine herself to the facts, not to bid for his pity or blame Humphrey unduly, acutely aware as she did so of her longing for the comfort of his love and sympathy. She looked away from him as she finished, wishing to hide from him the hurt and humiliation that the recital had caused her. He was silent, and at last she turned to him, to find that he was staring at her, his face set in a scowl, his cheeks darkly flushed.

"Hilary . . ." she had said, half in question, half in appeal.

Still he said nothing. She put her hand on his arm, but he shook it off.

"How the bastard must have been laughing at me today!" he shot out viciously.

"*Don't*, Hilary," she said sharply. "He'd promised not to tell you. I wanted to tell you myself."

"Well, you've told me, haven't you?" he said, his lips drawn back into a sneer.

She looked at him in bewilderment. She couldn't understand. Why should he behave as if she had wronged him in some way? Where was the sympathy and understanding she had counted on so securely? Half-ashamedly she began to plead for it.

"Hilary, you're all I've got now. Please . . ."

He interrupted her, rising abruptly to his feet.

"I'm going out," he muttered. "Don't wait up for me."

She followed him into the hall, but he snatched his hat from the stand and went out without looking at her, slamming the door behind him.

She had waited for him till after midnight, pretending to read, trying to control the sick suspense at her heart. Soon after she had gone to bed she heard him come in and had sat up in bed, straining her ears as his steps approached her room, ready to call "Hilary" if they should pause there. But they went on to his own room and she lay down again, staring into the darkness, her mind a tumult of bewilderment and unhappiness.

After a few hours she drifted into a short uneasy sleep and awoke to a neuralgic headache and to the sound of Hilary's bedroom door opening. His footsteps went past her room, down the stairs, and across the hall. She heard the front door close.

"Has Mr. Hilary gone out?" she enquired when Evelyn brought her tea.

"Yes, madam," said Evelyn. "He said he'd be in for breakfast."

"It's a lovely morning," said Viola, trying to speak casually. "I expect he's gone for a walk."

She was still trying to reassure herself when she turned from the window and absently took up the pile of letters from the table by her plate.

Bills, receipts, charitable appeals, an invitation to a bridge party, and a letter from Frances.

Frances didn't often write, but when she did her letters usually consisted of a category of her recent doings, without comment or description. She opened it absently, her mind still hovering anxiously over Hilary, then stood looking at it in amazement. The address at the top of the letter was that of a London block of flats. She frowned perplexedly as she began to read:

DEAR VIOLA,
You'll be surprised to hear from me from this address. I decided quite suddenly to come up to London, and I've found a very nice furnished flat—small, but up-to-date and central. I've not decided yet whether to stay here permanently, but I probably shall. You must come and see me here when next you're in town.
Your loving sister,

FRANCES

Viola stared at the letter, all thought of Hilary and Humphrey driven from her mind. What on earth had made Frances decide to go to London? Her letter gave no hint of it. She remembered that disturbing scene in Frances's bedroom, that strange outburst: "You're lucky to have something to be unhappy about. I wish to God I had."

She hadn't taken it very seriously at the time, or thought much about it afterwards. It was absurd to imagine that Frances—so dull and such a good sort—wasn't completely happy in her rut. She had a sudden vision of her—the pale worn face, with the faded hair taken back into an unfashionable bun, the invariable country tweeds and plain felt hats. She hadn't been to London except for rare day visits connected with her work since the war. There was something curiously simple and childlike about her. She had indeed never really left her childhood, with its sheltered atmosphere and ordered routine. The old house still guarded her, imposing on her its rules and regulations. Though the old people took no part in her work, it was done under their protection, with their approval. To everyone who knew her she was Miss Ellison of Campions, Colonel and Mrs. Ellison's daughter, almost indistinguishable from the background against which she existed. What would she find to do in London? What would London do to her? (Again the instinctive impulse to consult Humphrey, strangled hastily before realisation should hurt too deeply.) As if she hadn't enough to worry her just now, she thought with weary exasperation! Anyway, she told herself, it wasn't her business. Surely Frances was old enough to live in London if she wanted to. But was she? Was it her business? She remembered suddenly and irrelevantly how sweet and shy and lovely Frances had been as a young girl, how radiant with happiness during her short engagement to Robin. She would have made a perfect wife and mother. How wasteful life was of its best material!

Then the door opened and Hilary entered. One glance at him showed that the mood of last night still hung over him. His mouth was set in a tight twisted line, his eyes were angry and hostile.

"Good-morning, Hilary," she said.

The forced pleasantness of her manner jarred even on herself.

"Good-morning," he replied, without looking at her.

She poured him his coffee and he helped himself to bacon in silence.

"What do you make of that?" she asked, handing him Frances's letter across the table.

He read it, then handed it back to her.

"What is there to make of it?" he said without pretence of interest.

"Isn't it rather strange, her going to live in London after all these years?"

"I see no reason why she shouldn't, if she wants to."

His tone was short almost to discourtesy. She realised for the first time that Humphrey had acted as a restraining influence on him. He had never given way so openly to his moods when Humphrey was there.

They went on with the meal in silence.

Hilary was feeling ashamed of his curtness to her, but he couldn't help it. It was all so damnable. He'd just caught a glimpse of freedom—of sanity and wholesomeness and happiness—when the prison gates had closed on him again. "She's not, I suppose, what you'd call a lady." He saw Humphrey going from his mother to this street slut, whoever she was, and his flesh crept in horror and disgust. What had yesterday seemed natural, beautiful, was suddenly foul and besmirched. The insult was to his mother, but he felt it as if it were his own. His body was hot with shame, his nerves so raw that he could hardly bear to look at her. He had just reconciled himself to the fact of Humphrey's possessing his mother, when this horror presented itself—his mother and this trollop both his stepfather's property. Share and share alike. How long had it been going on? A wave of nausea swept over him. He pushed his plate away and put his head on his hands.

"Hilary, what is it?"

He controlled himself with an effort.

"Nothing," he said, and began to make a pretence of eating again.

She looked with compunction at the tense lines of his face. The news had upset him, but he might have shown her, she thought resentfully, a little more sympathy. It was all so unlike her idea of what their relations would be when she told him that she was going to leave Humphrey.

"You're spending this vacation at home, aren't you, Hilary?" she said.

"No, I shall probably be joining Fordwick," he replied. "I sent him a wire asking if I could."

"When?"

"This morning."

"You'll be going at once, then?"

"As soon as I know it's all right. There's nothing to stay here for, is there?"

She tried not to let him see how much he hurt her.

"But, Hilary, we have so much to settle together. I mean ... there's the question of where we're to live, for one thing. We shan't want to stay here."

"Here?" he gave a short laugh. "I should think not! We'll move South, of course. Somewhere near Thorneham."

The youthful arrogance with which he now disposed of her irked her almost as much as his previous indifference had done. There was even a hint of impatience in his tone, as if he already found her a tiresome responsibility, an obstacle in the path of his freedom. For the first time she saw her future relation with Hilary not as one of companionship and understanding, but as the unequal drag of age on youth, saw with sudden dismay that he might come actually to dislike her because of her real or imagined dependence on him, that the absence of Humphrey, instead of bringing them nearer together, might thrust them yet further apart.

"I don't know that I want to be near Thorneham," she said. "There are many more convenient places."

He scowled at her, his handsome young face set.

"It seems the obvious and sensible thing to go to Thorneham," he said. "You know the place and the people."

There was a suspicion of hectoring in his tone that galled her pride.

"I think I'm the best judge of that," she said rather sharply. "I'm still quite capable of seeing to my own business."

It was the first time he ever remembered her snubbing him, and the colour flooded his face. She was horrified at the situation that had suddenly arisen between them. We're making it hateful and ugly when it might be beautiful, she thought helplessly. We're bickering and snarling at each other. I'm losing grip of myself. I never did that when Humphrey was here.

"I'm sorry, Hilary," she said unsteadily. "I didn't mean that. I——"

Evelyn entered.

"Miss Monica's here," she said. "I've shown her into the morning-room."

"I'll go to her," said Viola wearily.

"It was Mr. Hilary she asked for," said Evelyn.

Hilary rose jerkily and went from the room.

Monica had come down to breakfast to find Hilary's letter awaiting her.

> I shall be in Reddington all these vacs, [he wrote], and we must see a lot of each other. I've never wanted to spend a vac. in Reddington before! There are heaps of things we must do together. I've always wanted to walk over Wealdon Moor but I've always been too lazy. You must come there with me now. We'll take a picnic lunch. I hated leaving you last Thursday. ...

She had to read it twice before she could believe it. It was as if those vague day-dreams that she had tried to suppress as weakness and self-indulgence had miraculously become part of real life, as if real life itself had become more real and alive than had seemed possible. Everything around her was different—the sky bluer, the sunlight more dazzling. Of course, if it hadn't been Hilary it wouldn't have meant so much, but Hilary was always so afraid of committing himself, so terrified of the responsibility involved in any personal relationship, that it meant everything from him. She closed her eyes for a moment and let the love of which she had been so afraid flood every corner of her being. She felt dazed and tremulous with joy. (But *that* couldn't happen to me ... not to *me*, part of her kept saying. The thing you want as much as that doesn't really happen to you. But there's his letter, replied the other part. He wouldn't have written that unless he'd meant it.)

She felt that her happiness must shine out of her face, and half expected Elaine or her mother to notice it and ask what had happened. They made no comment, however, and, glancing in the mirror over the mantelpiece, she was surprised to find that she looked just as usual. Her thoughts soared away to Hilary again. She longed to take care of him, to protect him from everything that could hurt him, longed to charm from his spirit the secret fears that possessed it, to make life simple and happy for him, as she knew she could if he would only let her. . . . Her joy was almost oppressive in its intensity. It had come so suddenly and unexpectedly. It seemed to be more than she could contain. . . . Hilary. . . . She saw him quite plainly . . . the fine delicate features, the sensitive lips, the dark brooding eyes. She had known from the beginning that, if only he would let her in behind his defences, she could stop things hurting him so desperately, so unnecessarily. And now he had let her in. She could do it. . . . It was the one thing in the whole world she wanted to do with her life. She thought of the things in which her interests had centred before she came to know him—her work, her examinations, her college friendships, her future career. They meant nothing now, nothing at all. She couldn't believe that they had ever mattered even in the slightest degree.

Elaine and Joey had finished breakfast and were setting off to work—Elaine as neat and smart and immaculately groomed as if she had spent hours over her toilet, Joey grumbling as usual. Joey was always grumbling in a vague good-natured sort of way that no one took any notice of, saying how much he hated the business and how much he wanted to go out to the colonies and take up farming.

"No, we've lost enough money on farming in this family," said Aggie for the hundredth time. "Besides, you're the only boy, and we ought to keep together."

Aggie had a rather pathetic idea that a family ought to "keep together." When she was young her family used to go about everywhere in a crowd. They had been famous for miles around as a "united family." She was always trying to get Elaine and Monica and Joey to go out with her, but they never would. "I think it's such a pity not to keep together," she would say plaintively.

"Mugging your life away in a beastly shop," they heard him say as he went into the hall.

Aggie, still wearing the overall with the hole under the arm, and with her hair as untidy as if she hadn't done it only a few minutes before, sat at the breakfast table, reading the serial of her morning paper. Monica sat opposite her, her eyes fixed on Hilary's letter, her whole being a paean of joy and thanksgiving. Aggie raised her eyes from the serial, and for a moment Monica thought she must be going to say, "Why, whatever's happened to you, Mon dear?" but she only said, "It's the limit the way they always stop these serial tales just when you want them to go on."

"I suppose that's the idea," said Monica absently.

"I suppose so," said Aggie. "Of course in a way you can see what's going to happen. His wife's going to leave him." That reminded her of something. "I wonder how your Aunt Viola will get on without your Uncle Humphrey."

Monica considered the question idly. Aunt Doreen had told them at the tea party on Saturday that Uncle Humphrey had fallen in love with a woman in London and that Aunt Viola was going to divorce him. It was a pity, but it didn't somehow seem to matter. Things that happened to middle-aged people never seemed quite real. Their lives were more or less over. She read her letter again and came to a sudden decision. After making any overture of friendliness—even the slightest—Hilary always suffered torments of uncertainty and humiliation till it was returned. He would be torturing himself now by fears lest he had said too much or too little, his quick pride ready to leap to arms at the faintest suspicion of a repulse. She would go to him at once and suggest that they should walk to Wealden Moor this afternoon. It would set his mind at rest. She couldn't bear to think of his remaining in suspense a moment longer than was necessary.

She rose hastily from the breakfast table.

"I'm going out, Mother," she said. "I won't be long."

"All right, dear," murmured Aggie, glad to be left undisturbed with her paper for a little longer. She'd found a murder case that was even more exciting than the serial.

Monica put on her hat and hurried through the streets to Elm Lodge. She had a sudden picture of Hilary's anxious strained face and the quick smile of relief that would flash upon it when he saw her.

The housemaid showed her into the morning-room, and she stood at the window, her heart beating unevenly, her love a flame that glowed and leapt within her.

Then the door opened and Hilary entered. They looked at each other in silence. She had known that he might be stiff and on his guard, resentful of himself and her for the unrestrained friendliness (and more than friendliness) of his letter, and that she could reassure and soothe him in a few moments. She could always break down the walls that he built around himself. She never took offence at the sulkiness that masked his secret self-distrust. But she saw at once that this was different. His eyes were hard and angry. There was an ugly twist to his lips.

"Well?" he said.

She began to tremble, but she met his gaze steadily enough.

"I came to say that I'm free this afternoon if you'd like to walk to Wealden Moor."

He stared at her.

"Wealden Moor?" he said as if he didn't understand. "I'm leaving Reddington this afternoon."

The colour had faded from her cheeks. It was with difficulty that she spoke in her usual low unemotional voice.

"I thought you said in your letter——"

He interrupted with a short laugh.

"Oh, that letter! I'm afraid I was half-shot when I wrote it. I don't even remember what I said in it."

There was no mistaking the cold dislike in his eyes, the bitter sneering lines of his mouth. She'd lost him. Or rather, she'd never had him. It had all been a mistake—she didn't understand how or why. He didn't want her. He never had wanted her. She'd been right in thinking that she wasn't the sort of person to whom—that happened. She'd been a fool ever to have imagined that she was. She must go back to the drab world to which she belonged. She hadn't the passport to the world of glamour and romance. The flaming sword—quite rightly—barred her way. She felt no resentment—only a deep heartache of unhappiness. She loved him so terribly. Her eyes dwelt on his angry tortured face, and she thought: I shall never love anyone as much as this all the rest of my life. She noticed that there was a button missing on his sports coat, and it made him seem unbearably pathetic and vulnerable and helpless. As she looked at him her love was like a sword cutting slowly, agonisingly, through her heart.

She took up her bag, which she had put down on the table.

"I'm sorry . . ." she said.

Then Viola entered with a telegram.

"There's a telegram for you, Hilary," she said.

She kissed Monica absently. "How are you, dear?"

Hilary tore open the telegram.

"It's from Fordwick," he said. "It's all right about my going. I'll start at once."

"I think I'll run up to London to see Frances, then," said Viola. "I'm a bit uneasy about her."

Hilary had turned on his heel and gone from the room.

"I must go back, too," said Monica. "I've got masses of work waiting for me."

She was relieved to find that she could speak and behave naturally. She felt shaken and just a little sick, but she was quite mistress of herself. "Goodbye, Aunt Viola."

"Goodbye, dear."

She walked slowly down the path and into the road again.

Chapter Twelve

VIOLA paid the taxi-man and stood for a moment looking up at the soaring block of flats. She could hardly believe that Frances was really living here. It was so impossible to picture her apart from the background of Campions.

Hilary had set off to join Fordwick almost immediately after Monica's visit yesterday, and Viola had spent the rest of the day forming plans and altering them, till she felt exhausted. It humiliated her to realise how much she had depended on Humphrey for the small ordinary decisions of life. She had always despised women who could do nothing without a man at their elbow to help and advise. She discovered now to her chagrin that she belonged to that class, and that the quick judgment on which she had prided herself was less stable and reliable than the slow deliberateness that had irritated her so in Humphrey.

The sight of a letter from her mother when she came down to breakfast that morning had increased her anxiety. How worried the old people must be about Frances! But when she opened it, she found that her mother referred to Frances's departure quite casually at the end of two pages of news about Carlo.

"Mr. Fenton has done wonders for the little chap. It was chiefly liver trouble, after all, and we've had to put him on a very strict diet. The poor darling does so miss his titbits, but we've explained to him that it's for his own good, and the little pet really seems to understand. He's so good, bless him! Mr. Mellor was very nice about our wanting to consult Mr. Fenton. He said that he was quite glad to have a second opinion himself, so there was no unpleasantness of any sort, which was a great relief to us.

"Frances has gone to London. We're glad for her to have a little pleasure, as, of course, it's very quiet here, and Father and I don't go about much nowadays. Mrs. Hayes is doing her work at the Women's Institute for her. She'll do her best, I'm sure, but she really has the oddest curtains at her windows this summer that you could possibly imagine."

If their mother didn't worry, Viola had told herself, putting the letter back into its envelope, there was no reason why she should. And yet somehow she couldn't help worrying. She kept thinking of Frances, with her faded auburn hair, her haggard lined face, and the look of childish innocence so oddly at variance with her years ... and had finally come to London in order to reassure herself.

She walked up the steps, through the swing doors and into a large hall, on one side of which was a reception desk and on the other an opulent display of fruit and flowers.

"Miss Ellison?" she said to the reception clerk.

He was a tall, heavily built young man, with aggressively striped trousers, black shiny hair, and plump pink cheeks like a baby's.

"Yes, she's in," he said, consulting a board behind him. Then he beckoned to a page, who did not appear to be more than ten but who took Viola into his charge with the bland impersonal manner of a cabinet minister.

He led her past what looked like a street of shops—more flowers and fruit, provisions, gowns—to a lift that stopped on the first floor.

"We change here," he explained and led her through a lounge, furnished with very small tables and very large chairs, where groups of people sat about, smoking and talking, to another lift, which took them up to the top of the building. Viola then followed him down a long narrow corridor—grey rubber floor, grey walls, grey ceiling, with doors of a drab green colour at regular intervals. From behind one came a burst of laughter, from another the grating sound of a cheap gramophone, from another the unctuous tones of a B.B.C. announcer. Round a corner and down another narrow grey passage broken by the line of green doors. To Viola the place seemed oppressive and prison-like.

At a door half-way down the second passage the page stopped, and Viola saw the number 553 on the door.

"This is the room, madam," he said, and retreated noiselessly along the rubber corridor.

Just at first Viola didn't recognise Frances in the woman who came to open the door. She looked younger, prettier, and yet somehow more worn.

They kissed each other, then Viola held her at arm's length and examined her. The faded auburn hair had been brightened and fashionably dressed. She wore a smart and youthful jumper suit, surprisingly short, with well-fitting high-heeled shoes. Gone were the baggy tweeds, the sloppy dresses made by the village dressmaker, the square "ward" shoes, and the general effect of dowdiness that had marked her attitude to dress. "Dear old Frances!' people used to say of her affectionately. "She simply doesn't care what she wears."

"You got my letter, didn't you?" she said.

"Yes," said Frances. "It was sweet of you. I was hoping you'd come. . . . Well, what do you think of the flat?"

Viola looked about her. It was a charming room, furnished in modern, but not aggressively modern, style. There was a divan in a recess that could be curtained off, several easy-chairs, a bookshelf, a gate-legged table, and a writing-desk. Bowls of flowers stood everywhere, sunshine poured in through the open windows, and the sound of the traffic far down in the street below arose as a pleasant muted murmur. Frances was talking in a new, quick, eager voice.

"It *does* seem so funny not to have a fireplace. That's a radiator just under the window, of course. It's the first time I've ever lived without a fireplace and a mantelpiece. I think I miss a mantelpiece even more than a fireplace. It's a sort of focus and so useful to put things on. And now do come and look at the kitchenette and bathroom. It was the kitchenette I really fell in love with."

Viola inspected the tiny white-tiled room, the ingenious little cupboards, the electric cooker and toaster, and small compact refrigerator. She inspected them absently, wondering how she could break down the hard bright barrier that Frances had interposed between them.

She powdered her face and readjusted her hat at the little mirror in the bathroom, then came back to the sitting-room, where Frances was spreading a gaily coloured tea-cloth upon the gate-legged table.

"Frances," she said suddenly, "do tell me, darling—I want to understand—what made you come here like this?"

Frances looked at her, standing motionless, the corners of the tablecloth still in her hands, and the hard brightness dropped from her suddenly, leaving something perplexed and faintly unhappy.

"I don't know," she said slowly. "Honestly, I don't know, Viola. I just felt I had to. I don't know why."

"Was it—was it anything to do with what I told you about Humphrey?"

"I don't know," said Frances again. "It might have been, but—I don't know. Suddenly, after you'd been over—do you remember?—and we'd had that talk in my bedroom, I began to realise that nothing had ever happened to me. I don't suppose you understand, because things have happened to you, but nothing's ever happened to me all my life. Losing Robin wasn't anything really. I tried to explain to you about that, didn't I? All my life, ever since I can remember, I've gone on living at home with Mother and Father and just doing things to fill up my time. Silly little things that I wasn't interested in and that anyone else could have done just as well and that really wouldn't have been missed if no one did them. And so——" She broke off helplessly. "Well, I can't explain, but I just couldn't go on any longer. I had to get away."

"But—Frances," said Viola gently, "what are you going to do here? I mean——"

She didn't quite know how to explain to Frances that if no one needed her in a little country village, no one was likely to need her in London, but the hard bright shell had enclosed her again. She was getting out the china with an unnecessary rattle—three cups and saucers, three plates. She glanced at the clock.

"Darling, you don't mind—do you?—but I've got someone else coming to tea."

"No, of course not," said Viola.

She felt relieved. Their neighbours in Thorneham often came to London. Frances wouldn't be cut off from her old friends. They would look her up and report to her parents how she was getting on. A weight of responsibility seemed to fall from her spirit.

"It isn't anyone you know," said Frances. She sounded a little constrained. "It's someone who was very kind to me when I arrived in London last week. There were such a lot of people and I couldn't find a porter to take my luggage from the van, and I was getting terribly flustered and this young man was so kind, Viola. He saw, I suppose, that I was upset by the crowds and that the porters took no notice of me, and he just fetched my bags out himself, got a porter, put me in a taxi and came with me here. So I asked him to tea today."

The weight of responsibility fastened itself upon Viola's spirit again.

"Then—you mean, he's a complete stranger?" she said.

A curious dreamy look came over Frances's face.

"In a way," she said, "but in a way he isn't a stranger at all. . . . Viola, he's awfully like Robin. I told you that I'd almost forgotten what Robin looked like, but as soon as I saw Richard I knew that Robin had looked just like that when first I met him."

"Richard?"

"That's his name. Richard Horrocks. He helped me settle in here, then took me out to tea. We got quite friendly and he asked me to call him Richard. You see . . . Frances, I told you—didn't I?—how bitter it made me to feel that I might have had a grown-up son just as you have Hilary; and, somehow, Richard seemed just as if he might have been my son—mine and Robin's. It seemed——" A light seemed to break over her worn features, softening and transforming them. "It seemed almost as if it had all been *meant*. As if it were Robin who'd told me to go to London and Richard had met me there to take care of me. . . ."

Viola looked at her anxiously.

"But, darling, you ought to be careful. You don't know anything about him, do you?"

Frances laughed—an excited unsteady laugh.

"Oh, Viola, wait till you *see* him. You won't talk like that then. . . . Besides, he told me all about himself. He sells cars on commission and has an invalid sister, poor boy. He sends her nearly all the money he earns. He's so unselfish and sweet, Frances. He's never had a mother—to remember, I mean. An aunt brought him up and she was very unkind and grudged every penny she had to spend on him. . . ."

Viola considered this moving story in silence, and the worried lines on her brow deepened. It was just the story to appeal to Frances, of course.

"Oh well," she said, dismissing it with a shrug. "You look very nice, anyway, darling. Where did you get your suit?"

A faint flush dyed Frances's thin cheeks.

"Do you like it?" She patted her hair self-consciously. "I couldn't help seeing that I looked—dreadful, when I got here. It didn't seem to matter what I looked like at Thorneham, but Richard says he'd like to take me about and show me London, and I felt I must try and look a bit better for his sake. You see . . . There's never been anyone before to care what I looked like. I bought the suit and had my hair done this morning, and—I did look so pale, Viola, and everyone seems to do it, though Mother would be dreadfully shocked, I suppose—I bought some rouge and powder at the hair place, and the girl there showed me how to put it on. I had what they call a face treatment, too, and I'm going to have another on Friday. The girl said that everyone had them nowadays. . . . Do you think it dreadful of me, Viola?"

"Of course not, darling," Viola reassured her, "but—about Richard——"

Frances glanced at the clock on the writing-desk.

"Oh, dear! I must hurry. He said he'd be here at half-past. Viola, be an angel and get out the cakes—will you?—while I put on the kettle. They're in the tin in that cupboard."

Richard Horrocks arrived at exactly half-past four, carrying a large sheaf of American Beauty roses. He was tall and blond, with regular features and wavy hair. He looked slightly taken aback at seeing Viola, but quickly recovered his poise.

"Mr. Horrocks. ... My sister, Mrs. Lessington," Frances introduced them, and added, "but you must call him Richard, mustn't she, Richard?"

"Rather!" said the visitor, with boyish enthusiasm.

Boyishness was evidently his strong suit. He was eager and frank and enthusiastic, with an attractive touch of shyness. His manner to Frances was a clever blend of protective devotion and respect. He spared just the right amount of attention for Viola, but Frances was evidently his chief concern.

She received the roses with tremulous delight.

"You shouldn't spend your money on me," she said. "You shouldn't really."

"But I wanted to," he protested, laughing. "I simply can't tell you how much I've been looking forward to this afternoon. I began to think this morning that it was never going to come. Won't you wear one of them?"

He broke off a rose and fastened it in her brooch.

"There!" He turned to Viola. "It suits her, doesn't it?"

Frances, flushed, her eyes alight, looked almost pretty.

"Oh, but you shouldn't, you shouldn't," she said. "Such lovely roses! And it'll only die on me.

"Well, it won't mind," he said gaily. "I'm sure it would rather die on you than in a vase with a lot of other roses."

"What nonsense he talks!" laughed Frances happily. "Now do sit down and let's have tea."

She took her place at the tea-table and began to pour out. She was glowing with a new radiance, a quivering eager happiness. It made her seem younger and at the same time, somehow, intolerably old. The nervous brightness that had replaced the old calm detachment was precarious, brittle, unreal. She was describing a visit she had had from her next-door neighbour the night before.

"She insisted on my going in to see her cactuses. I didn't want to. I hate cactuses. She had *hundreds* of them. They were everywhere.

It made me think of the reptile house in the Zoo. And she was exactly like a cactus herself."

Viola had never before seen Frances gay and animated like this. And the boy applied just the right touch of flattery, laughing delightedly at her jokes, displaying interest in every detail of her description, making her feel, Viola could see, young and charming and entertaining.

Viola studied him covertly. He was good-looking and well-built, but he wasn't quite as young as he seemed on first meeting. There were faintly graven lines on the regularly featured face that contradicted the youthfulness of his manner. His boyishness was just a trifle artificial, his smile too flashing, his laugh too frequent. He was perfectly at his ease even in his occasional displays of disarming youthful shyness. His light-coloured suit with its exaggerated waist-line only just escaped being flashy, and the wave in his bright yellow hair was evidently carefully tended. Robin ... Viola remembered dimly a shy courteous boy, rather self-conscious and not particularly good-looking. How on earth could Frances see any resemblance between them?

"And you must let me take you to the Zoo," he was saying.

"We used to go there when we were children, didn't we, Viola?" smiled Frances.

Yes, Viola remembered. ... Those two annual visits to London. The pantomime in winter. The Zoo in summer. Frances, a serious little girl in a sailor-suit, her hair hanging down her back in an ordered row of ringlets, drawing her anxiously back from the bars in the lion house ("Don't stand so near, Vi darling. He might be hungry"), holding her hand tightly in the crowd, comforting her when she suddenly found that she had lost her sixpence in the parrot house, insisting on giving her threepence from her own to make up. Frances had always been a "little mother"—ready to help and protect and console, recklessly generous with her possessions.

She looked at her now as, cheeks flushed, eyes feverishly bright, thin body tense and quivering, she hungrily drank in the flattery this youth poured out so expertly. Viola would have liked to wash her hands of the whole business with a contemptuous, "The old fool! It's not my business, anyway ...", but she couldn't, because Frances was Frances, the grave little elder sister who had stood between her and the unkindness of life for so many years.

He rose to go at last, after arranging to take Frances to a theatre the next night. She fluttered about him eagerly, brushing a thread of cotton off his coat with a proprietary air, laughingly refusing to allow him to help her wash up.

"No, it'll be something for me to do when you've gone."

He took his leave of Viola with a firm quick handclasp, meeting her eyes with his over-boyish air and flashing his bright smile at her.

As the door closed on him Frances turned to her.

"Isn't he charming, Viola?"

She was alight with happiness, and Viola felt a sudden compunction at the thought of even trying to extinguish it. It was years since she had seen Frances look happy.

"He's charming, of course," she said slowly, "but, honestly, Frances, you know nothing about him. I don't want to be unkind, darling, but do be careful. London's full of charming young adventurers."

Frances laughed—the gay radiant laugh of her girlhood.

"Oh, Viola, don't be so gloomy. Adventurer indeed! You talk as if I were a child. I'm a middle-aged woman and"—her voice grew serious—"I've found the son I might have had if I'd been luckier. Didn't you see the likeness to Robin?"

"Honestly, no."

"Well, of course, you could hardly be expected to. You never saw much of Robin, did you? But isn't it sweet of him, Viola, to want to take an old woman like me about? I got to know him quite well, you know, yesterday, and he *is* so sweet, and he's had such a hard life. I don't think he looks very strong, do you?"

She could talk of nothing but the guest, and hardly waited for Viola's comments or replies as she poured out her eager praises. Viola said little. Criticism and opposition would, she knew, only increase the infatuation and cause her to stifle any secret doubts she might have. Finally she began to talk about clothes, asking

Viola which were the best shops and what was being worn, but she had not, of course, really changed the subject. Richard mustn't be ashamed of her when he took her out. . . . So she would have striven to do credit to her son—hers and Robin's, for she had by now in some curious way completely identified the boy with her imaginary son.

Viola rose at last to take her leave—weary, baffled, and apprehensive.

"Don't bother to come down with me, Frances."

"Well, I won't, darling. I've got a lot to do. I'm not quite settled in yet."

Viola made a last attempt.

"Frances, darling, you will be careful, won't you?"

Frances laughed again—gaily, light-heartedly.

"You are a silly old goose, Viola. Of course I'll be careful. I always am careful. . . ."

Viola walked slowly down the long narrow grey corridor. It seemed even more depressing than it had seemed on her arrival. She supposed that now she must take the train back to Reddington—to the aching emptiness that her life had suddenly become, to the long stretch of minutes and hours and days all full of this heart-sick pain and regret. She clung even to her anxiety about Frances. At least it kept the thought of Humphrey away. . . . But she couldn't resist a sneaking envy of Frances. However illusive her happiness, at least she was happy. She believed in someone. She had something to look forward to tomorrow. . . .

As she passed through the entrance hall a tall man turned from the reception desk, and pleased recognition flashed into his eyes as they fell on her.

"Viola!" he said, coming forward to her.

"Why . . . Adrian!" she said, surprised to find how glad she was to see him.

"I was coming to call on Frances," he went on. "She's here, isn't she?"

"Yes. How did you know?"

The sight of him had calmed something of her unrest. His quiet air of breeding soothed the nerves that the bumptiousness of the boy upstairs had set ajar.

"It *is* good to see you," she added.

"It's good to see *you*," he returned. "I ran into the Longdons yesterday, and they told me Frances was here, so I thought I'd come and see her."

Again Viola told herself that she need not look on Frances as an innocent girl stranded in a wicked city. Her old friends would rally round her. She would probably soon tire of the boy and find fresh interests. There was nothing to worry about, so she wouldn't worry. ...

"She's in room 553," she smiled. "It's up two lifts and along two corridors, but you get to it in the end."

He hesitated.

"You're just going, aren't you?" he said.

"Yes, I've had tea with her."

"Are you going back to Reddington?"

She hesitated in her turn. She had meant to go back to Reddington, but she needn't. Why should she? Why not stay in London—for a short time, at any rate? In London, at least, she could fill every minute of her time, and leave no room for memories and regrets. And incidentally, of course, she could keep an eye on Frances.

"Just for tonight," she said. "I'm probably coming up in a day or two for a longish stay."

She saw the unguarded pleasure in his eyes.

"That's splendid! You've neglected this part of the world too long."

"I know. ... I'm going to mend my ways."

She thought of the things they could do together—concerts, theatres, exhibitions. They had been such close friends once. There was everything in him that she had missed in Humphrey.

"I shall see something of you, I hope, then. ... What time is your train?"

Again she readjusted her plans.

"There's quite a good one at nine-thirty."

"May I take you out to dinner, or are you engaged?"

"No, I'm not engaged. I'd love it. Somewhere in Soho. One of the places we used to go to. . . ."

"That'll be great," he beamed.

He turned towards the door with her. She looked up at him and laughed.

"But you'd come to see Frances," she reminded him.

He laughed, too.

"So I had," he said. "I'd quite forgotten. I'll have to come and see Frances another time."

Chapter Thirteen

HESTER moved to and fro about her bedroom, dusting and tidying mechanically. At first she simply hadn't been able to believe it. It wasn't that the man Humphrey had done something wicked. (He *had* done something wicked, of course, but guiltily she felt that she wouldn't have minded that very much. Men *were* wicked. You'd only to read the newspapers to find that out. Even the nicest men seemed to have a horrid side to them. Hester had long ago decided that she was glad she hadn't married.) It was that the child Humphrey, who had played with her in the garden and walked with her over the moor, who had crept into her bed for a story in the morning and said his prayers to her at night, had suddenly ceased to exist. What she had heard about the man Humphrey had killed him. The man Humphrey had once stayed with her for six weeks as a little boy. That was all there was to it now. ... And panic swept over her as she realised that her Escape had gone for ever. She had nowhere to retreat now when Harriet fussed and worried her. There was no part of her life now that didn't belong as much to Harriet as to herself. Desperately she tried to recover her dream, but her mind shrank back from it in revulsion. The man Humphrey had spoilt it—had left a smear of foulness over every part of it. She tried to summon a picture of the child Humphrey, but he always turned into the man Humphrey furtively entering the door of the flat where he kept his mistress. She tried over and over again, and he always turned into that, even before she'd been able to see him clearly as the child. A vague featureless childish shape, then the man, painfully vivid, slinking up a dark stairway to a half-open door.

Panic gripped her more tightly. How was she to go on to the end of her life belonging to Harriet like this, not having a single memory that Harriet didn't share? She passed her duster over the wardrobe, then opened the door and looked at the dresses hanging there. In Harriet's wardrobe hung identically the same dresses—same number, same material, same style.

Never in all her life had she had a dress that wasn't just like Harriet's . . . and she never would have. It was as if she had been born chained to Harriet. Revolt surged through her at the thought. She *hadn't* been born chained to Harriet. It was only because she was so weak that she had let Harriet dominate her so completely all these years. There was nothing to stop her walking out of the house now at this very minute and never coming back. She had enough money to live—very economically—by herself. There was certainly nothing to prevent her going into the town and buying a dress of her own choice, a dress that wasn't an exact replica of one of Harriet's. She closed the wardrobe door and stood there, staring into space, her heart beating unevenly, as the monstrous resolution formed itself in her mind. Then quickly, without giving it time to fade, she went into Harriet's bedroom and opened the drawer where she kept their money. After all, she told herself, it had been left to them jointly, though Harriet had always had charge of it. It was locked in the little black cash-box that Father had used for the shop in the old days in Parker Street, and the key was kept inside the Staffordshire china cow on the mantelpiece. She took the key, unlocked the box with trembling fingers, drew out two pound notes, and stuffed them into her purse. Then she locked the box again, replaced the key, and went noiselessly downstairs. For a few moments she stood in the hall listening. The only sound was that of Harriet's voice singing "Rock of Ages" as she swept and dusted the drawing-room. Harriet's voice had a range of two notes only, but she always sang as she went about her housework. Sometimes it got on Hester's nerves unbearably.

She took her hat and coat from the hat-stand and slipped them on, her eyes still fixed fearfully on the closed door of the drawing-room. She felt that she was doing something desperately wicked, something that would shake the whole world to its foundations when it became known. ("But I must have something of my own," she kept saying to herself. "I must have something of my own.")

She opened the door, called, "I'm just going out for a moment, Harriet," closed it quickly, and set off down the little path to the gate. Her heart was hammering in her thin chest. She was terrified at what she had done, yet doggedly determined to go through with it.

Harriet stopped singing and hurried across the hall to open the front door.

"Hester!" she called.

Hester apparently did not hear. She went on down the road with her scurrying nervous gait. Harriet looked after her, frowning perplexedly. She must be going to the little shop at the corner for something. That was as far as she ever went alone. But she might have asked her, Harriet, to go for her, or at any rate waited till she had finished the drawing-room and could go too. Harriet always felt vaguely anxious when Hester was out of her sight even for a moment. She was so absent-minded and so rash about crossing the road. She would stand on the kerb and let chance after chance go by and then dash across suddenly just when something was coming. There she was hurrying along. It would bring on her indigestion again—so soon after breakfast. And her hat was almost back-to-front. If only she had come to her and let her put her tidy before she started out! She simply wasn't fit to look after herself. She never had been, dear little Hester! . . . Harriet's thoughts brooded over her tenderly, anxiously. This dreadful news about Humphrey and Viola had made her feel that the rest of them must stand together, whatever happened. She and Hester, at any rate, had always been everything in the world to each other and always would be. . . . She'd finish the drawing-room, then she'd go and meet Hester on her return from the little shop.

Hester had boarded a tram to Market Square. She was still trembling and her heart was still beating unevenly. In vain she told herself that it was quite an ordinary and natural thing for a person to go into the town to buy a dress for herself. Hundreds of people did it every day. But she couldn't make it seem ordinary or natural. It was a flagrant act of defiance. It was a throwing-over of the habits and traditions of a lifetime. It was something that she had never done before, never, even in her wildest moments, contemplated doing. She sat there, tense and rigid, trying to conquer her terror of the crowded rocking tram, and to stifle the sudden desire to run back to Harriet for protection. ("I must have something of my own. . . ." "I must have something of my own. . . ." It seemed to keep time with the tram's swaying movement. "I must have something of my own . . .")

The tram stopped and a neighbour got in. She looked surprised to see Hester sitting there alone.

"I hope your sister's not ill, Miss Lessington," she said, as she passed down the tram.

Hester smiled with nervous brightness. "Oh no," she replied. "She's quite well, thank you."

At the Square she got out and looked about her uncertainly. There was Lessington's, with its plate-glass windows, its display of underclothes and shoes and blouses and jumpers, its cascades of colourful materials, its simpering wax models dressed in "The Latest Model," "Le Dernier Cri," "As Now Worn," and (rather oddly) "The Limit."

For the first time she began to consider where to buy the dress. Till now the stupendous fact of buying a dress at all had dwarfed every other consideration.

She decided not to go to Lessington's. It was so overpowering. The assistants were so grand and condescending. Even Harriet felt overawed by Lessington's nowadays and avoided shopping there. Besides, in Lessington's she might run into Joey, and that would never do. He would tell Aggie and Aggie would come round at once, agog with interest and curiosity, to find out why she had been alone.

She wandered slowly down Peel Street, looking into the shop windows as she went. They gave her back her reflection—a pale, thin, nervous-looking elderly woman in a brown coat that showed the net front of her dress and a brown hat worn rakishly on one side of her head. Feverishly she straightened it, taking out the hat-pin with trembling haste and jabbing it in again through her bun. . . . She'd gone on too far down the street now. It was petering out into rows of houses with an occasional sweet-shop and tobacconist's. She turned back towards the shopping district, walking slowly, peering shortsightedly into the shops, nervously shrinking from entering any of them. She was almost back at Lessington's. . . . She must do something soon. She couldn't just walk up and down Peel Street like this all morning. She dived with sudden desperate courage into the next dress-shop she passed and heaved a tremulous sigh of relief when she saw that the woman who came forward to serve her looked kind and plain and elderly.

"You're a bit out of breath, aren't you, madam?" she said. "Won't you sit down and rest for a few minutes?"

"No, thank you," said Hester, realising how breathless and unsteady her voice sounded though she hadn't been walking fast. "I'm quite all right. I—I want to buy a dress."

She looked round the shop. It was reassuringly dark and small and shabby. A headless model in a skimpy cotton dress reminded her of the little shop in Parker Street and sent a wave of comfort through her.

"I—I just want a dress," she said again, trying to speak calmly and authoritatively like Harriet.

"Yes, madam," said the woman. "An afternoon dress?"

"Yes, please," said Hester, accepting the suggestion gratefully. "An afternoon dress."

"About what price?"

"Oh . . . not very expensive," said Hester.

The woman opened a cupboard and showed a row of dresses hanging from a rod.

"I have a very good line at a guinea," she said. "Artificial silk. It wears very well, you know."

"Oh yes, of course," agreed Hester, trying to look knowledgeable about artificial silk. Really she didn't know anything at all about materials. Harriet always bought them.

The woman glanced speculatively at the brown dress with its plain V neck, filled up by the net front, and took from the stand a brown patterned one with a cross-over front.

"This isn't unlike the one you're wearing," she said.

"Oh, but I don't want one like the one I'm wearing," protested Hester.

What would be the use of having the sort of dress that Harriet would have chosen for her? Her eyes wandered along the line of dresses till it rested upon one of a glaring blue, the sort of blue that is used to depict the sky on cheap coloured postcards of Monte Carlo. It was made very stylishly, too, with a lot of little frills on the bodice and another little frill just below the waist. It was quite unlike anything that Harriet would have chosen.

"Is that the same price?"

The woman took it down.

"Yes, they're all a guinea. It's pretty, isn't it? Would you like to try it on? I'll put up the screen."

"Oh no," gasped Hester. The thought of taking off her dress and exposing herself in her underclothing before this strange woman horrified her. "I'll take it as it is. I'm sure it'll be all right."

"Well . . ." The woman held up the dress and looked first at it and then at Hester. "I think it's about your size. It may want shortening a bit. . . ."

"Yes, it's quite all right," said Hester nervously. "*Quite* all right. Thank you so much. . . ." She took out her purse and fumbled for one of the notes that she had taken from Harriet's drawer, then for a shilling. Her fingers felt cold and stiff as if they belonged to someone else.

The woman stood at the window and watched her scurry away with her parcel. Crackers, I shouldn't wonder, she thought. Then she shrugged and turned to put away the brown patterned dress. Crackers or not, she'd been easy enough to please. She wished a few more people were like her.

Now that Hester had actually bought the dress, terror seized her afresh, and she had a momentary temptation to throw it away somewhere, anywhere, and go home as if nothing had happened. But she couldn't do that. Something had happened. She'd been into the town alone. She'd taken the money from Harriet's cash-box. She'd have to give some explanation. And she didn't regret it, she told herself doggedly, holding tightly to her parcel as the crowd on the pavement outside Lessington's pushed and jostled her. She *had* to have something of her own, and even a dress that was too blue and too frilly for Harriet was better than nothing. How rude people were, bumping and banging into her! Surely they weren't quite as bad as that when Harriet was with her.

Suddenly she saw Doreen and Bridget emerge from a small hat-shop just across the road. Bridget carried a paper bag, obviously containing a hat. Doreen looked brightly triumphant, her mouth a small tight line, Bridget flushed and unhappy. Hester hastily turned away to gaze tensely and unseeingly at a wax model, clothed in corset, chemise, and stockings, which would normally have caused her acute embarrassment, and waited till she felt sure they would be out of sight. Then she made her way hurriedly to the tram stop.

Her expedition had taken longer than she had thought it would, and it was now the lunch hour. People crowded on to the tram in front of her. The conductor called "Full up" and pushed a fat man off the step almost on top of her. A woman behind her poked her shopping basket into her back. A child in arms, wedged tightly beside her, pulled at her hat. At last she managed to get into a tram, but she had to stand. She felt slightly sick with nervousness as she neared the stopping-place. What would Harriet say to her? What could she say to Harriet? Harriet would never understand, however much she explained to her, and anyway she never had been able to explain things to people. She got off the tram and walked slowly down the road, her heart redoubling its beats as she turned the corner that led to the house. She was trying to imagine the expression on Harriet's face as she opened the door to her. But Harriet was at the gate, and as soon as she saw her almost ran to meet her.

"Oh, darling," she said, "where have you been? I've been so anxious. Are you all right?"

There was no anger or irritation in her face—only the old loving anxiety, the deep protective tenderness.

"Yes," said Hester breathlessly. "Yes. I'm quite all right."

"I've been so anxious, dear. I went to the little shop and found you hadn't been there, and then Mrs. Green said she'd seen you on the tram. How tired you look! Come and sit down."

She drew Hester into the dining-room.

"There! Sit down and rest. I'll get a footstool so that you can put your feet up."

"No, no," said Hester wildly. "I don't want to put my feet up."

There it was, wrapping her round again, enclosing her like a soft warm haze, so that she hadn't any existence outside it, so that nothing, nothing, nothing, not even herself, really belonged to her. It was hopeless. She couldn't escape it however hard she tried. She sat down, because her knees were too unsteady to support her any longer, and clasped her parcel tightly to her breast. At least she had that. Or had she?

"Where have you been, darling?" said Harriet again as she fussed solicitously about her, putting a cushion behind her back, moving up a footstool, and lifting her feet on to it, though she took them off almost immediately. "You shouldn't go out alone, dear. It's too tiring for you. I'd have come with you if you'd only told me. I knew you were trying to save me trouble, but, darling, it's never any trouble to do anything for you, you know. ..."

Even now, of course, Harriet was too kind to reproach her, to dwell on the anxiety and suspense she must have suffered, but that didn't melt Hester towards her. It only seemed to emphasise the chains that bound her. She was kind to her because she was part of herself. ("I must have something of my own. ... I must, I must, I must.")

"I've bought a dress," she burst out defiantly. "That's why I went into the town. To buy a dress. A dress of my own."

Harriet's gaze was troubled, puzzled, but still unbearably kind.

"Why, darling? We were going to have the navy silk made up."

"I didn't want it," said Hester. "I didn't want the navy silk." Her voice rose shrilly. "I've bought this."

She tore open the parcel with unsteady fingers and took out the blue dress. It looked even bluer than it had looked in the shop.

Harriet turned her puzzled frown upon it.

"But, darling, isn't it a bit bright? ... And we never buy ready-made dresses, you know. Miss Porter's so much cheaper and finishes them off so well. Still ... perhaps for special occasions and for a little change ... I suppose I can get another there like it."

Even then it never occurred to Harriet that they weren't going to have two of them just alike. She never even considered the possibility of Hester's having a different dress from hers. It was an odd vagary, this of Hester's—to go into the town alone and buy a dress—but one mustn't make too much of it or say anything that might upset her ... dear little Hester!

Hester gazed at her with despairing eyes. So it was all going to be no use—this dreadful morning that had seemed like a thousand years. Harriet would get another dress just like the blue one and she wouldn't have anything of her own after all. Suddenly she remembered the money.

"I took the money for it out of your cash-box," she said. "I took two pounds."

Harriet did not look annoyed even at that—only faintly perplexed.

"But, of course, dear," she said, "the money belongs to both of us equally. I'd have given it you at once if you'd asked me and we could have gone into the town and bought the dresses together. It would have been much better really than having to make the two journeys. I'm sure that if they haven't another dress like that at the shop where you bought it, they'll change it for another that they have two of. And now, dear, you look so tired and unlike yourself, I want you to go upstairs and lie down till lunch-time. You'll get a nice half-hour's rest and I'll see to the lunch. ... You see, darling, you're not very strong and——"

Sudden recklessness swept over Hester.

"Stop!" she said, and was surprised to find that she was shouting at Harriet as if she were a long way off. "Stop! I can't bear it. ...

I've got to have something. ... You don't understand. I'm going away. Right away. By myself. I must. I can't go on living if I don't. ..."

"Yes, yes, darling," said Harriet soothingly. "You do need a holiday. I can see that. We were going away as usual in September, but we might just as well go earlier. ..."

Hester suddenly became very calm. "No, Harriet," she said in a quiet steady voice. "I'm sorry for the way I've behaved, but I really mean what I say. I'm going away for a holiday by myself."

Chapter Fourteen

ELAINE was just finishing breakfast when Aggie came into the kitchen, blinking sleepily and clutching a tumbled kimono about her. Her hair was bunched up behind into a tangle of hair-pins.

"I'm so sorry, darling," she said. "I must have overslept. It's funny because I so seldom do."

Elaine shrugged. She didn't mind getting her own breakfast—she preferred to do so, in fact, because the tea that Aggie made was generally tepid and the bacon she cooked either underdone or burnt—but she felt irritated by Aggie's quite genuine conviction that she always got up early to do it, when actually she overslept six mornings out of seven.

Aggie threw a propitiatory glance at her, wondering for the thousandth time how on earth the child managed to look so spick and span and fresh and neat at that hour in the morning. Funny to think that she had dressed and washed Elaine, when she was a little girl, and sent her off clean and tidy to school. At least, she supposed she had. She hadn't any very clear recollection of doing so, but then she had a very poor memory.

"I thought you were going to sew on the belt of that kimono," said Elaine. "It's been off for about a fortnight now."

Aggie looked down apologetically at the kimono, which, released from her clutching hand, gaped open down the front, showing her petticoat.

"Yes, I was, dear. I mean, I am. It just seems to slip my memory." She glanced out of the window. "Mrs. Markham's had her washing out for three days now, and it was raining all yesterday," she went on, in a transparent attempt to deflect Elaine's attention from her own shortcomings to those of Mrs. Markham—a large untidy woman, whose garden adjoined the bottom of theirs.

"Well, I suppose it's her own business," said Elaine shortly.

She was thinking, as she thought a dozen times a day, how she loathed it all—this living cheek by jowl with a lot of neighbours, the houses separated only by a thin wall, through which you could hear almost everything they said, the gardens by a low fence, over which they could (and did) look as often as they pleased, this prying into each other's affairs, this gloating over each other's makeshifts and deficiencies, this spying and counter-spying, this façade of pretences that deceived no one. ... She shrugged. Oh, well, she'd be out of it all now soon enough. ...

Aggie sighed and poured herself a cup of tea. Mrs. Markham's washing should have led on to how funny it was that she could never keep a maid, and the absorbing question as to whether or not she drank. But one couldn't go on discussing it in the face of Elaine's obvious indifference. It was odd, she thought wistfully, that none of her children ever seemed to want to talk about anything interesting.

Her kimono was gaping open again, showing the black cotton with which she'd stitched on the shoulder-strap of her white petticoat. She'd better go and change or Elaine would be starting on that next.

She drained her cup of tea hastily, and went to the door, saying casually, "Well, I'll just go and put something on."

Elaine, who had noticed the black cotton as soon as Aggie entered the room, said nothing. Perhaps Mother would be different if they had lots of money. Perhaps she'd be more like the exquisite fastidious mother of her imagination. And—she set her lips firmly—she would have lots of money before she'd finished. She'd only to play her cards properly, now that she'd made up her mind. She couldn't understand why she'd ever hesitated even for a moment.

Joey entered the room, buttoning up his waistcoat.

"Your bacon's in the pan," she said.

He went to the window.

"My God, what a morning!" he groaned.

Elaine looked out at the golden haze of sunlight.

"Seems all right to me," she said.

He wheeled round on her.

"All right? Good Lord, it's marvellous. . . . And I've got to spend it mugging at a desk, adding up rows of foul figures."

Elaine shrugged.

"Well, so have most of us, more or less."

"Yes," he said, "and they call it civilisation. It's slavery, that's what it is. Slavery. We might as well be galley slaves. Why, most of us hardly see daylight for half the year. And yet it's *our* world, isn't it? I mean——"

"You don't know what you do mean," said Elaine. "Anyway, stop tub-thumping and have your breakfast or you'll be late."

"I do know what I mean," he said heatedly. "The world was made for us, wasn't it? The sun and the grass and all the rest of it. So why shouldn't we enjoy it instead of spending our lives in prisons? Filthy, dark, underground prisons. An hour or two in the evening in the summer—that's all we get of something that *belongs* to us, that even savages have."

She looked at his strong thickset figure, his open ingenuous young face with its sulky scowl.

"I don't know what you're grousing about," she said. "You've got a decent job, which a lot of boys would give their eyes for, and you'll probably step into Uncle Humphrey's shoes in the end."

"As if I wanted his beastly shoes!" he growled. "Oh, he's all right. He's quite decent in himself. I'm not grumbling at him. I'd loath any indoor job just as much. It's all right for you. You like it. You've got more brains than I have, I suppose," he admitted grudgingly, "but it suffocates me. I can't breathe in the beastly place. Shut in all round by walls. . . ."

"Well, now you've got it off your chest, come and have your breakfast," said Elaine dryly. "We know it all by heart by this time, anyway."

He glowered at her.

"You think it just hot air, don't you?" he said. "Well, it's not. I'd rather be a farm labourer. That's the sort of life I'd like. Out of doors all day. Something to do with your muscles instead of pushing a beastly pen or squirming at beastly customers. . . . I know there's no money in it, you needn't tell me that, but I don't want money. I'd rather have a decent life without it than waste my life in a stiff collar and a bowler hat, chained to a desk or a counter—even if I was going to be a millionaire at the end, which I'm not."

"It all sounds very grand," said Elaine, "but what it boils down to, my lad, is that you're work-shy."

"I'm not," he said angrily. "I'd work like a nigger, if I could work on a farm. You know I did when I was a kid. It's the only part of my life I've enjoyed—helping Dad on the farm when I was a kid."

"And that landed us all nicely in Queer Street, didn't it?" said Elaine. She got up, put his bacon on a plate, and poured him out a cup of tea. "Here's your breakfast, and stop spouting. . . . Hello, here's the lady of leisure," she went on good-humouredly, as Monica entered.

She glanced at her speculatively as she spoke. Monica hadn't been herself lately. She'd been giving quite a passable performance of herself, but it didn't deceive Elaine. It deceived Mother, but anyone could deceive Mother. Mother was always so busy trying to see what was going on next door but one that she never saw what was going on right under her nose. It wasn't that Monica seemed depressed. She was, if anything, rather brighter and less silent than usual, but Elaine knew that she was unhappy. It was as if a light had gone out that always used to shine in her, even when she wasn't doing or saying anything. If it were anyone but Mon she would think that it was a love affair, but Mon had never had any use for men. Funny, thought Elaine, that neither she nor Mon had ever had any use for men. People took for granted that Monica wasn't interested in them, because she dressed so plainly and was always working for exams., but they would never believe that she, Elaine, wasn't. Just because she dressed well and made up her face they took for granted that it was done to attract men. If only they knew how she despised them—Tom Redfern, and the whole boiling of them! Even Mr. Randolph . . . though he, of course, would now imagine that she had fallen for him at last. She didn't mean to let any man mess up her life. What fools most women were, she thought contemptuously.

A shaft of sunlight fell on to Monica as she stood pouring out her tea. She was pale, and there were heavy shadows under her eyes. The kid hadn't slept properly for nights. She was worrying herself sick over something. Elaine looked at her with a softening of her hard young face, but it never occurred to her to try to win her confidence or find out what the trouble was. It wasn't her business. She couldn't bear people who poked their noses into your affairs under the guise of sympathy. She wouldn't thank anyone for coming mooning round her and asking what the matter was if she'd struck a rough patch, and neither would Mon. The kid had guts enough to stick it out—whatever it was.

"There's some bacon in the pan," she said.

"Don't want any, thanks," said Monica, cutting herself some bread. "What are you two quarrelling about?"

"Nothing," said Elaine. "Joey was just letting off steam, that's all."

Joey looked up from his plate.

"Oh yes," he said again, through a mouthful of bacon. "You think it's just hot air, but I tell you I've stood it as long as I can, and I'm not going to stand it any longer. I've thought more than once of taking the beastly bank-notes I'm supposed to put in the bank for him on Saturday, and cutting off to the colonies."

"You'd make a mess of it, if you tried," said Elaine calmly.

"No, I wouldn't. I'd manage it all right. I've thought it all out. I'm not such a fool as you think I am. I tell you, I've only got one life and I'm not going to waste much more of it. Why shouldn't I take what I want? *He* jolly well doesn't mind taking what *he* wants, does he? Going off with a——"

"Shut up, Joey," put in Monica quietly.

"Sorry," said Joey, somewhat abashed. "But" —whipping up his anger again—"I'm sick of being told that it's my duty to stick to the business. He's not so jolly keen on his duty himself, nowadays, is he?"

"He's always been decent to *us*," said Monica.

"Depends on what you call decent," said Joey, gulping down his tea. "Anyway, if he's got to have one of the family in the beastly show, why pick on me? Why can't that ass, Hilary, turn-to for a change and do a bit of work for once in his life and see how he likes it?"

Monica's face, bent over her plate, seemed suddenly to go pinched and drawn. Good Lord, it can't be Hilary, thought Elaine. But of course it can't. They hardly know each other. He's never been here and he's never at home when we go to Uncle Humphrey's. He's far too grand to notice any of us. I don't suppose she was even listening to what Joey said. It was just something she thought of that made her look like that. . . .

Still muttering, Joey snatched a last piece of bread, buttered it, and went out, slamming the hall door and running down the street, eating the bread and butter as he went.

"I ought to be off, too . . ." said Elaine, glancing at her watch.

"You don't suppose that Joey really thinks of taking Uncle Humphrey's money, do you?" said Monica.

"Course not. He's just a young fool letting off steam. It does him good. . . . One sees his point, of course. Older people are always dinning it into us to do our duty, so, when they go off the rails themselves, one feels—well, what's sauce for the goose is sauce for the gander."

Aggie entered. She'd done her hair and put on a skirt and jumper and looked comparatively tidy.

"What was Joey going on about?" she said.

"The usual thing," replied Elaine. "He says that he wants to be a farm labourer."

"It's so silly going on like that," said Aggie, pouring herself out another cup of tea. "It's your father all over again. Wouldn't look at anything but farming, and a nice mess it got him in."

"He's not really like Father," said Monica suddenly. "He's much stronger and more capable. I think he'd make a good farmer if he had a chance."

"Well, for heaven's sake don't tell him so," said Aggie. "He's got to stick to the business whether he likes it or not. After all," sententiously, "we can none of us do as we like."

"He says Uncle Humphrey's doing as he likes," said Elaine.

"Well——" said Aggie, torn between a desire to discuss this business of Humphrey and Viola and a feeling that it wasn't quite a suitable subject to discuss with young girls, though she had a vague and tantalising idea that Elaine knew far more about such matters than she did. She contented herself by saying, "I'm glad to say that there was never any trouble of that sort between your father and me, though I suppose"—generously—"we both had our faults."

"Surely not!" teased Monica, afraid that if she didn't say something quickly Elaine might get in with one of her sharp remarks that hurt Mother so much more than she had any idea of.

(She had so hoped that there might be a letter from Hilary today. She couldn't understand what had happened. Hadn't he meant anything he'd said in his letter? But it wasn't only his letter. It was all these weeks in Oxford, when their friendship had seemed to mean so much—to him as well as to her. She tried not to think of his eyes as she'd seen them last, angry, hostile, looking at her as if she were something loathsome.)

"I do think it's funny," Aggie was saying as she sat in her favourite attitude, elbows on table, both hands clasped round her cup of tea, "your Aunt Hester going away alone like this."

"How is it funny?" challenged Elaine.

"Well, it's just funny," said Aggie, "She never has done before."

"That's no reason why she shouldn't now, if she wants to," said Elaine.

She wasn't in the least interested in Aunt Hester. Why shouldn't the old fool go away alone—to Timbuctoo, or anywhere else she pleased?

"The family seems so scattered," went on Aggie. "Here's your Aunt Viola gone to stay in London."

"She's got a bit of sense, anyway," said Elaine. "I expect the whole thing's a godsend to her. Getting rid of a stiff like Uncle

Humphrey and escaping from a hole like Reddington at the same time. She'll be a fool if she ever comes back."

"It's a very nice town, Elaine," said Aggie, bridling, as she always did when Elaine sneered at Reddington. "Everyone says the public gardens are very pretty, and the new Town Hall's supposed to be quite an"—she paused, hunting in her mind for a phrase she had read in the local paper last week—"an architectural gem," she ended triumphantly. "And your Uncle Humphrey's a very good man. At least," she qualified her statement, "he always has been till now."

It can't be anything I've done, Monica was thinking. I haven't seen him since I got his letter. Could he have been annoyed at my going round to Elm Lodge like that? Oh, surely not. Besides, it wasn't just annoyance. It was—I can't bear to think of what it was. As if I were—horrible in some way. What could I have done to make him feel like that to me? He's been sulky and on edge with me before—generally because he thought he'd told me too much or shown me too plainly that he liked me—but he's always got over it almost at once. It's never been like this before. . . . Oh, God, let there be a letter from him by the eleven o'clock post. Please, God. I can't bear it if I don't hear from him soon.

Elaine came in from the hall with her hat and coat on.

"Cheer up, kid," she said to Monica. Monica started guiltily (that would be worse than anything—if people guessed), but Elaine went on, "You would eat cheese last night, and it always gives you colly-wobbles," and she breathed freely again.

"What are you going to do this morning, Mother?" went on Elaine, turning to Aggie, who had now opened the newspaper and was deep in the serial. She tore herself away from it reluctantly.

"Well, I thought I'd go into the town," she said. "I've got quite a bit of shopping to do."

"You won't go in that skirt, I hope," said Elaine severely.

"Well," said Aggie, "I had kind of thought of going in it, dear. It's quite a good one. At least it was when it was new."

"You mustn't *think* of going into the town in it," said Elaine severely. "It looks awful."

"I've only had it about a year, dear," put in Aggie deprecatingly.

"Well, it looks awful, anyway," said Elaine. Aggie couldn't keep her clothes any length of time without getting them all messed up. "If you go into the town, you must put on your blue coat and skirt."

"Very well, dear," agreed Aggie, anxious to return to the mysterious stranger, who would probably turn out to be the heroine's long-lost millionaire uncle.

"I'll skin you alive if you let her go out in that skirt," said Elaine to Monica.

Monica laughed. She was feeling relieved because Elaine hadn't, after all, suspected that anything was wrong.

"She won't dare to, now," she said.

She wondered why Elaine, who didn't care twopence for anyone in Reddington, was always so fussy about Aggie's appearance when she went out. Elaine herself did not realise how deep was the tenderness for Aggie that made her hate the thought of people's laughing at her.

"Goodbye," she called as she slammed the front door behind her, and set off briskly down the street towards the station.

She'd been trying not to think of her coming interview with Mr. Randolph. Not that there was anything to think about. It was all quite straightforward. She'd made up her mind suddenly the day she heard about Uncle Humphrey and Aunt Viola. It wasn't that the news about Uncle Humphrey and Aunt Viola had influenced her. She wasn't even particularly interested in it. She looked upon them as an elderly couple, and a love affair of any sort in connection with them seemed ridiculous. Moreover, she despised them for making a mess of things. She had no patience with people who made a mess of things. No, she wasn't influenced at all by what she had heard about them, but as soon as she heard it her own path seemed to lie quite clear in front of her. Whereas, before, Mr. Randolph's suggestion that she should become his mistress had seemed so impossible that she had not even considered it, it now, quite suddenly, became not only possible, but reasonable and inevitable. She must get away from Reddington and give the forces that surged within her scope to fulfil themselves, and this was the only way.

Although she had made up her mind as soon as she heard about Uncle Humphrey, she had put off telling Mr. Randolph till today. He had arranged to go to Paris by tonight's boat for three weeks, and on his return would start work at the London office. She meant to see as little of him as possible till she went to London. Everyone who was successful began in London, and from there—oh, she had no doubt of success. Consciousness of power, certainty of success, had been her secret consolation from childhood. And men weren't going to come into her life. She'd made up her mind as to that. Mr. Randolph would give her her start, but after that she would rely on herself. She didn't yet know exactly where the path she had chosen was to lead her, but she knew with absolute confidence that it would lead to success and wealth. She didn't want a soft life. She wanted to work and to work hard. The sort of life that other girls called a "good time" bored her. She looked forward into the future and saw herself, prosperous and securely established, driving down from London, after a hard week's work, to her country house. It was a large pleasant house with spacious lawns and a lot of trees and flowers. It was run efficiently by a staff of well-trained servants. Aggie presided over it, dignified and beautifully dressed, miraculously transformed into the mother of her dreams.

"I'll go to lunch now if I may," said Elaine.

Mr. Randolph looked up from his desk.

"Yes, that's quite all right." He hesitated. "I suppose you wouldn't care to have lunch with me?"

"Thanks, I have an engagement," said Elaine. Then she looked him straight in the eyes and said in the same cool voice, "If you still want me as your secretary in London, I'm quite willing to come."

Surprise seemed to make his protruding eyes start right out of his head.

"You—you've changed your mind?"

"Yes."

"I—I can't tell you how glad I am," he stammered. "Of course I still want you. I——"

He half rose from his seat, but her cold clear gaze disconcerted him and he sat down again. Evidently she wasn't going to allow any love-making. She never did, confound her! But it would be different when they were in London. She was as hard as nails, but she was straight. She wasn't the sort of girl to make a bargain and then back out of doing her share of it. And how lovely she was, with her ice-blue eyes, disdainful mouth, and long slender limbs! She turned him into a stuttering schoolboy. He'd never wanted anything in all his life as much as he wanted her.

She turned to the door.

"I'll go to lunch now, then."

"But look here——" he began. With any other girl in the world he would have played the masterful lover, taken her into his arms, willy-nilly, and beaten down her resistance with kisses, but this slip of a child could make him keep his distance by the flutter of an eyelid. He dared not even touch her. "Look here, I must see you. I——"

"You're going to Paris this afternoon," she reminded him quietly. "There'll be plenty of time to make arrangements when you come back. Good-morning."

She left him, baffled, excited, bewildered, wildly exultant.

She walked quickly down the road to Madame Bertier's hat shop. Her friendship with the little Frenchwoman had grown till now she went to the hat shop for her lunch every day, taking with her a packet of sandwiches and enjoying the coffee that Madame made over her little gas stove. Madame could cook delicious omelets, too, and sometimes they had these instead of sandwiches. Elaine helped Madame with her books, and in return Madame initiated Elaine into the mysteries of her trade.

"Ah, but you are so queek, so clevaire. And you have such chic," she would say. "You are wasted in an offeece. You should come into the dress business. You are made for it."

"Perhaps I shall one day," said Elaine dreamily. She looked at the kind white face beneath the sleek black hair, and went on, "I'm leaving Reddington soon. I'm going to London with Mr. Randolph."

Madame's face became grave and anxious. Elaine had told her some time ago of Mr. Randolph's proposal.

"Ees eet wise?" she said.

"I don't know," said Elaine. "But I can't stay here any longer. I must get away."

Madame sighed.

"Ah, but I know ze feeleeng so well," she said.

Chapter Fifteen

BRIDGET lifted the dress—of pale shell-pink net—over her head and
fastened the silver belt about her waist, throwing a mechanical
glance into the mirror as she straightened it. She didn't really care
what she looked like. She didn't care about anything now. ... She
hadn't seen Terry since the night he'd changed so suddenly after
talking to Mother in the drawing-room, but that alone wouldn't
have worried her. She understood Terry. He was sensitive and easily
offended, and—either on purpose or by accident—Mother must
have said something that had hurt him, but she could easily have
put that right if she'd wanted to. She could have soothed his ruffled
feelings and made things exactly as they had been before Mother
came down to the gate, all smiles and sweetness. The trouble was
that she didn't want to. She didn't care whether Terry was offended
or not. Her love for him had vanished as utterly as if it had never
existed.

When first Mother told her, she had just sat and stared at her
stupidly, thinking: But it can't mean *that*. It can't mean *that*: till
Mother had frowned and said, "Do stop gaping at me, my dear
child. You're surely not quite so ignorant as not to know that it
does happen sometimes."

Of course she knew that it happened—but not to Uncle Humphrey
and Aunt Viola, not to Terry and herself, for, if it had happened
to Uncle Humphrey and Aunt Viola, it had also happened in some
mysterious way to Terry and herself.

"After all," Mother went on, "the Massiters were divorced."

Sally Massiter had been a school friend of Bridget's at Harrogate.
She had hated her father—a smug oily little man who displayed

ingratiating manners to strangers but satisfied a secret lust for power by bullying his wife and children—and had come dancing joyously into the classroom one morning waving a letter from her mother. "The Blight's gone off with a dame. He wants us to divorce him. Isn't it heavenly?"

It had meant moving to a small house and struggling hard to make "both ends of the world's shortest alimony meet," as Sally put it, but she had not minded that. "It's like being let out of prison," she said.

But this wasn't like being let out of prison. It was like a prison closing round, cutting off light and air.

She sat with a set stony expression, trying instinctively to hide her feelings from Doreen's sharp eyes.

"We're not telling people just at present," said Doreen, "though of course they'll have to know soon. I must say, one would feel a little more sympathy with her if she hadn't always given herself such airs."

Bridget rose abruptly and went from the room. Doreen stared after her resentfully. Really, the child might have shown a little concern, asked a few questions, stayed to discuss the matter. But young people nowadays were so completely wrapped up in themselves that they had no interest in anyone or anything else. It was very disheartening.

Upstairs, Bridget stood by the window gazing out unseeingly at the garden. She remembered that when Doreen called her into the drawing-room she had been thinking, "I'll write to Terry and make it up." She wouldn't write to him now. She'd never write to him. She didn't want ever to see him again. . . . She didn't want ever to see Uncle Humphrey again either—all the rest of her life. She felt—though she knew it to be unreasonable—as though all his kindness had been an elaborate deception, as though he had deliberately tricked her into believing something that he knew to be false.

And today was Roy's twenty-first birthday and there was to be a dance at Furness House in his honour. She didn't dread it as much as she'd thought she would. She just didn't care. . . .

Doreen came into the room with a hair ornament of silver leaves that matched the belt. She had sent for it on approval from a shop in Burchester.

"It's a splendid match," she said, fastening it in the smooth fair hair.

She wasn't worrying about Bridget's being shy and quiet any more. That was evidently how Roy liked her. He'd rung up twice to make sure that she was coming and had sent a spray of expensive orchids from the best florist in the town.

"It just gives the finishing touch," she went on.

"But I thought we weren't going to have it," said Bridget. "I thought it was too expensive."

"Oh, well," replied Doreen evasively, "just for tonight. . . ."

Doreen had a habit of getting things from shops on approval, wearing them for some special occasion, arid returning them as unsuitable the next day. Ordinarily Bridget would have been wretched about it, but would not have dared to protest. She was dully surprised to discover quite suddenly that she wasn't afraid of Doreen any more.

She drew out the pins that fastened the wreath in place.

"I'm not going to wear it if we aren't paying for it."

"But, my dear child, don't be so ridiculous," protested Doreen. "It can't possibly do the thing any harm. I'll return it in exactly the same condition as it was sent to us. If it were damaged at all, of course, I'd pay for it."

"You'd have to, wouldn't you?" said Bridget, and added, "I'm not going to wear it, anyway."

Doreen was nonplussed for a moment, wondering whether to persist. Then she met Bridget's eye and decided not to risk defeat. There was something unfamiliar about the child. There had been for some time now. Not like her own darling little Baby-Bridget. . . . Oh, well, she thought sententiously, all daughters grow away from their mothers sooner or later, and one must just endure it. She could endure it very well—very well indeed—if Bridget grew away from her into Mrs. Roy Hamwell, and of late she'd been feeling very hopeful. She'd evidently been quite successful in scotching that ridiculous affair with Terence Wheeler. When she saw them standing there at the gate, looking at each other, she knew it was time to act and she had acted promptly and successfully. A girl needed a mother's help at the critical moments of her life. . . .

She only wished that she could go with Bridget tonight and keep an eye on her and perhaps give her a word of advice now and again, but it was strictly a young people's party—and a very exclusive one at that. Only a few Reddington people were being invited. Most of the guests were coming from London or the stately homes scattered about the Midlands where the Hamwells' friends and relations lived.

"Come downstairs and rest if you're ready, dear," she said. "It's not quite time for the taxi yet. Would you like something to eat?"

"No, thank you," said Bridget.

Yes, she looks very nice, thought Doreen. Her eyes and skin and hair are lovely, and that dress is so beautifully cut that she doesn't look fat in it. What a little fool she was about the hair ornament! I could easily have made her wear it, of course, but it would have been silly to have a scene just before the party. . . . And really she looks just as nice without it. A little listless and spiritless, perhaps. But that's only nervousness. These few minutes before the taxi comes are always rather trying. And a lot hinges on this party. She can't be quite such a fool as not to realise that.

They went down to the drawing-room, and there Doreen set to work to charm away Bridget's nervousness by pleasant desultory chatter.

"You know, dear, I really am thinking of getting rid of Annie. I'm certain she's been at the milk again. I put a little mark on the bottle and it's almost an inch below it now. And she was very impudent when I spoke to her about it."

"She's only been here two months, hasn't she?" said Bridget. "And you got rid of the last one because she ate the butter."

"Yes," said Doreen, mistaking Bridget's tone for one of sympathy. "They are impossible, aren't they? And the wages they ask are so utterly ridiculous. And, of course, while other people are so silly as to pay them, one can't stand out against it alone. Ten and six a week is as much as the best of them is worth, and a good deal more. When I was a child you could get them easily for £20 a year."

"Pity you can't get one for nothing," said Bridget.

"But, darling," said Doreen, a note of excitement in her voice, "I may perhaps get one for nothing. I only heard today. . . . Well, not an ordinary maid, of course, but almost as good. Mrs. Torrent told me about someone she'd heard of—a Miss Marcher—who's over seventy but quite strong. She's been left without a bean. I mean, she had all her money in some sort of family business that's gone smash and she's penniless. Her brothers can't do anything for her because, of course, they're in the soup themselves, and anyway they have their wives to look after. Mrs. Torrent was saying that she was thinking of trying to find some family to give the old thing her keep in exchange for housework."

This broke through Bridget's indifference. "But Mother," she protested, "you couldn't expect an old woman like that—and a lady—to do the house-work here!"

"But why not, darling?" said Doreen sweetly. "It would be a kindness to the poor old thing. That is what I'm thinking of chiefly, of course. One has a sort of duty to people in misfortune."

Bridget was silent, seeing an old woman badgered and harried relentlessly from task to task throughout the day. Mother would give her no rest. She never could bear to see servants sitting down and taking their ease even for a few minutes. One servant must always do the work of two, or she felt she wasn't getting her money's worth out of them. It was horrible . . . but, after all, it didn't really matter. Everything was horrible. . . .

"If she wants to live with the family, of course, that will be all right," went on Doreen. "I shan't mind that at all. It will save light and coal in the kitchen, and, anyway, old people don't eat much. . . . Here's the taxi at last, darling."

Bridget left her cloak in the cloakroom, where a crowd of very smart girls whom she did not know were laughing and talking and clustering round the mirror, and followed the maid to the billiard-room, where the dance was being held. The billiard-room was a later addition to the house and ran all down one side of it. Chairs, settees, and flowering plants were arranged along the walls, and at one end a french window, concealed by tall palms, led into the garden.

Mr. and Mrs. Hamwell, an impressively handsome couple, stood side by side to receive the guests, with Roy in the offing.

The first thought that leapt into Bridget's mind as Roy—slight, sinuous, with dark mocking eyes and arrogant self-assurance—stepped forward to greet her was that, miraculously, he wasn't spoilt like everything else. He hadn't, of course, belonged to the world of Uncle Humphrey and Aunt Viola. The black shadow that had engulfed them didn't even touch him. He stood for what was left; what hadn't been swallowed up in the abyss. Something of her unhappiness fell from her as their eyes met. Her youth responded eagerly to his. Nothing ever hurt him. Nothing ever worried him. He took what he wanted, carelessly, without question. That was what she was going to be like—now.

The orchestra struck up and he claimed her for the first dance, holding her with practised skill a little more tightly than was necessary and smiling down at her. Her depression vanished and a feeling of excitement surged over her.

"I was afraid till the very last minute that you wouldn't come," he was saying.

"Why should you think I wouldn't come?" she smiled.

For the first time there was a hint of coquetry in her manner.

"Well, you know what you are," he teased. "Not very easy to get hold of, are you?"

"You seem to be managing it all right now, anyhow," she said as his arm tightened round her.

"Oh yes ... I mean to manage all right," he said.

He always did "manage all right," of course. His money, his unquestioned position as an important member of the small community, together with his natural self-confidence, had given him an easy manner of command. The best tables at restaurants were his by right, waiters and porters waited on him with nimble deference. Because he never doubted that life should give him of its best, it always did give him of its best, and he took it as his due.

He was making fun of the guests, his mother, his sister, and the grim aristocratic-looking aunt who was staying with them. He always made fun of people, and he was so amusing that you had to laugh even if you were slightly shocked by the malice that underlay his mockery. Bridget responded, as she had never done before, capping jest with jest. It was as if the defences behind which she had happily sheltered all her life till now had been torn down and she had been driven into a strange world in which she had to use a new language.

Roy claimed her for dance after dance, and glances were exchanged on all sides. At supper she had two glasses of champagne, which brought the colour to her cheeks, brightened her eyes, and loosened her tongue still further.

Roy laughed at her delightedly. She felt for the first time in her life that she was being a success. She was actually being the sort of person Mother had always wanted her to be. The knowledge exhilarated her and she redoubled her efforts. Then suddenly she thought of Terry, Terry to whom one needn't talk, Terry who wasn't bright or animated or amusing or rich, and the cold dull ache fastened upon her heart again.

Roy filled up her glass, ignoring her protests. He couldn't have explained what had first made him fall in love with her. It was partly that she was so unlike the other girls he knew. They were all the same type—thin to emaciation, assured, sophisticated, cynical, daring. He liked them, he got on well with them, they were good fun, but he didn't want to marry one of them. And then he met Bridget—shy and sweet and unsophisticated, with her round dimpled childish face and grave blue eyes.

"She's amazing," he had said to his sister Margot. "I didn't know there was a shy girl left in the world. How on earth can she be that appalling woman's daughter?"

"I think she's more appalling than the mother," his sister had replied. "She's just like the fairy at the top of a German Christmas-tree or an angel on a cheap Christmas card or that wax doll I once had—do you remember?—that opened and shut its eyes and said 'Mama' and 'Papa.' I've heard of the type, of course, but I've never seen it before. I thought it went out with crinolines."

Margot was thin, dark eyed, affected a manner of weary disillusionment, and had never known a moment's shyness in her life. She had made a "good match" the year she left school.

Later, when Roy's first half-amused interest in Bridget changed to love, she was not unsympathetic.

"I do understand how you feel, Roy," she said. "She's the sort of woman a man would like to come back to after his love affairs. And she's the type that would always take you back. You could sob out your penitence on her bosom. So few of us have bosoms any more. They may be coming back, of course. Bridget may be the vanguard of a new bosomed female. Anyway, though I've not got one, I can quite see their charm. And she'd have lovely babies, if you want babies."

"I do."

"I know. Men so often do. And she'd never make scenes. And she'd run the house well and get on with the servants. It goes with bosoms. And, of course, she'll wear wonderfully. She'll be a handsome woman when the rest of us are shrivelled hags."

"It's all very well to make fun of it," laughed Roy.

"No, I'm not making fun of it, Roy," she protested. "If the worst comes to the worst and you marry her, I'll do my level best to like her. Ma won't be pleased, of course—she's such a dreadful snob—but, after all, Mrs. Humphrey's right out of the top drawer."

"There's a vague rumour about that they're separating."

"Who?"

"Mrs. and Mr. Humphrey."

"Oh, how thrilling! Do find out from Bridget if it's true."

But he hadn't mentioned it to Bridget, because he wasn't really interested in it. He was only interested in Bridget. Dimly he had sensed, behind the childish gaucherie that his sister laughed at, a stark goodness and sincerity, a simplicity that was incapable of shifts and lies and disloyalties. It would be nice to have a wife like that—a wife you could be sure of. Her shrinking from him and his mother's opposition had only increased his passion, and tonight her sudden mood of gaiety settled whatever doubt still lingered in his mind. She was adorable. It was partly the champagne, of course, but that only made it all the more amusing. . . . He had inevitably acquired a Prince-of-the-Blood-Royal attitude to life, and he had always taken for granted that, despite her avoidance of him, she would accept him if he actually proposed. And he decided quite suddenly to propose tonight. He was in a position to marry. He worked in his father's office and would eventually succeed to his father's position, his mother made him a handsome allowance, and a godmother's legacy had made him pleasantly independent of both of them. He was tired of living at home. His mother was amiable enough, but she kept an eye on his comings and goings and expected him to conform to a certain extent to the family routine. He had tried living in rooms and had found it unspeakably dreary. He wanted a home of his own—a pleasant semi-country house outside Reddington (like Furness Hall but on a smaller scale) where he would be master, and he wanted a wife to look after it and him—a kind placid dependable wife like Bridget, who would not enquire too closely into his doings and who could on occasion be amusing and entertaining, as Bridget was being now.

With the clairvoyance that accompanies some moods of exaltation, Bridget knew quite clearly that he was going to propose to her, and she no longer shrank from the idea. She remembered what Lucy had said ("It always goes. One should marry where one will be most comfortable when it goes."). Roy carried with him an atmosphere of luxury and wealth. Cars, servants, smart clothes. . . . They hadn't mattered before, but suddenly they mattered now. The thought of them helped to drown the thought of the little house where, in her dreams, she had swept and dusted and cooked Terry's dinner. Money did help you to forget, and Roy was kind and rather exciting, and it would be thrilling to go about with him, wearing expensive clothes, staying at expensive places.

The billiard-room seemed very hot after supper, though the french windows to the garden were open.

"Shall we go out?" said Roy, and drew her with him into the cool scented darkness.

Whispers, laughter, and the glimpses of light dresses, showed where other couples had sought privacy.

"Let's get away from the rabble," said Roy, leading her down a tree-bordered path to an enclosed garden, where the hedge formed a small recess in which was a garden seat. A marble statue shone faintly through the dusk.

"Supposed to be an Italian garden," said Roy with his slight drawl. "They had one somewhere where Ma was staying and she came home full of the idea, but the statue of the blowsy female's as far as she got."

Suddenly the laughter died out of his voice.

"Bridget," he said, "will you marry me?"

She said "Yes" on a sharp intake of breath and let him gather her into his arms and kiss her lips.

At home Doreen was indulging in a pleasant day-dream in which exactly this happened.

Chapter Sixteen

VIOLA sat in the lounge of the hotel, waiting for Adrian. She was trying to feel free and happy. There was, she knew, every reason why she should feel free and happy. She had broken away from the narrow provincial life that had always irked her. She could take up again the interests that she had sacrificed to Humphrey. Adrian was only too willing to lead her back into the world she had lost—the world of art and literature, of new movements, new names.

One of the reasons why she could not feel free and happy was that she was worried about Frances—Frances, thin and flushed and feverishly excited, going about everywhere with Richard Horrocks, to theatres, to restaurants, to distant road houses, taking dancing lessons, wearing fantastically smart clothes, sending extravagant sums of money to the invalid sister whose existence Viola had doubted from the first.

Viola had gone to see her several times, hoping to find her alone, but Richard Horrocks was always in attendance—sleek, dapper, just too immaculately turned out. His boyishness in particular jarred on Viola. He made childish jokes and puns and laughed at them uproariously. And his vitality gave neither himself nor Frances any rest. He dragged her here, there, and everywhere. Despite her obvious happiness, she looked sometimes worn almost to breaking point.

"How absurd you are!" she said, when Viola, finding her alone at last, remonstrated with her. "It just shows how little you know Richard. He's so sweet and unselfish. And such a boy."

"He's not such a boy," said Viola.

"He's only twenty-one."

"Twenty-one!" echoed Viola. "My dear, he's thirty if he's a' day."

"He's twenty-one, Viola."

"Well, if he's twenty-one, aren't you making yourself rather ridiculous by going about with him like this?"

But Frances only laughed. Her happiness protected her like an impenetrable shield.

"Of course not," she said. "Don't you see, it's that that makes it all right. He might be my son. It—it's just as if he were my son." She grew serious. "You know, Viola, I've always thought that the relation between a mother and son can be the most beautiful relation in the world. . . . And to me Richard is the son that Robin and I might have had. . . ."

"Well, you're heading for a breakdown," Viola warned her. "This rushing about all over the place is enough to kill anyone. And it's a kind of life you aren't used to."

"But I feel marvellous," said Frances. "I've not felt so well for years."

Viola tried attack from another quarter.

"What about this invalid sister of Richard's?" she said. "Have you ever seen her?"

"Of course not," said Frances. "She lives right up in Scotland. The doctor says that she must never come to London. But I've had the sweetest letters from her. . . . She's so grateful for the little I've been able to do for her and Richard."

The next time Viola met Frances, Richard was there too, and he was so quietly and deliberately rude to her that she decided to wash her hands of the whole business. After all, she told herself for the hundredth time, she wasn't responsible for Frances. But the next week she received a letter from the family solicitor asking her to call at his office. At first she thought he must have heard some rumours about her and Humphrey, but she found that he wanted to consult her about Frances. It appeared that Frances had sold so many of her securities recently that the old man was growing anxious.

"I don't like to worry your father and mother with the matter," he said, "but, at this rate, Miss Ellison will leave herself barely enough to live on. I have, of course, pointed that out to her, but she has ignored my advice. She is becoming, if I may say so, Mrs. Lessington, very unlike herself. Frankly, I'm uneasy about the matter. One hears—disquieting reports. But, as I said, I don't like to worry your parents."

Viola went straight to Frances's flat, insisted on seeing her alone, and charged Richard, perhaps rather too hotly, with being an unscrupulous adventurer. Her contempt broke down Frances's new gay imperturbability.

"How *dare* you speak of Richard like that?" she said hotly. "You've lost your own happiness and you're jealous of mine. That's what it is. My money's my own and it's unpardonable impertinence on your part to try to dictate what I shall or shall not do with it."

Viola felt helpless. She remembered reading in her schooldays Horace's account of the man who sat day after day in an empty theatre under the delusion that he was watching new and absorbing plays. Physicians cured him, and, in taking away the harmless delusion, deprived him of his only pleasure in life. Frances was happy for the first time for many years, and, had there been no danger, it would have been cruel to attempt to take away her delusion, but there was danger, very grave danger. In despair Viola consulted Adrian, but Adrian, quite at home in assessing the value of a picture, in picking out the probable "winners" from new and as yet unknown artists, was at a loss when confronted with a problem of this sort. Moreover, he instinctively shrank from it as involving responsibility. He had always avoided responsibility, and life so far had given him less than his fair share of it. He was well off, had no family ties, and his interests included few human relationships. His instinct was to shift the problem of Frances on to other shoulders.

"I think you'd better go down and see your father about it," he said. "It's his business, not yours. Anyway, I expect old Jenkins was exaggerating. It's a solicitor's job, you know, making mountains out of molehills. It's a shame to worry you with it."

His solicitude was all for her. For Frances, drained of vitality and money by the parasite that had fastened upon her, he felt no pity or compunction, only a fastidious disgust.

"After all," he went on, "she's perfectly right in saying that she can spend her own money as she likes. One can't interfere in other people's lives, my dear."

That's a comfortable theory, thought Viola somewhat bitterly. It's a good thing that everyone doesn't hold it. She felt again the sudden unguarded longing for Humphrey's help. Humphrey would probably have gone straight to the point and tackled the unspeakable Richard himself—a thing that none of the rest of them could do, as it seemed. She did not even know where Humphrey was. She had heard nothing from him since the letter telling her that he could not give her evidence for the divorce till the girl's return from Paris. There they all were, kicking their heels and waiting on the chit's pleasure. Apparently, even Humphrey didn't know her address. The welcome rush of anger against him flooded her heart. It was monstrous of him to put her into such a position. . . .

But, immediately, the only thing to do seemed to be to go down to Campions and see her father and mother. Presumably they still had some sort of authority over Frances. If they told her to come home she would obey them.

The visit, however, turned out to be a repetition of her former visit, when she had gone to tell them about Humphrey.

"Frances is quite old enough to look after herself, dear," said Mrs. Ellison, "and I think it does a woman good to have a man friend. After all, you say you're going about with Adrian, so what's the difference?"

"Mr. Jenkins says she's spending far more money than she ought to," said Viola. "It's no use my saying anything. She won't even listen to me. And this boy's *dreadful*. . . ."

"I don't know, dear," said Mrs. Ellison mildly. "Frances says he's very kind and helpful. I remember my sister and I generally disliked each other's men friends when we were girls. I think it's only natural. And Frances has always been so economical. I think it's rather good for one to have a little burst of extravagance occasionally."

"She looks wretchedly ill."

"She's never looked strong, of course. She's one of the wiry sort. Always looked so fragile and never had a day's illness in her life."

"But, Mother, don't you mind her living alone in London like this? Don't you miss her? Mayn't I tell her that you want her to come home?"

"Of course we miss her, dear," said Mrs. Ellison perfunctorily. "Such a dear girl and so wonderful in the village. The Women's Institute really hardly knows how to get on without her. Mrs. Hayes was saying only the other day how much they missed her. They'd had to fall back on a raffia demonstration again, because no one had arranged anything else. But it's years since Frances had a real holiday, and she does deserve it. I remember how I used to love a few weeks in London when I was young. We never go now, of course, because your father finds it so noisy."

Viola looked at her helplessly.

"But, Mother, all the money Frances is spending . . ."

"Well, darling, it's her own money. One always does spend a lot of money in London. I know I always used to. I remember once I bought a carriage dress that cost thirty pounds. It was grey cashmere, trimmed with black velvet and feather bordering. I felt so guilty when I told your father, but he was very nice about it. He said it was the prettiest dress he'd ever seen. He always liked me to have pretty things." For the first time a shade of anxiety clouded the placid old face. "Don't say anything to your father about this, dear. Honestly, I don't think there's anything to worry about."

Of course you don't, thought Viola, because, if you did, you'd have to worry, and you don't want to. Like Adrian, her mother and father had built up a little world of pretence as a refuge from the crudeness of real life, and they admitted nothing to it that they did not want to admit. The anxiety on her mother's face deepened.

"He really has enough to worry him just now," she went on. "First there was dear little Carlo's illness and the dry-rot in Rose Cottage and now—I don't think I told you in my letter, dear,

173

because it only began last week—the Buff Orpingtons are being taken from the orchard."

"A fox?" said Viola, surrendering to her mother's determination to see nothing beyond the limits of her own little world.

"I don't think so, dear. I think it's Major Grant's Alsatian. So do your father and Matthews. A fox kills for food, but this seems to kill for the sake of killing. I mean, their bodies are left there—just mauled, not eaten at all. It's dreadful." The horror that she had denied to Viola's account of Frances distorted the delicate features for a moment. "Your father told Major Grant about it—quite courteously, of course—and Major Grant was almost rude. It's very worrying. One doesn't quite know what to do. . . ." The little pretence world had its worries, of course, but they were little pretence worries, mock worries, like a child's toys. "I suppose the truth's sure to come out sooner or later, but meantime there's the loss of the poor hens and the unpleasantness with Major Grant."

Her mother referred once again to Frances when Viola said goodbye. She referred to her kindly, with an affectionate rallying smile.

"Now, don't worry any more about Frances, darling," she said. "I'm quite sure you're mistaken. I have such happy letters from her. . . . I expect you're a bit run-down and need a change. One does worry about such foolish things when one's run-down."

And there Viola had left matters. Frances, now completely under Richard's domination and infuriated by what Viola had said of him, avoided meeting her, and Adrian waved the matter aside. A symphony by a new composer was to be performed for the first time at Queen's Hall, and Adrian had heard privately that it would be one of the musical sensations of the century. It was, of course, far more important than that ridiculous affair of Frances and the boy what-was-his-name.

Viola had been with him to Queen's Hall to hear the symphony last Sunday. She had enjoyed it, but her mind had been running on other things all the time—on Humphrey and Frances and Hilary. She had had one or two postcards from Hilary since he had set off on his holiday with Fordwick—bald impersonal accounts of their movements. She hoped he was happy. She still felt ashamed of that rather ugly scene she had had with him before he went. She must try to be more patient when he came back, to remember that he was highly strung and easily upset. He was all she had left now. She had never before realised what a terrible thing loneliness was. That was why she felt so grateful to Adrian for his constant kindness and attention.

She glanced at the clock. It was five minutes to three. He had said that he would call for her at three. After the exhibition at the Leicester Galleries they were going on to his rooms, where he had asked a few friends to tea. It was somehow characteristic of Adrian to prefer a tea party to a cocktail party.

Her thoughts went to Humphrey again. ... Despite her efforts to harden her heart against him, she couldn't really believe that he was not distressed at the position in which he had placed her. Perhaps he was trying to get into touch with the girl. Perhaps he had by now managed to get into touch with her. Perhaps by the next post she would receive a letter addressed in his handwriting, and, opening it, would find the receipted hotel bill—the "evidence." Her heart began to hammer against her side at the thought, and she felt suddenly glad of this period of respite. What a fool she was! She had always despised people who didn't know what they wanted, and it was humiliating to discover that she was one of them.

She took up to the newspaper and tried to fix her mind on the leading article. Humphrey was always well up in the news of the day and would give her patient explanations and accounts of anything that she was too lazy to read for herself. Politics were to him something real and deeply interesting. To Adrian they were part of the ugly modern world that had to be shut out of his life. Adrian's room was full of journals of art and literature and music, but he prided himself on not taking in a daily newspaper. A faint aroma of the aesthetic movement of the nineties hung about him. He was well groomed and well tailored, but one could easily imagine him with long hair and a velvet coat.

There he was, just coming in—tall, thin, with an indefinable air of distinction. It struck her suddenly what a contrast he was to Humphrey in every way. She summoned the vision of Humphrey's thickset clumsy figure with its suggestion of sturdy peasant stock. Adrian's eyes roved round seeking her, and lit up as they fell on her. It consoled her in her new terror of loneliness that someone's eyes should do that—should pass absently over half a dozen women better looking and better dressed and light up when they rested on her. She noticed, as he came near, the sensitive lines of his thin clean-cut face, the kindness of his grey eyes, the almost womanly softness of the long mobile mouth. He was one of those men who are better-looking in middle age than in youth. His slight stoop and greying hair suited him. The elaborate courtesy of his manners, which had appeared stilted in his younger days, now blended charmingly with his personality. Greeting him, she found herself wondering how Hilary would get on with him.

"This is splendid," he was saying. "How well you look! Are you sure this isn't too early for you? Have you rested?"

She smiled.

"Quite. I don't have an after-lunch nap, if that's what you mean. It's too obvious a mark of middle age, don't you think?"

They went through the hall to the front door, and Adrian summoned a taxi. Viola would have liked to suggest walking through the park and taking a taxi at the other end, but she had learnt by experience how much it worried Adrian when she made any suggestion other than the one he had in mind. He wavered, hesitated, inclined first to one then to the other, decided on one, then wished he had decided on the other, was harassed and put out for hours afterwards. There was something faintly spinsterish about him. He hated to be jerked out of his rut. Sometimes this irritated Viola, at others it endeared him to her.

"What exactly are we going to see?" she asked, as they drove through the streets. "You did tell me, but I've forgotten."

"French Impressionists," he replied.

He began to talk about French Impressionism. Viola listened absently, but with something of the same indulgence with which she used to listen to Hilary's eager outpourings when he was a child. He cared so terribly about it and it seemed to matter so little.

She wished she could quench that nagging anxiety about Hilary. Of course, he was all right. He'd gone for a holiday with a college friend. He'd sent her some quite cheerful postcards. There was nothing to worry about. It was because they had had that ugly little quarrel before he went, that she was worried. He was so quickly up and down. Probably by now he had completely forgotten their disagreement and was enjoying the holiday whole-heartedly.

"What's the matter?" said Adrian with sudden compunction. He was always quickly sensitive to her moods. "Here I am, holding forth like a tub-thumper, and I believe you've got a headache and would really rather not come at all. Have you?"

"No ... not a bit," she assured him.

She wondered whether to tell him that she was worried about Hilary and decided not to. It would only worry him, too, and then she would have to reassure him as well as herself. When you told your troubles to some people, they were lifted clean from your shoulders to theirs. Others made your troubles theirs, yet somehow didn't relieve you of them, but gave you their anxiety to bear as well as your own.

Looking at the pictures with him, she remembered how they used to go round art exhibitions together, in the old days—she and Gray and Adrian. How eager and zestful they had been! What fierce arguments and discussions they had had! How lifeless this was, compared with it! And yet how near it made her feel to Adrian! How she clung to his friendship as the only thing left from the wreck of her happiness! He had made up his mind to buy one picture only, and he could not decide between two of them. He walked from one to the other. He asked her advice over and over again. When she advised him to buy one, he pointed out the merits of the other; when she advised him to buy that, he pointed out the merits of the first.

"Get both of them," she said, but he felt himself bound by his original decision to buy one only and would not even consider buying both. He was slow in everything he did, with a slowness quite unlike Humphrey's. There was purposefulness behind Humphrey's slowness, there was indecision behind Adrian's. But it was, after all, his very dependence on her that helped to console her for Humphrey's desertion.

"It's been splendid to have you here," he said. "I don't know when I've enjoyed an afternoon so much." He had done little but go from one of the two pictures to the other, standing irresolute for long periods in front of each. "I'd never have made up my mind without you," he went on, for she had at last in desperation insisted on his buying the first of the two pictures he had admired.

She was tired when she reached his rooms—too tired to do anything but lean back in an armchair and listen to the conversation around her. The guests were mostly of the same type as Adrian—dilettanti, deliberately withdrawing themselves from the rough contacts of everyday life, adept at discovering new talent of the more exotic type and assessing reputations, shudderingly disdainful of "commercial values." It was the world of cultured leisured patrons of the arts. Though Gray had been a creative artist, he had belonged to this world. Once it had seemed the only world worth belonging to.

The jargon had changed with the years, of course, but she could soon have picked it up again, if she had been interested. The trouble was that she wasn't interested. Through all the years of her exile in Reddington she had thought of this world as the one to which she really belonged, and now she found that she didn't even belong to this. While they discussed a recent exhibition of Wyndham Lewis's paintings, she found herself thinking of Reddington, wondering what the family was doing, pondering over the pieces of news that had reached her: Aunt Hester for the first time in her life had gone for a holiday alone. (Why on earth had she done that? She'd be lost without Harriet.) Bridget was engaged to Roy Hamwell. (That was disturbing news. He was attractive enough but dissolute and unreliable. Surely Doreen knew that. Why hadn't she warned the child? Humphrey would be worried when he heard about it). Monica was working very hard for her exam., hardly going out at all and looking pale and rundown. (Odd that a young girl like Monica had no thought or interest beyond her work.) Elaine was being moved to the London branch of Randolph's. (She must be very capable for them to want her at the London branch. But she'd be lonely in London. She knew no one there).

She had received a long letter from Aggie that morning in which she told her shortly about Elaine's promotion, and described at great length a quarrel that had taken place between Mr. and Mrs. Parmenter last night, as to whether they should have a plain or patterned paper on the dining-room walls when they had it "done up" next spring. Queenie had supported her father and it had ended in Mrs. Parmenter's having hysterics for half the night. She went on to relate that Mr. Bolton had won a prize for the best household hint that week in the local paper, and was as excited as a child. The hint was something to do with freshening up stale loaves (Aggie couldn't quite remember what it was) and the prize was half a guinea. Mr. Bolton had spent it on a new electric iron, which he'd been wanting for some time.

An incredible homesickness for Reddington assailed her. She was tired of strange faces and strange scenes. All this talk about symbolism, expressionism, rhythm, the subconscious, escapism, the Modigliani legend, bored her unutterably. She wanted to be in a place where everyone knew everyone else; where you recognised in the streets and in the trams the assistants who served you in the shops; where the upholsterer, meeting you in the town, would compliment you and himself on the appearance of your new dining-room curtains; where, when you dropped into a café for a cup of coffee in the morning, you knew people at all the tables round you; where the news even of a slight illness brought offers of help from all the neighbours; where the proprietor of the garage was really concerned if you had trouble with your car. She wondered how much the gala for the Cottage Hospital, which had been held last week, had made; whether they'd started yet on the much-discussed and long-postponed widening of Peel Street; whether the new Vicar of St. Matthew's (who was High), was hitting it off any better with his parishioners (who were Low); whether the new Allotments Scheme for the Unemployed was working well

(Lessington's had headed the subscription list for that). How she had longed to get away from it all and how she longed now to be part of it again!

Gradually the guests departed, leaving her alone with Adrian. He turned to her, his thin face alight with enthusiasm.

"Have you enjoyed it?" he said.

He was proud of having introduced her to his world, a world that was to him the only world in which it was possible to live. There was something so kind and good about him that her feelings of a minute ago seemed almost disloyal. Periods of transition, she told herself, were always trying. She had once heard that released prisoners felt occasionally a bewildered desire to return to their prisons.

"I've loved it, Adrian," she said. "Do tell me about the people who were here."

He told her about them one by one, describing their various interests. She listened absently.

"You'll like them when you get to know them," he said.

She had noticed before that he seemed to take for granted that their lives were going to lie together for the future. Did he think that she would marry him when she had divorced Humphrey? She had vaguely contemplated going abroad with Hilary after the divorce, but now she doubted whether Hilary would wish to go with her. She shrank from the thought of joining the army of lonely unattached women who spend their lives drifting aimlessly from place to place. Probably she would marry Adrian. She loved him, though it was more the love one had for a brother than a husband. Perhaps it would be more durable because of that.

He was showing her an etching that he had bought last week.

"It's a beautiful thing, isn't it?" he said. "He's not really well known yet, but I buy everything of his I can get hold of now."

She sensed a slight constraint in his manner and noticed that he glanced furtively at the clock.

"Are you thinking it's time I went?" she smiled.

"Of course not," he said, but he looked confused.

"Whose reputation are you considering," she teased him, "yours or mine?"

He flushed.

"Don't make fun of it, Viola. As a matter of fact it just occurred to me that—your husband" (he hated Humphrey so much that he would never say his name) "might possibly be having you watched."

A wave of anger swept through her.

"Humphrey's not like that," she burst out, then at sight of his bewilderment her anger faded. "I'm sorry, Adrian, but—honestly he isn't. Still ... I'd better go, perhaps. I'm terribly tired. Don't bother to come down. The porter will get me a taxi."

She turned to him suddenly, drew his head down, and kissed him. He had been so kind to her. Without him she would be so desperately lonely.

"My dear ..." he said unsteadily. "I've always loved you. You know that, don't you?"

She broke away from his embrace.

"I'm sorry. I shouldn't have done that. But you're such a dear. ... Goodbye, Adrian."

Chapter Seventeen

HESTER carefully selected another embroidery silk, threaded her needle, and started on the little bunch of flowers in the second corner. When she went away with Harriet, they always spent the evenings embroidering tray cloths for the Zenana Mission Sale of Work that was held at St. Mark's every November, and, though she was now alone, she hadn't quite been able to break herself of the habit. Besides, it gave her something to do, and she still felt too unsettled to enjoy a novel.

Harriet had been very kind about her coming away alone. She had been worried, of course, and rather hurt, but, once Hester had said firmly, "Please don't talk about it any more, Harriet. I'm going away, and I'm going away by myself. I've quite made up my mind," she had made no further remonstrances.

Relations between them had naturally been strained, and more than once Hester had weakened and almost given up her project, but a curious feeling of desperation upheld her.

"I can't go on for the rest of my life without something of my own . . ." she kept saying to herself.

The day before she went, Harriet began to pack for her, as usual, setting out the array of bottles (indigestion tablets, quinine tablets, aspirins, throat paint, cough lozenges) that they always took away, but Hester stopped her, speaking quietly and firmly.

"I'll pack my bag, Harriet. I'd rather, please."

So Harriet withdrew into her own bedroom, where she polished the chest of drawers with unnecessary violence (forgetting that she'd already polished it once that day), and wondered miserably what was making Hester so very peculiar, and whether she ought to consult a doctor about it. Why, Hester couldn't get on without her even at home. Everyone knew she couldn't. What would she do in a strange place? She'd never even bought her own railway ticket before. She tried to comfort herself by the reflection that she would probably come back after one day, but that wasn't really very comforting because dreadful things could happen even in a day, even in an hour, even in a second. She might fall down and break her leg. She might get run over. Her absent-mindedness made her so careless about crossing streets. And beneath all her anxiety was a feeling of desolation, a terrible hurt feeling, because Hester *wanted* to go away without her. . . .

Hester packed her bag and replaced the little bottles in the medicine cupboard. She wasn't going to take any of them. They were all part of Harriet, and she didn't want to have anything of Harriet with her. She packed the frilly blue dress that she had bought by herself in Reddington, her brown silk, and her best nightdress—the wincey one with lace at the neck. She was only going to be away for a week, so she wouldn't need many clothes.

They breakfasted in silence on the morning of her departure. Neither of them had slept; both looked tense and pale and anxious.

"I'll take your bag down to the tram, dear," said Harriet when Hester was ready.

But Hester refused to let her do that. She would rather take it to the tram herself, she said. She felt like a criminal because Harriet looked so unhappy and was being so kind, but even so she never wavered.

"Goodbye, dear," she said. "I'll be quite all right. You mustn't worry about me."

They kissed in a quick furtive fashion as if they were afraid of each other; then Hester went down to the gate, carrying the bag, and Harriet went up to the attic, from the windows of which she could see the corner where the tram stopped. She watched the thin figure mount the step and disappear inside.

The tram moved slowly off. . . . She wondered whether to go to her bedroom and have a good cry or start turning out the drawing-room, and finally decided to start turning out the drawing-room.

Hester went to the same seaside place that she and Harriet had always gone to—somehow she couldn't break so far away from tradition as to go anywhere else, even if she'd been able to think of anywhere else—but she didn't go to the same boarding-house. She hadn't made any arrangements before she went, so, stammering with nervousness, she had asked the taxi-man if he knew of a nice cheap boarding-house, and, after giving her a shrewd appraising glance, he had brought her to Laurel Bank. Laurel Bank was one of those double-fronted Victorian villas that have come down in the world but not lost their self-respect. The lace curtains at the windows were spotlessly clean. There was a neat row of geraniums leading from the gate to the bottom of the freshly scrubbed front-door steps, where a foot-scraper and a fibre mat made their mute appeal. The Misses Munnings, who kept the boarding-house, were indeed almost aggressively "house-proud." They spent most of their time clearing up after the guests—shaking cushions, dusting, polishing, putting things back into their places. The furniture consisted of a few good pieces from the Miss Munnings' old home (they had come down in the world like the house), with a make-weight of small bamboo tables and wicker chairs. The guests ate at one long table in the dining-room, with Miss Munnings at the head and Miss Flora Munnings at the foot. Miss Munnings was brisk and business-like and pleasant, chatting with the guests and making little jokes as she served the dishes. Miss Flora, on the other hand, was shy and quiet and mouse-like, speaking only when she was spoken to and then as little as possible, avoiding notice, slipping into the room for a meal at the last moment, and slipping away as soon as it was over. One met her sometimes, doing out the bedrooms or carrying bed linen across the landing, but she always seemed to vanish from sight the instant one set eyes on her. The pivot on which the whole house revolved was Mr. Cardigan, the Resident. He had been a friend of the Misses Munnings' father and had lived at the boarding-house ever since they had opened it. He sat next to Miss Munnings at meals and was given all the choicest tit-bits. He had cream on his fruit salad, where the others had custard. He occupied by right the only really comfortable chair in the drawing-room, and even newcomers seemed to know by some sixth sense that it was not for them. He often spent the evening with the sisters (he called them by their Christian names and referred to them as "the girls") in the tiny sitting-room that they had appropriated to their use, and that held the piano on which they had learnt music, their mother's rosewood writing-desk, and all the family photographs in silver frames.

Mr. Cardigan was a short square old man with white hair, a trim white beard, and very blue eyes. He ignored new guests till they had been there a week. At the end of a week he would unbend so far as to comment on the weather, after a fortnight he would discuss the political situation, and at the end of a month would crack little jokes. He would smile when people said how shy Miss Flora was. "Shy?" he would say. "You should see her alone with her sister and me. She's as gay as a little girl. She's a wonderful mimic, too. She can take people off so that you'd almost die with laughing." And so, when his laugh rang out from the sisters' sitting-room in the evening, the guests would wonder uncomfortably which of them Miss Flora was taking off.

Hester had entered this small community with shrinking timidity and apprehension. She seemed to have set out on a desperate adventure whose end no one could possibly foresee. During the first day she felt so homesick that more than once she nearly threw the whole thing up and went home, but her pride restrained her. She had come away to find something of her own, and she must stay till she'd found it. The visit, however, didn't seem to be fulfilling her hopes. There was nothing here to take the place of what Humphrey had spoilt. She wandered aimlessly along the promenade or sat in a corner of the drawing-room on the most uncomfortable chair she could find, because she wanted to be sure she was taking no one else's, and watched the other guests.

The other guests were not particularly interesting. There was a young couple who were out all day and a Mrs. Clarkesworth—a massive overdressed good-natured woman, whose chief topic of conversation was the misfortunes of her family. They seemed to have had more accidents, to have suffered more losses from fire and flood, to have contracted more malignant diseases, to have made more unfortunate speculations, to have been more cheated and defrauded and misused, than any other family imaginable. She took a gloomy pride in them. "We've had our share, I can tell you," she would say complacently. "They say, you know, that it never rains but it pours."

Hester listened to it all with deep interest, sitting on the uncomfortable chair, wearing the frilly blue dress, working at the tray cloth for the Zenana Mission Sale of Work, but, though the stories wrung her heart with pity for the unfortunate clan, it wasn't really anything that could belong specially to her. It couldn't take the place of the little boy Humphrey whom the man Humphrey had so ruthlessly destroyed. She'd thought that the holiday itself would be some precious secret possession, but it was turning out to be flat and dull—exactly like the sort of holiday she had with Harriet, only flatter and duller. . . . It was funny that she had longed to be alone and, now that she was alone, she felt tired and bored. It was partly, of course, that she wasn't feeling well. Her indigestion had been much worse since she came away. She'd thought that she'd almost enjoy having her indigestion all to herself without Harriet to follow her round with pills and advice, but she didn't. And she'd caught a cold when she was out on the front in the rain yesterday, which was already beginning to go to her chest, though she was pretending that it was a very slight one.

The only other occupant of the lounge was Mr. Cardigan, and he was asleep in his own armchair, snoring softly at intervals. There seemed something vaguely improper in being alone in a room with a sleeping man, and she wondered nervously whether she ought to stay there; but, after all, she assured herself, it *was* the drawing-room, and there was nowhere else to go except to her bedroom, where the only chair was an upright wooden one. The young couple, Mr. and Mrs. Wilmot, had been in the drawing-room for a few minutes after lunch, whispering together in the corner by the door, but they had gone out almost immediately. The general opinion was that they were a honeymoon couple, but if so they lacked the light-heartedness that is supposed to belong to that state. They looked absurdly young and yet somehow pathetic and frightened. They rarely spoke at meals. At other times they talked to each other urgently in undertones. They seldom smiled.

"They take the married state very seriously," commented Miss Munnings.

"Well, after all, you never know what'll happen," said Mrs. Clarkesworth. "It doesn't do to take anything too lightly. A second cousin of mine was killed by a fall of rock on his honeymoon."

Mr. Cardigan's snores grew louder. Hester's cold seemed to grow heavier. Her head throbbed and her back ached. It was dreadful, just sitting there and listening to Mr. Cardigan's snores. She decided suddenly to go upstairs and lie down on her bed. . . . She put the tray cloth into her work-bag and tiptoed softly to the door. She reached it safely without waking Mr. Cardigan. The snores continued uninterrupted. She could still hear them, growing gradually fainter, as she went up the stairs to her room.

There she drew the curtains and lay down on her bed. She had just dozed off when she was wakened by the door opening and shutting sharply. At first she thought that she was dreaming. Little Mrs. Wilmot couldn't really be standing in her bedroom, her hand at her breast, staring in terror at the closed door, couldn't really be turning to her and saying, "Oh, Miss Lessington. . . . Do forgive me. . . . I'm in such terrible trouble."

Hester sat up on the bed and blinked at her. No, of course, it couldn't be real. It was the sort of thing that could only happen in dreams. Perhaps her cold had made her a bit light-headed. . . . But Mrs. Wilmot came across the room and sat down on the bed by her. She had a pale pointed freckled face, and the short flannel skirt and plain jumper she wore emphasised her slight undeveloped figure. She put up a thin hand and pushed back a lock of sandy hair that was falling over her forehead. She looked like an ill-used frightened child.

"Oh, what must you think of me," she said breathlessly, "rushing into your room like this? But"—she threw another terrified glance at the door—"I had to. I had to."

Hester forgot to be shy and self-conscious. She even forgot her headache and the pain in her back. She forgot everything but the trembling girl by her side.

She slipped an arm round her reassuringly.

"What's the matter, my dear?" she said "Whatever's the matter?"

She could feel the quivering of the taut form against her and held it more tightly. "Don't be frightened. It's all right. Tell me what's happened. . . ."

Mrs. Wilmot raised blue frightened eyes to her.

"Oh, you're so kind. . . . It's—it's my husband. . . ."

"Your husband? But what's he done, my dear?"

"Nothing . . ." said the girl in a quick unsteady voice. "I don't mean—Peter isn't my husband really. . . . Oh, I know it sounds dreadful, but—we love each other, you see, and he's going out to Canada to a job next week, and I don't suppose we shall ever see each other again. We just had to do it—had to have one week to remember for the rest of our lives. I—I'd have gone with him altogether if it hadn't been for the children."

"Have you children?" put in Hester wonderingly.

"Yes. Three. And I couldn't leave them. I couldn't do that whatever happened. . . . And so——" A step came along the corridor, and she sat, frozen with terror, her blue eyes wide and staring, then, as it passed the door, relaxed into convulsive trembling. "I thought he'd seen me and was coming after me. . . . You see, I said I was going to spend the week with my sister. She knew and understood. She'd never give me away, but the other day as I was going out of the front door I saw Mrs. Blake passing the gate. She lives next door to us at home, and I suppose she'd come over on a day excursion. I hurried in again and hoped she hadn't seen me, but she must have done, and she must have told Ernest, because—he's here."

"Here?"

"Yes. I was just going downstairs, and I saw him coming in at the hall door. I don't think he saw me. I ran into the first door I saw, and it was yours. Oh, it was dreadful of me, I know. But if he sees me, or if he sees Peter——"

"Where's Peter?" said Hester.

"He's gone to the station to ask about trains. We were going tomorrow, you know. I'd stayed to rest in my bedroom because I was tired. Oh, what shall I do? I'm so frightened. . . ."

A strange exhilaration had seized Hester. No one in all her life till now had ever come to her for comfort or help. A great tenderness for this unhappy frightened child swept over her, filling her heart with warmth and radiance, a tenderness that she had never felt before except for the child Humphrey during those weeks that had now vanished out of her life. She forgot that she had never done anything without Harriet's help. She felt, quite suddenly, strong, capable, infinitely wise.

"Where is your husband now?" she said.

"I think he went into the drawing-room. Miss Munnings and Miss Flora have gone out. But—he'll wait till they come back. I know he will. . . . He's certain to find out now."

"What's your name—your real name?" said Hester.

"France."

"And what's your sister's name?"

"Susan. Susan Wilde."

"And what day was it this neighbour of yours saw you?"

"Last Tuesday."

Hester patted her shoulder.

"Now you're not to worry at all," she said. "You just stay here. Don't come out whatever happens. We shall just have to risk Peter's coming back. I think it will be all right, though."

She took her work-bag from the chest of drawers and, with another reassuring smile at the white desperate face, went out of the door and down the stairs. The strange new feeling of exhilaration still upheld her. It was as if all her life she had been waiting for something to happen to her and now at last it was happening. In the drawing-room Mr. Cardigan still dozed in his armchair, filling the air with gentle musical snores. On a chair near the window sat a tall heavily built man, with very black hair, bushy eyebrows, and a long tight mouth. He sat there, upright and motionless, like an implacable figure of fate. The dark, almost black, clothes emphasised the general impression of joylessness.

He half rose from his chair as Hester entered.

"Miss Munnings?" he said.

She smiled at him brightly.

"Oh no," she said. "My name's Miss Lessington."

He sat down again and continued to stare grimly in front of him. Hester took the chair next his, drew out her tray cloth, and set to work upon it.

"It's a lovely day, isn't it?" she said.

He made no answer.

"Have you come to stay here?" she went on.

"No," he answered without looking at her.

"Just dropped in for tea, then, I suppose?" she said. "So wise of you, I think. So much more peaceful to have it in a nice home-like place like this than in one of those noisy cafés in the town." She was amazed to hear herself chatting away like this. She could hardly believe indeed that it was herself.

Mr. Cardigan awoke and looked around him. It was one of the unwritten rules of the house that no one talked above a whisper in the drawing-room when he was having his afternoon nap there. He stood up, fixed his eyes on Hester in silent reproach, and went with slow dignity from the room. The two were left alone.

"Have you had a long journey?" went on Hester.

He turned to her.

"Do you know when the proprietress will be back?" he said.

"No," said Hester. "I rather think she's gone out to tea. She may not be back for some time. Not very many people are staying here just now, so she naturally takes the opportunity of getting out a little."

He looked at her thoughtfully with his deep-set angry eyes—as if it had suddenly occurred to him that perhaps she would do as well as Miss Munnings.

"You say that not many people are staying here?" he demanded.

"Not really very many just at present," said Hester in her new bright chatty voice. "I believe that more are expected next week."

"Is a"—he stopped, swallowed, and continued as if with an effort—"a Mrs. Wilmot staying here?"

Hester knit her brows. "No," she said. "I don't remember that name at all. No one new has been here for quite a long time. Two ladies came over just for the day last Tuesday, but neither of them was a Mrs. Wilmot. A Mrs. France, I believe it was with her sister, a Mrs. Wilde." She went on—gaily, artlessly garrulous. "I think that Mrs. Wilde knew Miss Munnings and brought her sister over just for a little outing, you know. They had lunch here, and then Mrs. France went out for a little blow by herself, because Mrs. Wilde had a headache. ... Such pleasant ladies, both of them."

His eyes were fixed on her, and she saw in them something of the fear and unhappiness that she had seen in the eyes of the woman upstairs.

"You're sure the name was—Mrs. France?" he said.

"Oh yes. Of course," said Hester innocently. "Do you know her? A very small lady. So charming. She was staying with her sister, and they just came over for the day."

His sombre eyes held hers, and she met them unflinchingly.

"She showed us a snapshot of her three children," she went on. "She's devoted to them. ..."

She saw that he believed her—believed her, perhaps, because he wanted to believe her, because he couldn't face life unless he did.

He rose from the chair.

"Thank you," he said. "I'll go now."

Hester opened her eyes wide.

"But I thought you wanted to see Miss Munnings," she said.

"It's not necessary, now," he said.

He was suddenly anxious to leave the house as soon as possible, to leave it before he had time to doubt her word, before some terrible irrevocable proof of his suspicions presented itself. He took his leave of her abruptly and strode quickly off down the street. Hester stood at the door and watched him till he was out of sight. As soon as he had vanished, Mr. Wilmot appeared round the other corner. They had missed each other only by a few moments. He looked, as ever, shabby and deprecating. About his whole figure was an air of acceptance and resignation. Life had treated him badly, but he wasn't resentful, because he'd never really expected it to treat him any other way. His worn young face was set in lines of determined, but unconvincing, cheerfulness. If she were watching for him out of her bedroom window, she mustn't see him looking despondent. It was their last day together. They mustn't waste it in lamentations. It was his job to cheer her up, not to add to her sorrow by his own. . . .

He looked slightly surprised to see Hester standing at the front door.

"She's in my room," said Hester. "The one at the top of the stairs. . . . You'd better go to her quickly."

And suddenly she became aware once more that her back was aching and that pains were shooting through her head.

Chapter Eighteen

"WHAT time did Roy say he'd be here?" said Doreen.

"Half-past three," replied Bridget.

"It's twenty-five past now, so I expect he'll be here any minute," said Doreen.

There was a note of tense unnatural brightness in her voice, and she glanced sharply at Bridget as she spoke, wishing that she would try to look a little more like a girl who is just going to meet her fiancé. Bridget had, of course, often visited Roy's home, but this would be the first time she had stayed there. She was feeling nervous and keyed-up. Doreen, too, was feeling nervous and a little sorry for herself. She had worked so hard to bring about this engagement, but now a faint uneasiness pervaded her mind whenever she thought of it. Bridget seemed so listless, so unaware of the importance of keeping a man interested, of propitiating his relations, of showing both them and him perpetually what a perfect wife she would make. An engagement was, after all, only an engagement. A girl couldn't afford to relax her efforts till she was actually married.

And there seemed to be a new streak of hardness in Bridget that made it very difficult to help and advise her.

"Please, Mother, I'd rather not talk about it," she would say shortly when Doreen tried to explain to her (quite kindly) that she ought to flatter Roy more and make herself more pleasant to his mother and sister. Oh well, that's what always happens, I suppose, Doreen thought pathetically. One works oneself to skin and bone for one's children, and gets no gratitude from them.

The actual announcement of the engagement, however, had fulfilled her highest hopes. It had been the sensation of Reddington.

Nothing else was talked of for quite three days. Everyone congratulated her. Her friends treated her with new respect. She was aware, of course, that less complimentary things were said behind her back, chiefly by mothers who would have liked to secure Roy Hamwell for their own daughters, but that only intensified the triumph. Any unqualified success arouses jealousy. And she had need of a little triumph and success, for she had worries enough just now. Miss Marcher had arrived and was almost incredibly slow and stupid. Doreen prided herself on never losing her temper, but it was all she could do to keep it with the exasperating old woman. She was deaf and short-sighted and took as long to turn out a room as most people would take over a whole house.

The clock struck the half-hour. Bridget drew on her gloves.

"You won't forget to give my love to Mrs. Hamwell, will you, darling?" said Doreen.

"No," said Bridget, looking out of the window.

She wished that Roy would come. She'd been dreading the visit all day, but now suddenly she was anxious for it. She wanted to get away from home even for a few days—away from her mother's terrible brightness and its tense underlying anxiety. ("You know, darling, an engaged girl's position isn't easy, but I'm sure that you'll show Roy and his people what a dear bright helpful little girl my Baby-Bridget is.") Away from the sight of poor Miss Marcher, patiently scrubbing and dusting with gnarled rheumatic hands, her frail old figure bent nearly double over buckets of coal and pails of water. ("No, Bridget, I don't wish you to help her. We must start as we mean to go on. She's quite strong. She said she was. She said she enjoyed work.")

"Tell her that I saw her in the town on Monday," went on Doreen, "and that I thought she looked perfectly charming in that black-and-white dress."

Bridget was silent. Of all the humiliations to which her engagement exposed her, none was worse than her mother's ceaseless toadying to Mrs. Hamwell and the arrogant contempt with which Mrs. Hamwell received it. The sudden hatred of both of them that sometimes flared up in her heart frightened her. She had never hated people like that—wickedly, for no reason at all—before. It was as if, with her engagement, some evil spell had been laid on her.

Roy's small green saloon car had drawn up at the gate, and Doreen went quickly into the hall to open the door. There was real pleasure in the smile with which she welcomed him. Roy was just the sort of boy she had always wanted to marry when she was young, but no one of that sort had come her way and so she had had to make the best of a Parish Church curate.

"Come in, my dear," she said, flashing an arch smile at him. "It's quite a long time since I saw you."

He smiled back at her. Her obvious admiration of him flattered him. He did not himself underestimate his good looks and charm, and he did not like others to underestimate them. He was fully conscious of the honour he did her in singling out her daughter as his wife. She was a pleasant, nice-looking little woman, and he sometimes idly defended her when his mother and sister ridiculed her, as they so frequently did.

"You see far too much of me," he said, displaying all his easy charm for her benefit. "Besides, we're in-laws to be and ought to hate each other." She laughed gaily. "I'm sorry I'm late. If Bridget's ready . . ."

Bridget came into the hall.

"I'm quite ready."

He kissed her—decorously, because Doreen was watching with a fond maternal smile, but lingeringly. She had the most kissable mouth he had ever encountered—soft and full and sweet.

"She's a cold-blooded little creature," he said. "I can't teach her to kiss properly. At the best she pecks like a maiden aunt. Come on, darling. I promised Mother we'd be home for tea."

He helped her into the car and they drove off through the streets. The fresh air, the speed, the relief at having escaped from Doreen for a day or two raised Bridget's spirits. Terry himself had helped to make things easier. She had called to see Lucy last week, and Lucy had congratulated her enthusiastically on her engagement.

"I think it's splendid, Bridget," she said. "So sensible of you.

Something that will ensure you a Rolls and peaches out of season when the glamour's faded. And you won't forget your old friends, will you?"

"Of course not."

"I mean, you'll introduce me to someone with money—won't you?—so that I can go and do likewise. I want to get out of this hole. It's on my nerves."

Aunt Agatha, it seemed, was going to take Lucy away for a holiday, and Mrs. Wheeler was sulking at being left out of it.

"She's trying to make herself really ill so that I can't go," grumbled Lucy, "and I bet you anything she'll succeed. Mind you, it's not all beer and skittles going away with Aunt Agatha. It means dancing attendance on the old devil from morning to night, but at least it's a change and she does things in style."

"And Terry . . .?" said Bridget, trying to speak calmly and to still the sudden beating of her heart.

"Oh, Terry!" said Lucy in a tone of disgust. "He's as much of a wet as ever. Mooching about with his birds and stamps and country walks. He doesn't even belong to a tennis club. Honestly, Bridget, when I think of what a brother might do for a girl, I could kill him. I know of girls who've had marvellous chances through their brothers' getting to know decent people. Maisy Farmer married a lieutenant-colonel that her brother got to know at golf. Though I don't suppose *he'd* ever get to know anyone useful whatever he did. And he's such a fool about Aunt Agatha. He deserves all he gets from her."

"I think you're a *beast*, Lucy," said Bridget hotly.

Lucy laughed.

"I know I am. But anyway, I'm honest about it, aren't I? I don't pretend to be sweet and long-suffering. . . . Do you know, Bridget, I believe Terry quite fell for you just before you got engaged to Roy Hamwell. I ragged him about it till I really thought he was going to murder me."

Bridget thought of the days when Lucy had seemed the most wonderful person in the world, when she had been proud to be chosen to walk round the playground with her at "break," when she had been so much excited at the prospect of going to tea with her that she had hardly slept at all the night before. A heavy desolation swept over her. People changed. There was nothing solid in life to hold on to, nothing. . . .

As she was going away she met Terry at the gate. The sight of him set her heart racing again. He was passing her without looking at her, but she stopped.

"Terry . . ." she said.

He stared at her in silence for a few moments, then went on, his face white and set. A couple of passers-by grinned. Bridget walked on, trembling with anger.

All right. She'd done with him. She'd never try to make friends with him again. . . . If he could treat her like this it only proved how unhappy they'd have been; proved once and for all that it couldn't have lasted.

"Let's go the longer way round," she said to Roy. "It's such a nice day."

The longer way round meant not passing Uncle Humphrey's house, and to pass Uncle Humphrey's house now brought a curious constriction to her chest—a sensation that in her childhood she had associated with the dentist's waiting-room and called a "dentist pain." Roy smiled to himself, thinking that she wanted to prolong the drive for the sake of being alone with him. She was such a deliciously shy little thing. She gave him a superior-male feeling that none of the other girls he knew—all smart and sophisticated and independent—gave him. And she was so ridiculously prudish, shrinking even from the sort of love-making that most girls took for granted, imagining, apparently, that a kiss was the utmost length to which an engaged couple could go—and a particularly unexciting sort of kiss at that. This sometimes amused and touched him, sometimes irritated him. It was as well, of course, that one's wife should be modest, but there were several things about her that would have to be changed when she became his wife. However, he wasn't going to worry about that just yet. He was quite satisfied with her as she was for the present. She was sweet and amenable, and her freshness and simplicity still made a strong appeal to his prematurely jaded senses.

She glanced at him covertly as they drove through the town. She could not be quite indifferent to his good looks, his admiration of her, his mercurial high spirits, and the carefree atmosphere of luxury he carried about with him. After all, it would be pleasant to have everything you wanted, dresses, servants, cars. You couldn't rely on people, and that only left things. Things couldn't fail you. . . .

Her "dentist pain" increased as they approached Furness Hall. Nothing, she thought despairingly, would ever make her feel at home with Roy's people.

She was rather glad to find that the drawing-room was full of guests. Mrs. Hamwell came forward to receive her and graciously offered her cheek. Mrs. Hamwell was a tall majestic woman, handsome in a conventionally aristocratic style and dressed in the heavily expensive fashion usually affected by that particular type. Among her equals she was quite good company, humorous in a dry, rather cruel, manner; utterly devoid of sympathy and understanding, but shrewd, well-informed, and entertaining. To her inferiors she could be—and frequently was—devastatingly rude, but in such a quiet matter-of-fact way that the victim only realised afterwards the full offensiveness of what she had said or done. It was easy to see that Roy had inherited from his mother the touch of arrogance which underlay his friendliness. It was easy also to see that it was Mrs. Hamwell on whom Doreen ineffectually and from a far, far distance modelled her social behaviour.

Bridget sat down in a corner of the room, and an aunt of Roy's, who was staying in the house, came to sit next to her. She was a stout little person with a vivacious manner—one of those people who talk incessantly without saying anything. Bridget heaved a sigh of relief. One needn't talk to her. One needn't even listen. Her eyes roved round the room. Most of the guests were personal friends of the Hamwells who had motored over from a distance, but here and there she recognised a well-known Reddington figure—the Rector, tall and thin and stooping, discoursing on the political situation in a singing intonation suggestive of the Litany;

the head master of Reddington Grammar School, a small dreamy man with a large fussy wife (they had come from a country town in Surrey and cherished a fierce secret contempt of the Midlands); Dr. Tatsfield, the fashionable Reddington doctor, whose good looks and charm of manner covered a growing tale of faulty diagnoses. Servants moved to and fro with plates and trays. When the guests had gone, the ladies would take out their embroidery and work to an accompaniment of desultory chatter till it was time to dress for dinner. Bridget tried to think how lovely it was going to be to have everything done for you by servants, but somehow she couldn't put any conviction into the thought, because she still couldn't quite forget the little house in which she had bustled about so busily from morning to night. What was the fun, she thought rebelliously, of having a house of your own if you just sat about and let the servants do all the interesting things for you—even to putting coal on the fire? It was just like living in an hotel. It *was* like an hotel, too, she thought, looking about the room. The curtains were elaborately pelmeted and had obviously been made and put up by professionals. Bridget had planned cretonne curtains for the little house, with a small flowered pattern and frills at the top—the sort you could run up on a machine.

Roy's aunt had gone now, leaving in her place a military-looking man with a monocle and a moustache whom Bridget had not met before. He was stiff and pompous and not very easy to talk to. He made her feel stupid. But, of course, she *was* stupid, she admitted ruefully to herself. She always had been stupid. And Roy wouldn't really like having a stupid wife. It would annoy him, just as having a stupid daughter had always annoyed Mother. He'd said one or two things already that showed that he wished she weren't quite so stupid. It wouldn't have mattered with Terry, because Terry was stupid, too. She never felt that she had to talk to Terry when they were alone together. They would have been quite content to sit in silence by the fire in the evenings, she sewing, he reading. But it was silly to think of that now, especially as he'd shown her plainly now how much he disliked her, how much he'd probably always disliked her.

Mr. Hamwell—a tall spare man with a deeply lined face—had come into the room and was greeting the guests with weary impersonal courtesy. The tense lines of his face seldom relaxed into a smile. It was common knowledge in Reddington that he and his wife lived as strangers, meeting, as a general rule, only at dinner and treating each other with studied politeness. Roy had told Bridget that he remembered Homeric rows between them when he was a child before they arrived at this state of armed neutrality. He stood in awe of his father and did not dare to scamp his work at the office, but he spent as much time as possible away from home. It was a strange trio, thought Bridget, to inhabit the spacious house so obviously built for a Victorian quiverful—Mrs. Hamwell, alone in her magnificent drawing-room; Mr. Hamwell, alone in his magnificent study; Roy, always out with his "crowd." All studiously polite to each other. All strangers to each other. She looked about the luxurious room, with its gay chattering occupants, and was aware of a curious undertone of unhappiness.

Mr. Hamwell came across to her and greeted her with formal courtliness. She felt that he despised her because she was going to marry Roy, and rather liked him for it.

The guests gradually departed. Mr. Hamwell went back to his study. Mrs. Hamwell, stifling a yawn, rang for a servant to get out her tapestry frame. The aunt settled down to a game of patience. Roy had arranged to take Bridget out to a dance at one of the new road-houses that had recently sprung up in the neighbourhood of Reddington and were very fashionable among the younger set. He looked at his watch.

"Time you went and got dressed, my lamb," he said to Bridget.

"You'll have to teach Roy to spend his evenings at home," said Mrs. Hamwell, with a touch of malice in her voice.

Roy followed Bridget to the foot of the stairs.

"What are you going to wear?" he said.

"My pink dress ..." she said uncertainly.

"Haven't you brought your black one?"

"Yes."

"Well, put that on. And don't wear any jewellery with it."

Secretly she rather resented the lordly way in which he flung his orders at her, but her innate humility prevented her from making any objection. After all, he did know better about everything than she did. . . .

The Green Lizard was one of the newest and most up to date of the road-houses. It did a decorous trade in teas and lunches during the week, but only on Saturday nights did it really come into its own. Then the big dance-hall was opened, with the gallery for the jazz band and the tables in small recesses partitioned off by imitation panelling all round the side. It was a good floor and a good band, and people came to it from miles around. They brought their own drinks and sat at the little tables in the alcoves and ended up with eggs and bacon in the early morning and felt gay and modern and pleasantly dissipated.

Roy's party occupied two of the alcoves and shouted pleasantries to each other over the partition when they were not dancing. They had brought between them a formidable array of bottles, and several of them were already slightly tipsy. Wherever Roy went he seemed to be accompanied by this gang of noisy young people. They were all so much alike that Bridget even now could never be quite sure which was which. They all talked at the same time and screamed with laughter and played practical jokes on each other. Bridget sat there, trying ineffectually to mix with them, trying, still more ineffectually, to conquer the bleak feeling of homesickness that nagged at her heart. She didn't even know what she was homesick for. She certainly didn't want to go back to Doreen and Miss Marcher. Usually Roy helped her to mix with the "crowd," drawing her into the conversation and teasing her affectionately, but tonight he was leaving her severely alone. He was annoyed, she knew, because she had not responded with sufficient ardour to his love-making on the way down. He had danced with her twice, but now, as the music for the third dance struck up, he caught hold of the wrist of a dark slender girl, whose name was Eileen Durham but whom everyone called "Prickles," swung her to her feet in his cavalier male-conqueror fashion, and began to dance with her. He held her very tightly and bent his head down till his cheek touched her smooth curls, whispering into her ear, flirting with her ostentatiously. Bridget knew that he was trying to make her feel jealous; knew, guiltily, that she ought to be feeling jealous, even tried unsuccessfully to feel jealous. And with the knowledge that she couldn't feel jealous came suddenly and in a blinding flash of illumination the knowledge that she couldn't marry him. She had been mad ever to think that she could. She tried to trace the madness to its source ... and found it, somewhat to her surprise, in the fact that Uncle Humphrey was in love with another woman and that Aunt Viola was going to divorce him. It was as if she had been in a boat in a quiet stream and an electric launch had passed whose backwash had driven her boat from its course and nearly upset it. The stream had now grown calm again. The boat had righted itself and regained its course. ... She could think of Uncle Humphrey and Aunt Viola without any feeling but one of pity—pity and a faint contempt. How foolish they had been! She and Terry wouldn't be as foolish as that. Her love for Terry returned like a sudden burst of sunlight, flooding every corner of her heart, melting away all her fear and unhappiness. She couldn't tell Roy tonight, of course, but she'd tell him first thing tomorrow. Then she'd go straight to Terry and then to her mother. Mother would be angry, but she didn't care. She felt as if an intolerable burden had fallen from her shoulders. The sheer relief of it was ecstasy.

A tall thickset man with an untidy shock of red hair, called Alex—one of the "crowd"—came up to her and jerked her unceremoniously to her feet.

"Come on," he said, "Roy's pinched my girl, so I'm going to pinch his."

She tried to resist, but, though he was tipsy—he was always the first of the "crowd" to get tipsy—he was strong enough and she had to give in. He steered her unsteadily round the room, banging into several of the other couples, leering down at her amorously and pressing large hot hands against her back. His alcohol-laden breath made her feel slightly sick! When the end of the dance came, she made her way to Roy, who was following his new partner to one of the alcoves.

"Roy," she said, intercepting him, "let's go home now."

He stared at her coldly. "Prickles" had proved unexpectedly alluring, unexpectedly accommodating, and he had for the moment no thought for anyone or anything else.

"I've got a headache . . ." went on Bridget.

"My God! D'you think I'm going home for that?"

"Alex is making a nuisance of himself."

He sneered.

"Well, it seems to me you're very capable of taking care of yourself."

He went off to join "Prickles," and Bridget sat down for a moment with a group of the "crowd," hoping that Alex would forget about her. He was at present engaged in pouring gin from a bottle into two glasses and spilling most of it on to the table. The room was unbearably hot and noisy. The door into the garden was just near, and on a sudden impulse she slipped out, closing it behind her. It was like going into another world. The garden lay, dim and silent, beneath a sky silvered with stars. The cool scented air caressed her hot cheeks. It was bliss to be alone there—alone with the new radiance that filled her soul and body. She felt a faint compunction about Roy—but only a very faint one. He had tired of her already, though he wouldn't own it even to himself. Certainly, he'd have tired of her long before they could be married. . . . She walked down a flagged path between ghost-like ranks of flowers. A faint breeze brought with it the fragrance of night-scented stock. At the end of the path a little wooden gate led into the Car Park. She could see Roy's green car at the far end. She couldn't bear to return to the heat and noise of the dance-hall just yet. She must be alone with her new-found peace for a few moments longer. No one would think of looking for her in Roy's car. . . . She opened the door and sank down into the cushioned seat. Almost immediately she heard Alex's voice outside.

"Grand idea, Baby!" he was saying thickly. "I'd have thought of it myself if you hadn't done it first. Here's a drink for you."

He fumbled at the handle of the door, dropped the glass he was carrying, and began to giggle foolishly.

"All gone!" he said. "Never mind. We can do without drinks, can't we, Baby?"

"Please go away," said Bridget. "I want to be alone."

He clambered into the car by her, shut the door, and put his arm round her, drawing her to him.

"Now we're all right, aren't we?" he said. "In the bastard's own car, too. That's a good joke. He's got Prickles in the summer-house and I've got you here. She's my girl and you're his, but we've swopped, haven't we? That's fair enough, isn't it? Exchange no robbery. Come on. Let's pay the swine out in his own coin."

She pushed him away from her, managed to open the door, and slipped out from beside him. He caught at her dress, and she heard it tear away from the gathers behind as she escaped. She went out of the big gates and walked down the road towards the village. She didn't feel frightened or unhappy. It was all over now. She'd finished with it for ever—Roy and the "crowd" and her old bewildered self. She felt as if she'd awakened from a nightmare. There was a telephone-box just outside the village. Lucy, of course, was away with Aunt Agatha. Terry and his mother would be alone in the house.

He answered almost as soon as she rang.

"It's Bridget," she said. "Have you gone to bed yet?"

"No . . . I've been in the shed. I've only just come into the house." His voice was anxious. "Is anything the matter, Bridget?"

"No. Not really. Will you come out and fetch me home, Terry?"

"Of course. . . . Where are you?"

"I'm at the telephone-box near the Green Lizard. The one on the main road. I'll stay here till you come."

Chapter Nineteen

"I THINK he took that first movement too quickly," said Adrian.

He and Viola had been to hear a new pianist at the Aeolian Hall, and were walking down Bond Street towards the 'bus stop.

"Perhaps he did," agreed Viola.

She enjoyed going to concerts and picture shows with Adrian, but found the lengthy postmortems, to which he always subjected them, rather wearisome.

"And I don't think he got quite the full effect of the arpeggios in the second," he said thoughtfully.

"No ..." agreed Viola and went on, "Adrian, do look at that old woman. She's exactly like Jemima Puddle Duck."

He threw an absent glance in the direction of the stout shawled figure, and continued, "I remember hearing Rachmaninoff play it at the Queen's Hall in 1936, and I'm sure he took that first movement more slowly."

Viola sighed. She had learned by experience that it was impossible to distract him once he was well under weigh with the post-mortems.

A slight drizzle came on, turning gradually to a steady rain.

"We'd better get a taxi," he said, and stood on the curb waiting to signal one. But it was a busy time of day, and, even when a taxi-man saw his signal, someone else seemed always to step into it as soon as it slowed down.

"It's like the man at the pool of Bethsaida, isn't it?" said Viola.

She had noticed before that taxi-men and waiters were inclined to ignore Adrian's efforts to attract attention. It was as if they perceived the secret strain of timidity in his character. She was tempted to try herself to signal a taxi but knew that Adrian wouldn't like it. He was very old-fashioned in his attitude to women. They had to be guarded and sheltered from the rough contacts of life. I suppose he imagines, thought Viola, that we'd just sit with our hands folded and starve if we hadn't a man to look after us. And, of course, she admitted ruefully, some of us would.

A taxi had drawn up at last, and Adrian handed her into it.

"I hope you've not got wet," he said solicitously.

"No," she said, "only a few drops on my stockings. They'll be dry before we get in. What about you?"

"I'm quite all right," he said, but she knew he was rather uneasy. He was always afraid of catching cold and was careful to avoid draughts and to change his clothes when he had been out in the rain. He was nervous of infection, too, and generally put a formalin tablet into his mouth before joining any large gathering. He had been distressed that Viola refused to follow his example, and invariably handed her his little enamelled box before they entered concert-hall, theatre, or picture gallery.

"You don't know what you're breathing in these places," he would say. "It's only common sense to take a few simple precautions."

The rain had stopped when they reached his rooms and the sun had come out again, flooding the pleasant spacious sitting-room, shining on to a tall cloisonné vase that stood on the floor against the cream-coloured wall and dimming the flame beneath the silver kettle, which his landlady had lighted as soon as she heard him come in. Adrian always made the tea himself, carefully washing out teapot and teacups with hot water first. He said that tea should be made immediately the water boiled—not a moment before or after—and that servants, however well-meaning, could never be trusted to do it.

"Now, Adrian," said Viola, taking up a copy of the *Connoisseur* from the table, "go and change your socks. I'm quite dry and I shall be all right here till you come back."

She knew that he had been worried about his damp socks all the way home. He was obviously relieved by her suggestion.

"Well, if you're sure you don't mind," he said. "I won't be a minute."

When he had gone she put down the paper and wandered about the room, absently examining his treasures. He had unerring taste and an expert's knowledge of antiques. Some of the pieces of furniture in his room were almost museum pieces, and the china in the cupboards with rounded tops let into the wall on either side of the fireplace had been slowly and laboriously collected at sales all over the country. He had found that Chelsea China inkstand in a remote village in Cornwall and gone to York specially for the Bristol tea-set.

The general effect of the room was that of the eighteenth century—Sheraton, Hepplewhite, Chippendale, Adam mantelpiece, elaborately moulded cornices—and, indeed, the eighteenth century, with its cultured leisure and mannered elegance, was Adrian's spiritual home. Viola sometimes thought that Horace Walpole must have been rather like Adrian. He came in now, closing the door behind him and smiling at her.

"Sorry to have kept you waiting, my dear. I'll make the tea."

He had quite lost his former nervousness about her coming alone to his rooms, and had accepted her assurances that Humphrey "wasn't like that." She watched his kindly sensitive face bent intently over his tea-making, and an almost maternal tenderness for him stirred at her heart. How good he was, how kind and considerate and thoughtful!

"I'm certain that he should have taken that first movement more slowly," he said. "I've got a record of it played by Cortot. Shall I put it on?"

"Yes, do," she said perfunctorily.

He put on the record and sat listening intently, sipping China tea from the Scale-blue Worcester teacup. He always washed up his tea things himself, just as he always dusted his ornaments and furniture himself. No one else was ever allowed to touch them. Sometimes Viola imagined him dusting them lingeringly, tenderly, but very thoroughly. He was careful, he had told her, to have his dusters boiled with disinfectant at regular intervals. He had an odd vague terror of germs. She was honestly fond of him, sincerely grateful to him, but it was hard not to let something of the ludicrous colour her vision of him sometimes.

"You see," he said, "Cortot takes it much more slowly. I was sure he did."

The gramophone slowed down and he got up to change the needle.

"Would you like to have the whole thing over again really slowly?" he said. "One can take in the details so much better."

He loved to play over his records of classical music with the indicator at the extreme slow position, listening with grave appreciation to each note. Viola found the process irritating, but it gave him such pleasure that she could never bear to spoil it by showing her irritation.

He put on the record and sat listening attentively. Viola's thoughts wandered away to Frances. She had not seen her recently, because to visit her meant meeting Richard Horrocks, and Frances refused to come to see Viola unless Richard were included in the invitation. But Viola rang her up every morning, and Frances was apparently well and happy. Perhaps she had been foolish to worry about her. Perhaps she had even misjudged Richard, though she couldn't seriously believe that she had done that. ... Her thoughts went home to Reddington. She had tried hard not to think of it as home, but she couldn't stop. She was an alien both here and in her mother's house. It was to that ugly Victorian villa in the Midlands that her homing thoughts kept turning. She had had a letter from Harriet that morning, telling her that Hester had come back from her holiday with a temperature of over a hundred and the worst cold she'd ever had in her life. She was still in bed, but the doctor had said that she might get up for a few hours tomorrow. "The whole Thing was *Madness*," wrote Harriet in a letter full of anxiety and italics and capital letters.

She had heard from Doreen, too—an odd mysterious letter, begging her not to believe any report she might hear to the effect that Bridget's engagement had been broken off. She and Roy had had a slight misunderstanding, a "lovers' quarrel," but there was nothing more to it than that. . . . She had had another card from Hilary, another bare bald statement of where they'd been today and where they were going tomorrow. She wished uneasily that the boy would tell her more. She had had, also, a short note from her mother. It *was* Major Grant's Alsatian, after all. He'd been caught in the very act of worrying sheep on Hurst's farm, and had had to be destroyed. She was sorry for Major Grant, of course, but he had rather put people's backs up by being so disagreeable about it at the beginning. . . . She had not heard from Humphrey yet, but that was one of the things she dared not think of.

The record had come to an end at last, and Adrian closed the gramophone, the look of rapt appreciation still on his face.

"It's the only way of understanding the value of each separate note," he said. "I still can't think why he took that movement so quickly. There seems no reason for it at all."

Viola said nothing. She felt that there was nothing further to be said on the subject. He handed her a box of cigarettes, but she did not take one. Adrian did not smoke himself, and she knew that he secretly disliked other people to smoke in his room. He always protested, with his unfailing formal courtesy, when anyone smoked in a non-smoking railway carriage.

"It doesn't matter, surely, Adrian," Viola would remonstrate, "We're getting out in a moment."

"My dear, it's the principle of the thing," he would reply.

For the sake of the "principle of the thing," also, he would invariably complain, even though he had suffered no inconvenience, when the occupants of the other rooms in the buildings infringed in any small particular the rules laid down by the owner. "I'm the last person in the world to want to make trouble," he would say, and in his case the generally meaningless formula was perfectly true. For all his culture and aesthetic interests and financial independence, there was a pathos about him that touched Viola's heart. He had hosts of acquaintances but no real friends. He was lonely and longed for companionship, but shrank from the responsibility that human contact inevitably brings with it. He was acutely sensitive, but in some ways curiously lacking in perception.

Viola had come to know him well in these last few weeks, and her feelings for him had crystallised into this motherly tenderness that she had never felt before for anyone but Hilary. There was in both of them a strain of weakness that had nothing contemptible about it. Adrian loved her, she knew, but, without realising it, he depended on her, rested on her strength. She remembered Olive Schreiner's cry, "I don't want to be loved up to. I want to be loved down to."

"When shall I see you again?" he said as she took her leave. "What about lunch tomorrow?"

They arranged to meet at the Berkeley for lunch the next day, and she set off for her hotel.

She went straight to the desk, as she always did, hoping that there might be a letter from Humphrey.

"I'm afraid there's bad news for you, Mrs. Lessington," said the clerk. "We've been trying to find you all the afternoon. It's your sister. . . ."

Viola's heart missed a beat.

"My sister?"

"She's had an accident. Nothing serious, I believe. But she's been taken to hospital, and they've been trying to get into touch with you."

At the hospital she was shown into a waiting-room whose only other occupant was Richard Horrocks.

On the table in front of him was a bunch of carnations and a carton obviously containing grapes. He looked tense and anxious and her heart softened towards him. Perhaps he was really fond of Frances, after all.

"What's happened, Richard?" she said breathlessly. "I've only just heard."

He fixed troubled blue eyes on her.

"I wasn't there," he said. "I didn't hear till some time after it happened. She was knocked down by a car in the street just outside the flat. . . . I was going to tea with her and I found she wasn't in her room, and after a bit I went down to the office and they told me. . . . I came straight on here. I really don't know anything more.

They said there was no immediate danger, but they wouldn't let me see her yet."

A nurse came in and said to Viola, "Will you come now, please?"

"Do ask her if she'll see me," pleaded Richard. "I won't excite her. I'll only stay a few minutes. I—I feel sure she'd want to see me."

"I'll ask her," said Viola. She felt more kindly towards him than she would have believed possible. "I'm sure she would like to see you for a moment if it could be managed." She glanced enquiringly at the nurse.

"We'll see about it," said the nurse non-committally.

"Please tell me how badly she's hurt," said Viola, as she followed the nurse out into the corridor.

"Three of her ribs are broken and her head's cut," said the nurse. "But, of course, it's the shock that's the most serious thing in a case like this."

"Do you think that the young man could see her for a moment after I've been in?" said Viola. "He's a great friend of hers, and I'm sure she'd like to see him."

"We'll see," said the nurse.

She led Viola into a long ward, curtained off into cubicles, and drew back one of the pale-green curtains.

"I've brought you a visitor," she said with professional breeziness.

Frances lay beneath the neat smooth coverlet, her head swathed in bandages. Her face looked incredibly thin and white and worn.

"Darling," she said in a whisper, "I'm so glad you've come."

"You mustn't stay long," said the nurse, and went away, drawing the curtains together after her.

Viola stooped down and gently kissed the pale sunken cheek.

"What *have* you been doing to yourself, dearest?" she said.

"I don't know," said Frances. "I didn't know anything till I found myself here."

"Richard's in the waiting-room," went on Viola. "He's brought you some flowers. Would you like to see him for a moment?"

To her surprise, a look of terror flashed into Frances's eyes.

"No, *no!*" she said. She clasped Viola's hand convulsively. "Don't let him come. Please don't let him come."

"Of course not, darling," said Viola reassuringly.

"I don't want him. You won't let him come, will you?"

"No, dearest, of course not. We won't even talk about it."

Frances lay for some moments in silence with closed eyes, then said in a faint far-away voice.

"I must talk about it, Viola. I must tell you now how it happened. If I don't tell you now, I shall never be able to tell you. I shall be too ashamed. And I want to tell you. I want you to know. You'll understand. I feel sure you'll understand."

She closed her eyes again, and a flicker of pain passed over her face.

"Don't tell me now, dear," said Viola. "You ought to be resting . . ."

"No. I must tell you. Richard was coming to tea——"

"He told me."

"And I'd gone out to get some cakes, and, as I came back to the lift through the lounge, he was there, sitting with a friend and talking. They were behind the screen. The one near the lift. They didn't see me. I caught my name and stopped. They were laughing. Viola, I've got to tell you this. No, don't try to stop me. It'll be better when I've told you. . . ."

Viola pressed her hand.

"Very well, dear. Tell me. I won't interrupt."

Frances continued, bringing out each word as if with an effort, speaking in a whisper so low that Viola had to bend her head to catch the words.

"They were—laughing at me. Richard was telling him about all the money I'd given him. And about the sister. He hasn't got a sister really. He was making fun of me. He called me an old hag. He said he deserved every penny of it for going about with me. He—" her voice sank till it was almost inaudible—"when we were alone, Viola, he used to call me Mother. I asked him to, because he'd always seemed like my son. He told this other man and they both laughed. He imitated me. Oh, Viola, I'm so ashamed——"

She stopped.

Viola bent down to kiss the wasted hand, leaving it wet with her tears.

"Don't cry, darling," said Frances. "I feel better now I've told you. But then I felt ... I think I really went mad. I just wanted to get away from him. I didn't care where. I ran out of the place and into the street and a car was passing. I didn't do it on purpose, Viola. You do believe that, don't you?"

"Of course I do, darling. ..."

Frances let her head fall sideways on to the pillow with a little shuddering sigh.

"I've been so silly, haven't I?"

Viola's heart was torn by an agony of pity.

"Darling ..."

"We'll never talk of it again," went on Frances, "and I'll never tell anyone else. ..."

The nurse drew back the curtain.

"I'm afraid you must go now," she said.

Viola bent down and kissed the blue-veined temple beneath the bandage.

"Goodbye, dearest," she said. "I'll come tomorrow."

"I oughtn't really to have let you stay so long," said the nurse as they walked back along the corridor, "but she was so anxious to see you. I'm afraid she mustn't see the young man now."

"I'll tell him," said Viola grimly.

She went into the waiting-room, closing the door behind her.

Richard started forward eagerly.

"How is she?" he said. "Mayn't I see her just for a second?"

Viola looked at him in silence. She felt a hot stifling anger and with it a surging sense of triumph. He had nearly killed Frances, but Frances had escaped from him for ever.

"She doesn't want to see you," she said slowly.

His eyes met hers levelly, registering distress, compunction, and youthful gallantry. She realised that behind their affectation of candour there had always been the hard challenging brazenness of the habitual liar.

"Not want . . .? But, of course, she's in such pain, isn't she? I can't bear to think of it. How did it happen? She isn't too terribly hurt, is she?"

"She doesn't want to see you," said Viola, "because she heard everything you said to your friend in the lounge this afternoon."

He stared at her, open-mouthed, and as he stared he seemed to shrink and dwindle. His air of glorious youth fell from him, leaving something small and mean and malevolent in its place. His hard blue expressionless eyes, however, still held hers unflinchingly.

"I haven't the faintest idea what you mean," he said. "I wasn't in the lounge at all this afternoon. I went straight to her room from the street and found her not there."

"You'll be very lucky," said Viola, "if we don't sue you for getting money under false pretensions."

She was pretty sure it would be impossible to do that, but she wanted to frighten him and she succeeded. The colour drained from his face. His eyes slid from hers at last.

"You must be mad," he muttered. "I don't know what you mean. I haven't the slightest idea what you're talking about."

"You'd better go quickly," said Viola, "and if you make any sort of attempt to communicate with her again, I'll put the police on to you."

He went out like a beaten dog, his lips drawn back in a snarl, his face unrecognisable under its grey mask of terror.

His carnations and grapes still lay side by side on the table.

Chapter Twenty

" 'IGHLY strung, 'e is, too," said the little man with the ginger moustache proudly. " 'Ighly strung as a pedigree dog."

The brown mongrel looked up at him and wagged its tail as if pleased by the compliment.

"Why, 'e was in a motor-bike accident a while back," went on the man with increasing pride, "an' you've only gotter put him in a side-car an' 'e turns all of a tremble. 'Ighly strung, that's wot 'e is." He looked at the motor-cycle combination by the hedge and cocked an eye at the pale young man who stood with a hand on the saddle. "That yours?" he said.

The pale young man nodded.

"Well, let's put 'im in an' you can watch 'im," suggested the owner of the mongrel. "All of a tremble, 'e goes. You can see 'im trembling. Same as a jelly. It's 'is nerves."

He picked up the brown mongrel and set him in the side-car. The group watched expectantly. The brown mongrel sat, placid and unmoved, its tongue lolling out in a vacuous grin. The little man with the ginger moustache was for a moment obviously nonplussed. " 'E's always done it afore," he said. Then his pride of possession came to his rescue and he smiled complacently. "Well, it shows 'is courage, don't it?" he demanded.

Hilary wandered away from the group. The incident had turned his thoughts to Monica. In the old days he would have stored it up in order to describe it to her and to watch the sudden smile that would have lit up her grave little face. But he had drawn a curtain in his mind over Monica and all she stood for, so that he needn't think of it. He was trying, indeed, not to think of anything, to go on from moment to moment as if nothing existed but the immediate present.

He didn't know whether Fordwick had asked Bruce Lovel to join him before or after he had received his wire, but, in either case, he had used him deliberately to punish him for his original refusal. Bruce Lovel was a pale insignificant-looking youth, as negative in character as he was in appearance. He had been at school with Fordwick, and Fordwick had good-humouredly taken him under his wing when he came up to Oxford. He toadied to Fordwick shamelessly, accepting snubs and slights almost with gratitude, running errands, obeying orders, constituting himself Fordwick's unofficial fag.

"He enjoys being kicked," Fordwick said scornfully to Hilary, "but he's useful."

Certainly, when Hilary was present, Fordwick had always treated Bruce with studied contempt, and Hilary, who disliked him intensely, had ignored him.

He had been taken aback, therefore, to find Bruce installed as Fordwick's boon companion when he joined him for the motor tour. It was Hilary now who was treated as the unwanted third, the hanger-on. Bruce was consulted, deferred to. He and Fordwick had innumerable private jokes between them from which Hilary was excluded. Bruce, of course, was quick to take his cue from Fordwick and obviously enjoyed being in a position to snub with impunity someone who till now had snubbed him as a matter of course. Several times Hilary had considered leaving them and going off on his own, but had always decided not to, partly because he had nowhere to go—he couldn't endure the thought of going tamely home—and partly because he didn't want to let Fordwick down. Bruce was leaving them at the end of three weeks, and Fordwick and Hilary were to finish the holiday together. Occasionally Fordwick, choosing a moment when Bruce was not there, would suddenly become friendly and pleasant again, implying that he found Bruce a bore and was looking forward to the last few days alone with Hilary. Hilary could see that Fordwick had been disconcerted by the indifference with which he had accepted the situation. He had obviously expected a scene—reproaches, appeals, perhaps even tears. Hilary himself didn't quite understand his indifference. It was as if something in him had been so stunned by the shock of the discovery of Humphrey's infidelity to his mother that after the first sick revulsion he hadn't been able to feel anything very deeply.

He could even notice dispassionately that Fordwick, who had once seemed perfect in every way, had a discordant rasping voice and doubtful table manners.

The three had made their way by easy stages through Scotland, staying at Pitlochry, Lairg, and Oban, had come back through the Lake District, and were now staying at a country inn near Coventry. Bruce was returning home today, and Fordwick and Hilary had arranged to take him to the station after lunch and then go on to Devonshire in order to spend a week-end on Dartmoor before they separated. To Hilary the whole trip had seemed unreal. He had once had a dream in which he wandered in a dim valley between tall precipices, groping his way through the mist, and, despite the open sunlit country around them, he had felt all the time as if he were back in that dream. Now that they were in the Midlands, in the neighbourhood of his home, he felt restless and ill at ease, as if afraid that at any minute the numbed part of him might awake to agonised life.

They had celebrated their last night together yesterday by going into Coventry to the second house of a music-hall, where Fordwick had taken a box. They had dinner at an hotel near, and both Fordwick and Bruce had a good deal too much to drink. Bruce very easily became tipsy, and his tipsiness generally took the form of incessant peals of hysterical laughter. Fordwick's took more unpleasant forms, as a rule, but last night he had contented himself by keeping up a running commentary on the performance at the top of his voice and blowing a whistle (which he had brought with him for the purpose) whenever he approved of any particular turn. The rest of the audience was obviously annoyed, and finally the manager came to their box to ask them to refrain from further interruptions. Fordwick offered to fight him, Bruce neighed with laughter, and the manager, sending for a couple of attendants, had them ignominiously ejected—Fordwick hitting out blindly and ineffectually as he went, Bruce still helpless with mirth. Hilary's flesh crept with shame whenever he thought of the incident, but he was convinced that things would be better after today. It was Bruce who had been the jarring element and brought out all Fordwick's worst characteristics. When Bruce had gone, the old magic would reassert itself and the friendship would become once more rich and satisfying, sweetening the new secret bitterness that he carried at his heart.

Fordwick and Bruce were coming out of the hotel now with their suitcases. The group round the door moved aside for them. The mongrel jumped out of the side-car.

Bruce began to arrange the cases in the back of the car, and Fordwick came to Hilary, slipping an arm round his shoulders:

"It'll be nice to be on our own again, won't it, old man?"

The touch of Fordwick's arm on his shoulder used to send a thrill of pride through him, but now he had to steady his nerves to hide their shrinking. Despairingly, he wondered what was happening. Was everything in life turning sour on him—even this friendship that had once meant so much? Again he told himself that it would be all right when Bruce had gone. In any case he realised that his punishment at Fordwick's hands was now over. It was with the old friendly intimate smile that Fordwick invited him to take the front seat beside him, which Bruce had always occupied till now when Fordwick drove.

"Get in behind with your luggage, young Bruce," he said shortly.

Bruce got in sulkily. He had taken all Fordwick's attentions at their face value and was surprised and hurt by his sudden change of attitude. He slumped into the back seat and sat there, silent and scowling. Hilary, too, was silent. He was conscious of humiliation rather than pleasure. He felt like a dog who had been beaten for some misdemeanour, ignored for a time, and finally restored to its master's favour. He knew that Fordwick had taken a malicious pleasure in the snubs and slights he had administered and had enjoyed the thought of his imagined sufferings.

They set off through the village and along the country road. Hilary glanced at Fordwick's thickset figure—the ruddy sunburnt skin, the hawk-like nose, the vividly blue eyes, the square jutting chin. He wore a blue sports shirt and one of the violently checked tweed coats that he always affected. Isolated memories of his kindness and generosity came to Hilary's mind, blotting out the memory of the last weeks. He remembered how Fordwick had helped to nurse him through that bad attack of 'flu, how patient and considerate he had been during the period of convalescence, when Hilary had been querulous and unreasonable . . . remembered the book of old bird prints that he had given him after a quarrel that had been entirely Hilary's fault . . . remembered the time when he had retraced alone a long country walk they had taken in order to find a cigarette-case that Hilary had lost. And he was his most attractive self again—affectionate, good-tempered, boyishly high-spirited. Gradually Hilary began to yield to the old spell, to return to the old allegiance. After all, what else in life was left to him?

They were passing an orchard now—long straight lines of trees, old and gnarled but heavily laden with fruit. Fordwick stopped the car and looked up at the trees.

"Make one's mouth water, don't they?" he said. Then: "Come on! Let's get some. It's years since I robbed an orchard."

His excitement was infectious. Bruce lost his petulance and leapt out eagerly. Only Hilary hesitated.

"Come on, you old funk!" teased Fordwick. "What are you frightened of?"

"I'm not frightened," said Hilary, "but—suppose someone came . . ."

"They won't see us for dust if they do," said Fordwick. "Anyway if we're collared we'll pay for the beastly things."

He burrowed among the accumulation of odds and ends at the back of the car and brought out the basket in which they generally packed their picnic lunches.

"This'll do. Get a move on, or Bruce'll miss his train and we'll be saddled with the blighter till tomorrow."

Bruce grinned doubtfully at this joke and followed him over the five-barred gate. Hilary went last. It was, of course, only a schoolboy escapade, but he had an instinctive distaste for it.

"This looks all right," said Fordwick, stopping beneath one of the trees.

He jumped, caught the lowest branch with his hands and swung himself up. He was unusually agile, despite his heavy build. He mounted higher.

"There are some whoppers up here," he called. "I'll fill my pockets first, then I'll drop them down to you and you can put them in the basket. Mind how you catch them. We don't want them all bruised. And keep an eye on the gate."

A rain of the ripe red apples began to fall, which Hilary and Bruce caught as best they could, Bruce giggling nervously.

"We've got as many as the basket'll hold," said Hilary at last.

"Right!" said Fordwick. "I'm just coming down."

He swung himself down from branch to branch. Hilary tried to repress a suspicion that he had suggested the exploit merely in order to display his skill in tree-climbing.

"Come on," he said rather impatiently.

Fordwick hung for a second or two on the lowest branch, then dropped to the ground, making a neat landing.

They had been so intent on watching his manœuvring of the last branch that they had forgotten to watch the gate, and now became suddenly aware of a man in gaiters and stout farmer's boots standing just behind them. He was slight of build, with a thin bronzed face, which was set in tense angry lines.

"Well, I've caught you good an' proper," he said slowly. "And what d'you think you're doin', may I ask?"

Fordwick straightened his coat about his shoulders, brushed the lichen from his trousers, then looked the man insolently up and down.

"There's no necessity to use that tone, my man," he drawled. "Any damage we've done we're naturally quite willing to pay for."

"Oh, you are, are you?" said the man. "That's an easy way out for you, isn't it?"

"It's an excellent way out for you, my good friend," said Fordwick, changing his manner to one of airy amusement. "You've only to name any price in reason and we'll pay it. I'm sure that's not an offer you often get for your lousy apples. You're lucky to have caught us."

But it was obvious that his tone only angered the man further.

"Oh no, you don't," he said. "You come to the police, that's what you do. Thieving, that's what it is. And we'll see what the magistrates have to say about it. And if you try an' make off I'll have your car stopped before you've gone two miles. A pity them as thinks they're gentlemen don't know how to behave as such. Come on, now."

He placed his hand roughly on Fordwick's shoulder, and Fordwick lost his temper.

"Take your hands off me, you filthy swine!" he shouted, his face purple with rage.

There was a scuffle and Fordwick hit out savagely with his fist. The man fell back, his head met the trunk of the tree with a sickening crack, and he dropped to the ground, lying there in a crumpled heap.

The three of them stood silent, motionless, staring down at the figure on the ground. It made Hilary think of some ghastly waxwork tableau. Even Fordwick's heavy breathing that cut rhythmically across the silence seemed unreal, mechanical. It was Bruce who broke the spell.

"You've killed him," he cried on a high-pitched hysterical note. "You've killed him."

"Shut up," said Fordwick between his teeth. "Shut up or I'll brain you. D'you want the whole village here?" His ruddy cheeks had paled and he was trembling. "Of course he's not dead. He's only stunned. Feel his heart. Go on," he rasped. "Do as I tell you. Feel his heart."

Sobbing under his breath, Bruce knelt down on the grass and slipped his hand beneath the man's coat. His hand was shaking so much that he could not have felt whether the heart was beating or not.

"No, it isn't," he sobbed. "You've killed him. My God! You've killed him."

He stood up and looked round the peaceful sunlit orchard, his eyes blank with terror. There was a trickle of saliva at the corner of his mouth.

"Come on," he quavered. "Let's clear off before anyone sees us."

"But we can't leave him like this," expostulated Hilary.

"Of course we can, you blasted fool!" spat out Fordwick. "Are you crazy? D'you want to go to jail? And look here." His eyes shifted from one to the other. "We stand together in this, d'you hear? We undertake not to give each other away whatever happens. If there's any question of it, we weren't here at all. We didn't come this way. We went round by Dunchurch. I know someone there I can fix all right if it's necessary. Come on, for God's sake, and let's drive like hell."

They went back to the gate, leaving the motionless figure still lying beneath the apple tree. Bruce was still sobbing beneath his breath, saying "My God, you've killed him," over and over again.

At the gate Hilary stopped. "I'm not coming with you," he said.

"What d'you mean, you crazy loon?" asked Fordwick, staring at him.

"I'm not coming. I'm not leaving the man like this."

"Well, we're not waiting for you."

"I don't want you to. I hope to hell I never see either of you again."

Fordwick thrust his white sweat-bedewed face close to Hilary's.

"If you give me away——" he threatened savagely.

"I shan't give you away," said Hilary. "What d'you take me for?"

"I take you for an even bloodier fool than I thought you were, and let me tell you this—if you do give me away, I'll get even with you if I have to spend the rest of my life doing it."

Hilary looked at him contemptuously and said nothing. Fordwick glanced cautiously up and down the empty road then climbed over the gate and pulled Bruce after him.

"It's your last chance," he said to Hilary. "Are you taking it?"

"No."

"All right. If you get yourself into a mess we won't help you out. We'll swear you went off on your own this afternoon."

"You can."

Fordwick pushed Bruce into the back of the car and took the driver's seat. The engine started with a roar and they set off down the road at a terrific speed. Just before they vanished from sight, Fordwick said something to Bruce over his shoulder, and Bruce took Hilary's suitcase and threw it out on to the roadside.

Hilary stood there, looking after them, wondering detachedly how he had ever thought that Fordwick was brave and handsome and fascinating. He was a pasteboard figure from a child's toy melodrama. There was nothing real about him. Whenever Hilary met him again he would see the white sweat-bedewed face and shaking lips ... see him creeping furtively out of a sunny orchard. ...

He walked slowly back to the inert figure beneath the apple tree.

It still lay there, twisted unnaturally, the face bloodless, the mouth open, an ominous patch of dried blood where the head had caught the tree-trunk. Suddenly panic seized him, and it was all he could do not to run down the road after Fordwick, shouting crazedly to him to stop. A black mist seemed to descend on everything. He was in the grip of a nightmare terror such as he had never known in all his life before. Then through the darkness came a ray of light. And the ray of light was the thought of Humphrey. ... Humphrey, solid, safe, reliable, with that quiet good-humour that never failed, that stark goodness and kindliness that underlay every word and look. Humphrey's broad shoulders were made to bear burdens easily, effortlessly—other people's as well as his own. His separation from Viola suddenly meant nothing at all. It was no one's business but theirs. Humphrey was still immovably, triumphantly himself. The thought brought back the innocent golden quality to the summer's day and restored to him his strength and purpose. He bent down and straightened the unconscious figure, then slipped his hand under the coat till he felt the slow beating of his heart. He could see a small green gate in the wall at the further end of the orchard. He made his way to it and found that it led into the farmhouse garden. He opened it and walked down a path bordered with pinks and violas to the door of the farmhouse. A woman in an apron, her sleeves rolled up to her elbows, answered his knock. She was little more than a girl, sturdy and sunburnt. She looked at him with level unsmiling eyes.

"Yes?" she said.

"I'm afraid your husband's had an accident," said Hilary. "He's in the orchard. If you'll tell me where the nearest doctor lives I'll go and fetch him as quickly as I can."

The doctor stood in the stone-flagged kitchen, his eyes fixed curiously on Hilary. The woman was upstairs with her husband.

"No, he's not seriously hurt. He was knocked out and there's some concussion, but it's just a question of complete rest—for the present, at any rate. What exactly happened? You didn't do it, did you? You don't look as if you had a punch like that."

"No, I didn't exactly do it," said Hilary, "but I take full responsibility." He felt ridiculously like the hero of a cheap school story as he said it. The Good Boy who would rather Take a Beating than Tell Tales. "I'll leave you my name and address," he went on. "I expect my stepfather will come down and see about it."

The very saying of it brought with it a miraculous sense of relief.

The doctor looked doubtfully at the name and address.

"I don't know that I oughtn't to get in touch with the police at once," he said. He gave Hilary a long penetrating look, then smiled suddenly. "But I'm going to trust you. You won't let me down, will you?"

"Rather not," said Hilary earnestly.

He left his last five-pound note with the doctor as a guarantee of good faith and went out into the country road, along which he had driven so gaily with Fordwick only a short time before. He picked up his suitcase from the roadside and stood waiting for the Coventry 'bus, which, the doctor had told him, was due in a few minutes.

Despite the experience he had just passed through, he felt strangely happy and at peace. He would take the train to Reddington from

Coventry and see Humphrey at once. Then he'd go to Monica. He'd tell her about the dog in the sidecar. He wanted to see her smile again.

Chapter Twenty-One

VIOLA stood and looked for a moment at the little pile of letters by her plate. On the top was the inevitable postcard from Hilary. She smiled ruefully as she read it. The bald statements implied, she supposed, that he was enjoying the trip so much that he had no time for writing. He was devoted to Fordwick, of course. She herself had thought Fordwick rather attractive when he came down to see them last summer, but Humphrey, she remembered, had disliked him intensely.

She turned the envelopes over one by one . . . Frances, her mother, Madame Bertier, bills, receipts, appeals for charities. . . . Then her knees began to tremble and she sat down suddenly. The last envelope was addressed to her in Humphrey's writing. It had come at last, then. Inside she would find the receipted hotel bill. There was a feeling of tightness in her chest, and the hand that held the envelope shook uncontrollably. She made an effort to master herself and laid the letter aside. She wouldn't open it yet. She'd wait till she felt calmer and more able to tackle it.

She opened the letter from her mother. Frances's accident had brought Mrs. Ellison posthaste to London. A broken rib was something definite, something that demanded a mother's care and presence. One couldn't pretend that a broken rib didn't exist. Mrs. Ellison hadn't even tried to pretend that it didn't exist. She came up by the next train in a flame of motherly love and anxiety. Frances was her little girl again—her little girl needing comfort and nursing and petting. Viola felt that she had misjudged her. It was just a question of values. Some things didn't matter and others did. Broken ribs were among the ones that did. . . . She was staying at an hotel near the hospital and visiting Frances every day. The doctor had said that Frances could go home at the end of ten days. She was, she wrote, quite enjoying her visit to London and looking up all her old friends there. She rang up Father every evening, and he was quite all right, though, of course, looking forward very much to her and Frances's return.

As soon as her mother had arrived to take charge Viola had returned to Reddington. She was heartsick with longing for the little provincial town and for her own home, tired to death of London, of pottering about with Adrian to concerts and picture galleries and theatres. Even Adrian himself had begun to get slightly on her nerves. She wanted to be back in her rut, to lose herself in the little household and social duties that had made up her life for so many years. Her homesickness for this ugly house and for the life she had always imagined she despised had surprised and humbled her. How little one knew of oneself after all! She remembered with amazed incredulity the feeling of freedom that had come to her when she realised that she could leave Reddington for ever. She had tried freedom and it had proved stale and profitless. She wanted her prison, her chains, again. Was it that she was particularly spiritless, she wondered (who was it who had said "There is no freedom for the weak"?), or was it that the glamour of freedom lay chiefly in its inaccessibility? Was she like the child who pursues and catches a butterfly only to find it crushed and maimed, its grace and loveliness fled? She glanced at Humphrey's letter again and smiled—a twisted bitter smile. Evidently freedom was to be hers whether she wanted it or not.

She put aside several bills and receipts, then, taking a deep breath, opened the envelope with suddenly steady fingers.

DEAR VIOLA [she read],
May I come to see you this afternoon as I should like to talk matters over with you? I'll be with you about five if that will be convenient. If not, will you telephone me at the shop?
    Yours,

HUMPHREY

She put down the letter and stared in front of her. He was in Reddington, then, at the shop. What did he want to discuss with her? What was there to discuss? She got up and went to the window and stood there, looking out unseeingly. She was sick and tired of the long-drawn-out suspense. Was she never to win through to the peace of mind that she had once taken for granted so casually as part of her daily life? It would be better, she tried to console herself, when it was all over and Humphrey irrevocably lost to her. But she knew in her heart that it wouldn't be. It would never be better. . . .

She rang the bell, and Evelyn came in to clear away the almost untouched breakfast. Evelyn and Cook knew now, of course, that something was wrong, though Viola had told them nothing definite. It was difficult to tell them the facts of the case (which was all she knew herself) without seeming to blame Humphrey, and she did not want to do that. She wondered how much they knew or guessed—more, probably, than she realised. Did they gloat over the situation, or were they perplexed and sorry? She shook her head impatiently. What did it matter what they thought? Couldn't she let her mind dwell on something other than Humphrey for even a minute?

"You've not had much breakfast, madam," said Evelyn.

"No . . . I wasn't very hungry," said Viola, trying to speak in her usual voice.

"And you're not looking yourself, either, madam," went on Evelyn. "Don't you think you'd better see the doctor?"

The kindness of the woman's voice got behind Viola's defences, and to her horror she felt her eyes swim suddenly with tears.

"No. I'm all right, thank you, Evelyn," she forced herself to say, without turning round.

Evelyn went out, closing the door behind her.

Viola looked at the clock. It was nine o'clock. Humphrey was coming at five. Eight hours. Four hundred and eighty minutes. An eternity. . . . How could she live through it, with this sick weight of apprehension at her heart, each moment dragging like an hour?

Absently she opened Madame Bertier's letter. It reminded her that she had ordered a copy of a model hat some weeks ago and that it was now ready. She remembered that Madame Bertier had written before to remind her of this when she was in London. She decided to go into Burchester for the hat. It would make the time pass more quickly. Mr. Randolph's office was quite near Madame Bertier's. She would ask Elaine to lunch with her.

Elaine was waiting for her in the doorway of the restaurant. She looked, as ever, neat and well turned out and extremely pretty. The small cap-like hat, perched on her mass of fair curls, would have looked absurd, Viola thought, by itself as a mere hat, but on Elaine it gave just the right touch of youthful smartness. Viola was always secretly amused by her niece's air of poise and sophistication, but she did not resent it as did others of the family. ("*Me* to be patronised by a chit like that!" Doreen would say indignantly.) There was something gallant and courageous about it, and today she noticed a new element—a tremulous youthful excitement that was barely concealed by the assumption of maturity and nonchalance.

"There you are, my dear," she said. "How nice to see you! I rang up to book a table."

They entered the restaurant, and the waiter led them to the corner table that Viola had reserved. As they sat down Viola saw Elaine's cool appraising glance flick her over and rest for some seconds on her hat.

"Isn't it right?" she smiled apologetically. "I bought it in London in rather a hurry."

"It's too old for you," said Elaine critically.

"I *am* old, my dear."

"Not as old as that," retorted Elaine. "It's that velvet swathing that makes it look so old. If you'd let me take it off and put just a band of corded ribbon—much narrower, of course—and lower the crown just a fraction of an inch. . . ."

"It would be sweet of you," said Viola.

She felt vaguely touched, though she knew Elaine's interest to be quite impersonal. It was, she thought with a sigh, because of her new loneliness that she was so touched nowadays by any little kindness. Once, secure in the knowledge of Humphrey's devotion, it would have meant nothing to her.

"How's the family?" she went on.

"All right," said Elaine. "Mon's working far too hard. Even Mother's getting all het-up about it. She just slogs away all day and every day and hardly ever goes out. She's beginning to look a wreck, but it's no good talking to her. . . . You know," a dreamy expression came into her face, "I could make Mon look lovely if she'd let me, but she just won't be bothered. She hasn't any idea beyond tweeds and won't let anyone else have one for her. Oh," as she suddenly remembered something, "and there's Joey."

"Joey?"

"Yes," Elaine looked slightly embarrassed. "Uncle Humphrey's coming back to Reddington today, isn't he?"

At the thought of her coming interview with Humphrey, Viola's whole body seemed to turn cold, but she answered calmly enough, "I believe so."

"Well . . . Joey's going to tackle him and say he wants to leave the business, and Mother told me to ask you to ask Uncle Humphrey to be very firm with him. There's nothing else he *can* do. He's still got that crazy idea about farming. . . . Mother says that if Uncle Humphrey's very firm and says he mustn't leave the business and rubs it in what a mess Father made of farming, she thinks it'll be all right. But," her embarrassment returned, "Mother oughtn't to have—— Perhaps you——"

"Yes, I shall be seeing him today," said Viola. "I'll try and remember."

"That's all right, then. Mother said I was to be sure to tell you."

Once more Viola became aware of the new excitement beneath the youthful armour of assurance.

"What are you feeling so pleased about?" she said suddenly.

Elaine laughed—her rare laugh, clear and sweet and childish. "How did you know I was feeling pleased?"

"You look pleased. It shines right through you."

"I meant to tell you," said Elaine. "I haven't told anyone yet but Mon. It only happened yesterday."

"Who's the lucky man?"

Disdain clouded the radiance.

"Oh, *that*! Good gracious, it's not *that* ... It's Madame Bertier."

"Madame Bertier?"

"Yes. ..." Elaine leant confidingly over the table. "I called to have lunch with her yesterday—I often do, you know. We have sandwiches together—and she'd just heard that an old friend of her father's had died and left her all his money and she's going to London. Her things are too good for Burchester, anyway. Burchester isn't any better than Reddington in that way. It doesn't want or deserve anything better than," her lips curled scornfully, "Lessington's hat department. Sorry, Aunt Viola, but you know what I mean. And—this is the thrilling part, Aunt Viola—she's asked me to go there with her."

"But I thought you were going to London as Mr. Randolph's secretary."

Disdain—it was almost disgust this time—once more wrinkled up Elaine's small white nose.

"Oh, him! He's still in Paris. I don't think I'd ever have done that when it came to the point. ... He's got sticking-out eyes and his neck's too fat," she added irrelevantly.

Viola smiled.

"So when is Madame moving?"

"As soon as she can fix it up. She's gone to London today to look round. She says she won't take anything definitely till I've seen it. It's very important to have just the right shop in just the right place. Of course, the money may not run to the ideal place, but she's going to get as near it as she can. When she asked me to go with her I nearly died of joy."

Viola was silent. Her first thought had been that she must ask Humphrey to help them, to see that they weren't cheated over the purchase of the new shop, to put some money into the business on Elaine's behalf if the enterprise seemed sound. Then, with the familiar twist at her heart, she remembered. . . . She had no claim on Humphrey now, no responsibility for his family.

She looked at Elaine and thought how absurd it was for a girl as pretty as this to be contemplating a business career.

Elaine glanced up and met her eyes.

"I know what you're thinking," she said sternly.

"What am I thinking?" challenged Viola.

"You're thinking that I'm sure to marry. Just because I'm pretty. Weren't you?"

Viola shrugged.

"Well . . ." she said. "It's a generally accepted theory that pretty girls do marry."

"But why should they?" persisted Elaine with increasing severity. "I don't see what it's got to do with it. It makes me furious when people talk like that. Just as if every girl was loping round with her tongue hanging out waiting for someone to marry her. Like those dreadful advertisements that tell you what soap and scent and shoe polish to use to catch a husband. As if you *wanted* to! Mind you, men are useful to cart you about and give you a good time. The mistake is to take them seriously, and I'm never going to do that. . . . I'm going to have an exciting life with lots of hard work and failures and successes. I'm going to mix with people and move about and travel. I'm not going to waste it cooped up in the four walls of a house waiting for a man to come home to his dinner—cooking his meals and darning his socks and wiping his children's noses. Why should a man have all the fun and a woman none? And how many marriages do turn out well? There isn't a single married woman I know I'd change places with. I——" She stopped and the colour flooded her cheeks. "I'm sorry, Aunt Viola. I forgot. I didn't mean——"

"I know you didn't, my dear. It's all right. Go on."

But the interruption had checked the flow of Elaine's eloquence.

"I know some women are born marryers—Bridget is, for instance—but I'm not."

"I haven't seen Bridget since I came back," said Viola. "I met her mother yesterday, and she said that her engagement wasn't broken off."

Elaine laughed.

"It's a sort of Alice Through the Looking-Glass engagement," she said. "Bridget says that she's engaged to Terry Wheeler and Aunt Doreen says she's engaged to Roy Hamwell, and Roy Hamwell's announced his engagement to Eileen Durham, but Aunt Doreen still persists that he's engaged to Bridget. She cries and says that Bridget's broken her heart. She never seems to think of Bridget's."

Viola frowned anxiously. "I must go and see them. . . ."

"Now, Aunt Viola," admonished Elaine, "don't try and straighten out people's muddles for them. It's always a waste of time and energy."

"You're a cold-blooded little creature," said Viola.

"I know I am. I glory in it. . . ." She glanced at her watch. "I must go now. . . . Thanks for a lovely lunch, Aunt Viola. And you must come and buy a hat from us when we're settled. We'll make you look ten years younger, not ten years older."

His key turned in the lock at the stroke of five. Viola was waiting in the drawing-room. She had resisted the temptation to make herself look attractive, the rather cheap impulse to show him what he was losing. She wore the skirt and jumper she had put on in the morning and had used no rouge. She looked, she knew, middle-aged and haggard.

He closed the door behind him and stood there, fixing his eyes on her across the room. For a moment neither of them spoke, then she said "Well?" in a voice that sounded startlingly deep and harsh.

He took a letter from his pocket and, coming across the room, handed it to her.

"I'd like you to read that, if you will."

At first she could not read the words through the mist that swam before her eyes. Was it the "evidence"? Need he have turned the sword in her heart by bringing it like this in person? Then the words became clear.

Humphrey, I was married to Tony yesterday. The child is his, not yours. I ought to have told you before. Goodbye, my dear. You've been very sweet to me and I shall always be grateful.

LILY

The letter fell from her inert fingers on to the ground at her feet and lay there. A wave of faintness swept over her and she caught hold of a chair-back for support. He was at her side in a moment.

"Viola. ..."

She mastered herself.

"I'm quite all right," she said.

She sat down, battling against the riot of emotions that surged over her. She felt furious with herself for giving way like this. She had meant to be so cold and calm, so completely mistress of the situation—whatever the situation should turn out to be.

He picked up the letter and read the words again in silence. His first feeling on receiving it had been one of relief, but beneath the relief was a bitter-sweet regret, an aching compunction. He would never see Lily again. He would never know for certain whether the child was his or Tony's, whether she had given herself to him in an unavailing attempt to forget her real lover, or whether, realising that Viola held the foremost place in his heart, she was deliberately sacrificing her happiness to his. He had never met Tony. He could not even be sure that she had actually married him. She might, in her gay careless pride, have decided to go through with the affair alone rather than saddle any man with the responsibility of it.

Viola noticed the deep lines of strain and weariness on his face, and pity for him gripped her heart despite herself.

"What does this mean—to us?" she said at last in a low voice.

He stood on the hearthrug and looked down at her.

"That's what we have to discuss," he said.

There was a silence—so long that she had to break it.

"Well?" she said again.

He spoke slowly, as if with an effort.

"It's—altered things, of course," he said. "I can't expect you to feel to me as you felt before. If you wish to be free—and I've given you every reason to wish to be free—we can still go on with it. I can still let you have official evidence for divorce."

"I see ..." she said slowly.

His eyes were fixed on her steadily.

"There may be—someone else," he said.

She thought of Adrian—struggled to see him as a hero of romance, but could only see him standing on the kerb in the rain, worrying about his wet feet and trying ineffectually to summon a taxi.

"No," she said, "there's no one else."

"But even so," he persisted, "you may prefer to go through with it."

She made an impatient gesture.

"Leave me out of it for the present," she said. "What do you yourself feel?"

There was a pause before he answered, then he said:

"I'm not much good at expressing myself, but I'd give everything I possess and everything I'm ever likely to possess to be back where we were before this happened."

At his words all her unhappiness fell from her, and a great peace flooded her soul.

"Well?" he went on, "It's for you to decide. I don't feel that I've the right even to ask you to take me back."

"No, no," she said quickly. "You mustn't ever feel like that. It was my fault, too. I've realised that lately. I've realised a lot of things that I was too stupid to see before."

In the silence that followed she choked back a dozen questions. What was the girl like? Did he love her very much? Was he very sorry about the child? The episode—closed now for ever—was his, sacred and inviolable. She must not force him to any disloyalty or betrayal, must not handle it with curious prying fingers. She thought of Lily now, not with superiority or disgust, but with humility, dimly aware that it must have been some lack in herself that had made him turn to her for comfort.

"We needn't ever talk about it again," she went on, "unless you want to, but you mustn't ever feel that it was—your fault. I was jealous and stupid and conceited. I thought I was—quite a different sort of person from the person I really am. And I don't want you ever to let your thought of me spoil your memories of her. Do you know what I mean? I can't express it properly."

Now that the tension and suspense were over, an inexpressible weariness possessed her. She felt almost too tired to speak.

"You're very generous," he said.

She felt grateful to him for keeping his emotions beneath a strong guard, for making no demands on her, for not even touching her.

"Then we just settle down again as we were?" he went on.

"Please."

"Or would you like to go away for a little?"

She conquered a sudden desire to laugh hysterically at this.

"No. I've been away. I hated it. I've been longing to get home."

"So have I," he said simply.

It was at this point that Hilary burst in upon them. He hammered imperiously on the front door and seemed to enter the drawing-room almost as soon as Evelyn opened it. He was obviously in a state of uncontrollable excitement. He was trembling and his eyes were feverishly bright. During the journey home, panic had seized him again. Suppose the man died, after all. Suppose Fordwick managed to put the blame on to him. . . . He had hurried through the streets from the station in a state of terror, the rope already at his neck.

"Thank God!" he said as his eyes fell on Humphrey. "I thought I might have to chase all the way up to London after you."

Then he sank into a chair and covered his face with his hands, shivering convulsively.

Humphrey went across to him and put a hand on his shoulder.

"Pull yourself together," he said quietly, "and tell us what's happened."

The story tumbled out—so incoherently at first that neither of them could make much of it. Humphrey let him tell it his own way without comment, then began to question him in a matter-of-fact business-like fashion that soon got the story clear.

He pulled out his watch.

"I could get down there in about an hour by car, I suppose. I'll start at once."

"I'm frightfully sorry," said Hilary.

"That's all right," said Humphrey easily. "It doesn't appear to have been your fault, and there's nothing for you to worry about."

"No . . ." agreed Hilary, drawing a deep breath. "I don't feel that there is now. I knew it would be all right once I'd told you," he added ingenuously.

"It'll be a question of compensation chiefly, I suppose," went on Humphrey.

"I'm sorry about that too," put in Hilary. "I dare say Fordwick will help. He's quite well off."

"We'll leave him out of it for the present," said Humphrey dryly. "The man was furious."

"Well, I shall have to exert what small amount of tact I have to soothe him down," smiled Humphrey.

Hilary's strained features relaxed into an answering smile. Humphrey's cool clear sanity had robbed the situation of its nightmare quality. His fears of a short time ago seemed ridiculous.

"Shall I come with you?" he asked.

"I think not, thanks," said Humphrey. "If you want something to do, go and get the car out. It's not been used lately and it may take some starting."

"I suppose I shouldn't be any use?" said Viola when Hilary had gone to the garage. She felt a faint compunction that Humphrey should have to take on this responsibility so soon after their reconciliation.

"I think not, my dear. I'd rather tackle it alone."

She went with him into the hall.

"Shall you be back tonight?" she asked.

"Yes, but I may be late. Don't wait up for me."

That seemed to make everything normal and safe and happy again. She tried conscientiously to feel worried about this mess that Hilary had got himself into, but somehow she couldn't manage to. Humphrey was so eminently capable of dealing with it.

Hilary drove the car round to the front door.

"She started like a bird," he said. "I've topped up the radiator. Everything else seems all right."

Humphrey took his seat at the wheel and drove off, turning at the gate to give them his usual casual salute.

They watched till he was out of sight, then went back to the drawing-room.

"I never thought I'd find him here," said Hilary. "Had he come to talk things over?"

"Yes."

She didn't want to jeopardise her new-found peace by discussing the situation with Hilary. Hilary's emotional reactions might jangle the atmosphere, might disperse the calm quiet happiness that filled her soul and body. It was strange to think how short a time ago it was since she had looked to Hilary (ineffectually enough) for support and comfort, since he had loomed so large upon the horizon of her life. Now he seemed a tiresome child, for whom she was, nevertheless, responsible.

But he asked no further questions, did not indeed appear to be particularly interested. Secretly he was feeling slightly contemptuous of her. Fancy letting a decent chap like Humphrey go, as she had done, without raising a finger to stop him!

"Would you like some tea, Hilary?" she said, rousing herself from her dreams.

"No, thanks." He went to the mirror over the mantelpiece, smoothed back his hair, and straightened his tie. "I'm just going over to Aunt Aggie's. I want to see Monica."

Chapter Twenty-Two

THE drawing-room was full of subdued chatter that rose and fell like the sound of distant waves. Viola was pouring out tea at the low round tea-table, and Evelyn was carrying plates and cups of tea among the visitors. It was, on the surface, one of the usual family tea-parties that Viola had always given at regular intervals, but beneath it everyone was aware of a deeper significance. It celebrated her reconciliation with Humphrey, marked the resumption of their normal life together. That resumption Viola had found unexpectedly easy. She had been afraid that the weeks of separation would stand between them, alienating them from each other, but instead they seemed to draw them closer together. Both had suffered deeply, and their suffering formed a bond between them. Perhaps that had been the original cause of the trouble, she thought. Their life together had been too easy, and so they had lost their hold on reality and slipped apart without realising it.

Harriet, sitting on the settee next to her, was describing at great length Hester's narrow escape from pneumonia.

"It's a miracle she didn't get it. Her colds always go straight to her chest, but I've never known her have one quite as bad as that before. She came home with it right on her." She glanced with tender anxiety at Hester, who was talking to Aggie at the other side of the room. "She's better now, of course, but I'm being very careful of her. I take her breakfast to bed every morning, and I'm very particular about her not getting overtired. ... I do think it's always so important after an illness—don't you?—not to get overtired. And she gets tired very easily. I remember when she was a child——"

Viola listened absently. She was thinking about the letter she had had from Frances that morning, written from Campions.

"I'm so glad to be home again. I'd forgotten how much I loved it. I think that for years I'd been growing—blunt, if that doesn't sound too silly. Like a knife whose edge is all worn away. I couldn't feel happy or unhappy. And now I'm alive again—and happy." At the end was a P.S. "Darling, he wasn't really a bit like Robin, was he? The strange part of it all is that Robin himself seemed to come back to me while I was in hospital. He's quite real again to me now. I can't think how I ever thought that Richard was like him."

She had had a letter from Adrian, too. Adrian was in Paris, consoling himself with the Monets and Gauguins of the Luxembourg, and the Lepères and Simons of the Petit Palais. He imagined himself to be heartbroken, but Viola could read a faint unconscious relief between the lines. ("Perhaps, after all, I could not have made you happy, though it has been the dearest wish of my life.") Adrian and his type really preferred a shattered dream of romance to a flesh-and-blood woman who would inevitably bring complications into their ordered lives. He had, moreover, a natural air of melancholy wistfulness that fitted in well with the picture.

Doreen sat apart, wearing an air of tragedy. Doreen was playing the Tragic Mother these days. Never in all her life would she forget that dreadful night when Bridget arrived home with Terry Wheeler, dishevelled, her dress torn, radiantly happy, enclosed in an armour against which tears, anger, and reproaches beat in vain. She was going to marry Terry, she said. She didn't care how long she had to wait. They loved each other and that was all that mattered. Terry, usually so shy and silent, shared her strange exaltation. They treated her kindly and patiently, as though she were an unreasonable child for whom allowances must be made. As soon as Terry had gone, Roy arrived in a state of maudlin penitence, slightly unsteady in speech and movement. Bridget dealt with him too, calmly, coolly, efficiently. She was sorry, but she didn't love him and couldn't marry him. She gave him back his ring. "We'd never have been happy," she said, "and you know it in your heart." He wept and protested, and Bridget took him to the front door and dismissed him, still with that firm kindness, as if her serenity were so secure that nothing could shake it.

"You're wonderful—wonderful," said Roy thickly, standing on the step in the moonlight, the tears streaming down his cheeks.

"And you're drunk," said Bridget. "Do be careful how you drive home."

She came back to the drawing-room, and Doreen continued her hysterical assault.

"You've ruined me, you wicked girl!" she sobbed.

"Don't be silly, Mother," said Bridget. "I haven't ruined you."

"You must be mad," went on Doreen. "It will take me months to undo this night's work."

"You'll never undo it," said Bridget confidently, "if you mean breaking off my engagement to Terry. We belong to each other now for ever and ever."

Doreen stared at her in angry amazement. Where was her docile Baby-Bridget, the shy obedient little girl who had always tried so hard to please her? She had vanished, and this calm, determined, assured young woman had taken her place.

"It's no use talking about it," Bridget had continued. "I'm going to bed now. I'm sorry, Mother, but you mustn't interfere in my affairs any more."

Doreen had stared at her in incredulous fury. *Interfere!* The impertinence of the child! When had she ever "interfered" in her life?

She knew, of course, that it would be uphill work to regain the ground she had lost, but she didn't at that point altogether despair. The days that followed, however, wore down her spirit. That maddening calm and confidence still possessed Bridget. She refused to make any overtures to Roy, refused even to write to him. She did write to Mrs. Hamwell to apologise for cutting her visit short so unceremoniously, but it was a formal impenitent letter that, in Doreen's opinion, could only make matters worse.

Roy called once more, but Bridget would not see him, and he was sulky and aloof with Doreen, refusing to yield to her arch charm.

The day after he called she met Mrs. Hamwell in the Market Square, and Mrs. Hamwell cut her dead. Doreen went home and wept desolately. "I've given up my whole life to you," she said to Bridget. "I've sacrificed everything for you. I've *lived* for nothing but you, and you repay me by *ruining* me like this."

"I haven't ruined you, Mother," said Bridget patiently, "and I don't see that it really matters whether Mrs. Hamwell bows to you or not. She never did much more than that, anyway, did she? And I think she's a very disagreeable conceited woman. Personally I'd rather she cut me than not."

Bridget was relieved by the announcement of Roy's engagement to Eileen Durham.

"Well, I couldn't marry him now, anyway," she said.

"You could," said Doreen tearfully, "if you played your cards properly. He's only done it in pique. She's caught him on the rebound. You'll regret all your life throwing over a good man like Roy for that waster Terry Wheeler."

Bridget was so surprised by this aspect of the case that she could think of no rejoinder.

Doreen began to pin her faith on Humphrey's return.

"Wait till your Uncle Humphrey comes back," she said. "He'll put his foot down. I shall ask him to go and have a straight talk with Roy. In any case, *he* won't let you throw yourself away on a nobody like Terry Wheeler."

"Uncle Humphrey has nothing to do with it," said Bridget, forgetting how much Humphrey had had to do with it.

As soon as Doreen heard that Humphrey was back at the shop she went to see him, tight-lipped and determined.

"This must be stopped, Humphrey," she said. "Stopped at once and at all costs. The child has no father, and it's your duty to prevent her from ruining her whole life. She adores Roy really. They had a lovers' quarrel and both of them went off in a pique and got engaged to someone else. And they're both too proud to make it up. That's four lives *ruined*," her voice rose dramatically, "for the sake of a girl's whim. I'm all mother, you know, Humphrey. I can honestly say that no mother has ever *lived* for her child as

I have for Bridget. And I can't stand by and see her life wrecked like this. You must help me, Humphrey. She's always taken notice of what you say."

Humphrey had been kind but non-committal. He would have a talk with Bridget. He wouldn't promise more than that. Feeling a little more hopeful, Doreen sent Bridget down to his office at Lessington's. The story she brought back was at first incredible. Doreen, in fact, had refused to believe it till she had had confirmation from Humphrey himself. It seemed that Joey, too, had been to him, grumbling about his work, and, instead of giving the boy a good talking to and sending him away with a flea in his ear (as Doreen put it), Humphrey had listened sympathetically and had finally cabled to an old friend of his who was a farmer in South Africa, asking if he would take Joey as a pupil. And he had not only listened sympathetically to Bridget, too, but he had offered to give Terry the position in Lessington's that he had meant Joey to have, to put him through Lessington's, in fact, as if he were his own son.

"He's mad," said Doreen with the calmness of despair, when she was at last convinced that this was true. "He's crazy. This trouble with your Aunt Viola has turned his brain. . . . Well, I shall never give my consent to the marriage. Never. My conscience wouldn't allow me to."

But she knew that she would have to give her consent. She couldn't stand out against public opinion. Bridget and Terry were treated everywhere as an engaged couple, and it was taken for granted that they would be married as soon as Terry was earning enough to justify it. He had begun his work at Lessington's and was evidently getting on well there. He had already lost the surly hang-dog air that had once characterised him. It seemed to have melted away in the radiance that encompassed both him and Bridget. He was becoming what Doreen indignantly called "uppish." And as if all that weren't enough, there had been that ridiculous affair of Miss Marcher. Miss Marcher had fainted one morning as she was scrubbing the cellar steps, had fallen down on to the stone floor below and been removed to hospital with a broken leg. And to Doreen's amazement, she found that people were blaming her for it. Actually blaming *her* for it. Saying untrue and unkind things about her "working the poor old woman to death," when she'd taken her in and given her a home out of sheer kindness of heart, and even now rang up the hospital, whenever she happened to remember, to ask how she was. It was almost a lesson never to try to help anyone again. Kindness was always misunderstood and misrepresented. Looking back over the past few weeks, Doreen wondered whether it would have been possible for anyone to have tried so hard to help others and have received so little gratitude. It was the selfish people who came off best, after all, she thought bitterly. She had stopped reasoning and pleading with Bridget now. She just sat about, wearing a tragic expression, but even that wasn't very satisfactory, because Bridget didn't seem to notice. She was hardly ever at home, rushing off somewhere or other every minute with Terry or his common sister—what was she called? Lucy or some equally common name. It seemed that the common sister had gone away for a holiday with the common aunt, and that they had quarrelled and Lucy had come home alone and had decided to get a job. She was actually going as an assistant to one of the big stores in London, where she would live in a hostel. That was the sort of family-in-law she was going to have. Shop assistants! She hardly dared show her face in Reddington now, what with Mrs. Hamwell and the Wheelers and the dreadful people who were misrepresenting her kindness to Miss Marcher. But a few days ago a small ray of light had broken through the gloom. An old school friend, who had a house in Bexhill, had written asking her to pay her a visit, and Doreen thought that she really did need a change. She had met Viola the morning she received the note, and Viola had agreed that it would be an excellent plan and had offered to have Bridget to stay with her and Humphrey while she was away. Moreover, the friend had said, "As one grows older one makes few new friends, and I often think how nice it would be if you could come and live down here, too. Perhaps, when dear Bridget has made her grand marriage" (Doreen winced at that), "you will think about it."

And Doreen was thinking about it very seriously. She had come to the conclusion that she was too fine grained for the coarse Midlands. Hadn't some poet or other said that the Midlands were "sodden and unkind"? She didn't know about "sodden" but they were certainly "unkind." The South was notoriously more congenial to sensitive people. She'd have a look round while she was staying with Dorothy. A boarding-house might be the best solution. In a boarding-house one wasn't troubled with servants, and she'd always hated servants. Bridget was coming to stay at Viola's this evening so as to leave Doreen freer to make her preparations for the visit. Certainly Bridget wasn't much company nowadays, and she'd as soon be alone. She glanced round the room. There was Aunt Hester sitting staring in front of her with a vacant look on her face. Poor old thing! She really had been very ill. Doreen had been to see her several times while she was in bed, and had once even been tempted to buy her some flowers but had recollected in time that she probably had plenty.

"I hope you're keeping better, Aunt Hester," she said kindly.

"Yes, thank you," said Hester, "I'm quite well now."

She had awakened with a start from her dreams at the sound of Doreen's voice. She hadn't told Harriet—or anyone—about her new Escape, of course, but she could take refuge in it now whenever she liked ... hold Mrs. Wilmot's quivering form in her arms, go down to confront that bleak figure in the over-furnished little drawing-room. . . . She could live again every word, every movement, every thought. It never occurred to her to wonder what had happened afterwards—whether Mr. Wilmot's suspicions had really been lulled, how husband and wife had got on together, how the lover had fared. The little episode existed in her mind perfect and complete in itself, as if none of the actors in it had any reality outside. It was her Escape, the one part in her whole life in which Harriet had no share, the part that gave her her identity, that made her a separate being. It filled the place that those weeks of Humphrey's visit used to fill, and she never to the end of her life realised that it had in it the very element that had spoilt the other memory for her.

The door opened, and Hilary and Monica entered. They were glowing and flushed with exercise.

"We're not very late, are we?" said Hilary. "We ran all the way down from the moor."

He came to Viola for a cup of tea and took it over to Monica in the window recess. Monica, despite the inevitable tweed costume, looked radiantly pretty, her cheeks rosy, her dark eyes bright. Her small round face was as grave as ever, but the light beneath seemed to shine now very near the surface, and, as Hilary handed her the cup, broke through in a sudden vivid smile at something he said.

Viola watched them thoughtfully. Now that she had stopped worrying about Hilary he seemed to have become more normal—less neurotic and excitable. There were none of the old "scenes." He was pleasant, good-tempered, and, strange for him, seemed contented and happy. Perhaps the fright he'd had about the farmer had been a salutary lesson, though it was difficult to see why it should have had just that effect on him. Humphrey had found the man determined to "have the law on them," but, with a certain amount of difficulty, had managed to soothe his outraged feelings and to persuade him to accept pecuniary compensation. He had gone down to see him again, and the two had got on very well together. Finally Humphrey had arranged to send Joey down there to get licked into shape till arrangements should have been made for his going abroad. Joey, they heard, was "shaping well" and enjoying the life. Humphrey had written a formal impersonal note to Fordwick to tell him that the farmer had not been seriously injured, but had had no reply.

Viola's eyes still rested on them. They were sitting on the window-seat with a plate of sandwiches between them, talking and laughing together as if they were the only people in the room. Something of possessive jealousy stirred at her heart. It was, of course, good for Hilary to have a girl friend, and Monica was a nice steady girl who would do him no harm, but she hoped she wasn't taking it seriously. She certainly wasn't good enough for Hilary. . . . Oh dear, she caught herself up, I mustn't be *that* sort of mother. I've loved his not being interested in girls, but I suppose it's only natural that he should be. . . . Anyway, I can leave Humphrey to deal with anything that needs dealing with. It had been heaven to leave things to Humphrey again. And Humphrey had certainly been busy since he came back, disentangling the family muddles—Joey, Bridget, Hilary.

Aggie was sitting by the fireplace, enjoying the iced cake and the festive atmosphere—she loved tea-parties—but feeling slightly nervous. Elaine had said that she might get away from the office in time to come on to Aunt Viola's for tea, or, on the other hand, she might not. It would depend on how much work there was. And Aggie, just before setting out, had yielded to the sudden temptation to put on a yellow silk bow that she had bought secretly at Lessington's the other day. It was very dressy and had only cost one-and-eleven, and Aggie thought that it just brightened up the navy-blue dress which she'd always thought looked so dull and dowdy. That temptation had, in the way of temptations generally, led to another, and at the very last minute she had hastily pinned the bunch of brightly coloured fir cones in the front of her hat. She thought that, with the bow, it improved her appearance immensely, but she knew that it would annoy Elaine, and she was hoping guiltily that Randoph's had had a very busy day, so that she would have time to go home and take off both bow and posy before Elaine saw them. Elaine, however, hadn't been quite so stern lately. This morning she'd said, "Mother, I *do* wish you'd mend that hole under the arm of your overall," but she'd said it quite kindly. Aggie had promised to mend it, but it was somehow very difficult to remember to mend a hole that only other people saw. ... Elaine had been quite nice about Nero, too. She'd found him lying on the sofa after supper last night and she'd said "Hello, you mangy old horror!" almost affectionately, as she lifted him down. Perhaps it was because she was leaving home so soon and going to London to that hat-shop. Aggie disapproved strongly of the hat-shop. What on earth did a girl like Elaine want with a hat-shop? It would have been so much better to go to London as Mr. Randolph's secretary, if she must go to London. Aggie had always had a sneaking hope that Mr. Randolph would turn out to be Mr. Right. It would have been so nice to have one of them married and he'd have been such an exciting son-in-law.

Then there would have been babies and family parties and that sort of thing. Aggie loved babies and family parties. She had taken for granted that Humphrey would try to persuade her to give up the idea of the hat-shop, but instead of that, he had helped them to buy it and had even put some money into it. It was dreadful the way the family was breaking up. Joey working on a farm just like a common labourer, Elaine off to London, Mon hardly ever in the house these days and going back to Oxford next week. Aggie felt pathetic and aggrieved. What was the good of having children if they all went off and left you like this? She wished she could have kept just one for company, but evidently she wasn't even to do that. Still, she reminded herself consolingly, worse things than that could happen to people. Mrs. Mumbles had told her only this morning over the eleven o'clock cup of tea about a woman whose six children had all died of different diseases in the same month. Even if only three had died in the same year (Mrs. Mumbles was a little inclined to exaggerate), she was better off than that, at any rate. She must tell them to write regularly and perhaps one day she'd go out to South Africa to stay with Joey and see the Statue of Liberty one heard so much about. Or was that in Australia? And perhaps she'd go to London to stay with Elaine and they'd go to theatres together, and Elaine would be nice to her because there wouldn't be Nero and Mrs. Mumbles and the neighbours and the hole in her overall to irritate her. (She really must try to remember to mend that hole before she went to bed.) She was just wandering happily about London with Elaine, when Elaine herself passed the window with Humphrey, and her spirits at once sank down into the depths. For Elaine gave her a keen glance through the window that stripped her in a flicker of an eyelash of both bow and posy. Oh dear! She wished she hadn't risked it. . . .

They heard voices in the hall, then Elaine came in alone.

"Uncle Humphrey's just gone up to wash," she said. "I'm not very late, am I?"

She kissed Viola, looked at Aggie, who pretended to be so much engrossed in what Doreen was saying that she hadn't seen her enter the room, then went across to the window recess to Hilary and

Monica. Queer how both those two had suddenly turned into human beings, she thought amusedly, as Hilary leapt to his feet and went to get her a cup of tea.

She had hardly been able to believe her eyes the first evening Hilary had come to the house asking for Monica, but it had happened so often since that she had grown quite accustomed to it.

And last night Monica had rather shyly asked her to help her choose a new dress. "A—a sort of afternoon dress," she had explained. "Something not quite as plain as my others."

So it must have been Hilary all along. Poor old Mon! Any girl who married Hilary was asking for trouble, but then most girls seemed to go about asking for trouble. Perhaps Monica would humanise him. She seemed to have started the process. Elaine took a sandwich from the plate Hilary offered her—little realising that, instead of feeling vastly superior, as she imagined, he was feeling nervous and awkward and very much in awe of her. She replied absently to his polite enquiries about her health. What a sketch Mother looked! Where on earth had she got that ghastly bow and that unspeakable blodge of cones stuck anyhow in front of her hat? It simply wasn't any use trying to make her look decent. Heaven only knew what sort of a fright she'd make of herself when she was left alone. Poor old Mum! Elaine couldn't feel really angry with her. She couldn't really feel angry with anyone. Mr. Randolph had come back last night and she'd told him this afternoon that she was going to London but not with him, and that she was leaving Randolph's at the end of the week. He'd goggled and spluttered and blustered. He'd begged and pleaded and almost wept, and she'd wiped the floor with him. She'd enjoyed wiping the floor with him. His neck had got fatter while he was away, and his eyes seemed to stick out further. She knew that, even if Madame Bertier hadn't asked her to join with her in the hat-shop, she would never have been able to go through with it. She had enjoyed the scene with him immensely. It had given her an exhilarating sense of power. Even in his anger he had been afraid of annoying her. Even when he was urging her and pleading with her, he had hardly dared to touch her. She had two more days to put in at the office, and she knew that he would spend them in sulking. He amused her when he sulked, but it was nice to feel that she would never see him again after this week. Once more she wondered what there was about men that made women lose their heads over them. She had never been able to understand it. Hilary, Terry, Roy Hamwell, Uncle Humphrey . . . each had a woman to lose her head over him for no reason at all.

Humphrey came into the room and glanced around him. There was a pleasant tea-party atmosphere in the room, a sustained murmur of conversation—discussions of the idiosyncrasies of neighbours ("Mrs. Bolton's taken up the Hay diet. Such a pity, because he makes such delicious pastry"), of the cheapness of the new greengrocer's shop that had just opened in the Market Square ("They always start like that," said Doreen darkly. "Then they begin putting their prices up"), of the jerry-built houses in the new Garden Estate ("They say if you knock an ordinary nail in the wall it goes right through to the next house"), of the Town Council's habit of perpetually taking up the main roads ("If it isn't gas it's water. Or if it isn't water it's electricity. It's never down more than two weeks together"), and of the latest effort of the local Operatic Society ("She pays half their expenses and so she always insists on having the best part, but she can't sing a note. It was ludicrous last week").

Humphrey's eyes met Viola's across the room in a swift intimate smile. The new understanding between them, the deep tried love that now united them, was like a warm glow at his heart. He took his cup from her and went to stand by the mantelpiece.

Elaine came over to sit by Aggie.

"Where did you get that bow?" she demanded.

"At Lessington's," said Aggie, looking at Humphrey for protection.

"Why do you *sell* such dreadful things, Uncle Humphrey?" said Elaine sternly.

"It's very nice," he smiled. "Don't bully her."

Doreen was telling Viola that she'd never felt really well in Reddington. "I shall have to see how Bexhill suits me. . . ."

Humphrey glanced round the room again. It seemed only a few days ago since Viola's last family tea-party. Impossible to believe that since then they had decided to get a divorce and then decided not to. It had made little impression on the family, he thought, with a dry smile. Of course, there had been rather an unusual crop of other family excitements to put it in the shade. Bridget's engagements, Hester's unprecedented holiday by herself, Frances's escapade. . . . They had provided sufficient excitement in themselves and had mercifully kept people's attention away from his affair. His affair, in fact, seemed to have made no stir at all in the family, and for that he was duly thankful.

"Do have one of those little rock buns, Humphrey," Viola was saying. "You said you liked them last time Cook made them, so she's made them again specially."

With an attentiveness that secretly amused Humphrey, Hilary leapt to his feet and brought him the cake-stand.

"Did you enjoy your holiday, Aunt Hester?" Monica said.

"Yes, thank you," said Hester dreamily. "It was very nice."

"What did you do?"

"Oh, nothing. . . ."

"Do?" put in Harriet grimly. "She as near as possible caught her death, that's what she did."

"Nonsense," smiled Hester. "It was just an ordinary bad cold."

"You know, dear," said Aggie, patting the bow and taking courage from Humphrey's nearness, "they *are* being worn. The girl said so."

"You're just the limit, Mother," said Elaine, but there was a note almost of tenderness in her voice.

"I took it back to the shop," Doreen was saying. "I said, 'Weigh it yourself. It's almost a whole ounce under weight.' "

Through the window they saw Terry and Bridget. Terry carried her suitcase and was just opening the gate. They walked very slowly up to the front door, their heads close together.

THE END